Jon Stenhugg is the pen name of a Swedish author, born in California, U.S.A., and who graduated from Stockholm University, Sweden, with a degree in Education, Psychology and Statistics.

He taught Education and Psychology to teacher trainees at Stockholm School of Education for thirteen years, with time out for a few years of administrative service at the Swedish National Board of Education and the University of Falun. After that he worked for a number of years in the private sector, as a sole proprietor of a firm in the computer industry. He began to write this novel in 2005 while living and working in Ireland.

THE SECOND CHILD

JON STENHUGG

To Nicola Barr,

SilverWood

Published in 2015 by SilverWood Books

SilverWood Books Ltd
14 Small Street, Bristol, BS1 1DE
www.silverwoodbooks.co.uk

ISBN 978-1-78132-330-4 (paperback)
ISBN 978-1-78132-331-1 (ebook)

British Library Cataloguing in Publication Data
A CIP catalogue record for this book is available from
the British Library

Set in Adobe Garamond Pro and Berthold Akzidenz Grotesk by SilverWood Books
Printed on responsibly sourced paper

Only puny secrets need protection.
Big secrets are protected by public incredulity.

Marshall McLuhan, *Take Today: The Executive as Dropout*

Prologue

Nuremberg Prison, Germany
14 October, 1946

The trial was over. The men sentenced to hang in the gray stone prison the following day shivered in their whitewashed cells.

U.S. Army Lt. John Hurtree shook the rain from his hat and checked in with the Office of the Provost Marshal. He removed his long brown trench coat and laid it on the table. The Corporal frisked Hurtree's wiry body. The box under his arm was next. The guard logged the contents into the journal, 'Photographs', beside Hurtree's name and rank.

Hurtree followed the echoing boots of a young soldier to the wing where the prisoners awaited their fate. A soldier stood outside each cell. Sweaty despair tainted the air, mixed with the smell of freshly waxed floors.

The chill of the morning grew for Hurtree when he entered the cell of the prisoner who had requested his presence, Prisoner 13, Hermann Schwerlieb, previously Reichsmarshall for the short-lived Third German Empire.

Hurtree shifted the box from under his arm and the two men sat in Schwerlieb's cell. Hurtree took the only chair, narrowing his bright blue eyes on the man opposite, and placed the box on a simple wooden table between them.

Schwerlieb sat on the metal military cot covered with drab army blankets. The whitewashed granite walls reflected the harsh light from a single electric bulb dangling from the ceiling, high overhead. Impossible to reach. The soldier outside the open door watched in silence as the prisoner spoke.

"As you know, Lieutenant Hurtree, I am to be killed as a common criminal. Me. Hitler's successor. I ran the whole country when he was ill. And now to be hanged as if I had been caught for some monstrous crime. It's not possible for me to understand. This whole trial was a farce and our sentences a political crime. Imagine if we had won the war and executed Churchill this way. Even the German people would have disapproved of that. In spite of what the British did to Dresden."

Hurtree listened to the ranting for several minutes. He noticed Schwerlieb was much thinner since their last meeting. He was tall and heavy, but the obese midriff of the drunken morphine addict was gone.

Schwerlieb turned away from the door and the soldier guarding it. He lowered his voice and pleaded, "I want a favor from you, Lieutenant Hurtree. I would like to die as a soldier. Be shot by a firing squad. I can accept that. You can arrange it."

"No." Hurtree shook his head. "I'm absolutely sure it cannot be done. You are all sentenced to death by hanging. Was that all?"

"No." Schwerlieb wiped sweat from his hands on his white cotton dungarees. "I asked you to bring the photographs you showed me during our interviews. I see you have done so. I would like to look at some of these photos one last time, if I may."

Hurtree took the box from the table and placed it on his lap. "Which ones?"

"I will search for the ones I would like to see."

Hurtree looked away, seeking a reply on the wall beside him. He found none. "You don't have much time," he said at last, and slid the box over to Schwerlieb.

Schwerlieb removed the lid. His expression warmed several times when he examined the photographs. He shook his head as he relived the dialogue surrounding the events while the picture was taken. He leafed through several more pictures, then took one in both hands and removed it. His face broke out in a wide smile.

Hurtree stretched his neck and noted it was the picture of the children, the subject of many hours of interrogation before the trial. He studied Schwerlieb's face, seeking anything to explain the interest in the image of the children. Schwerlieb scanned the photograph at length, and Hurtree could see the warmth of reminiscence soften Schwerlieb's chiseled face.

"It's a nice picture," Hurtree coaxed. He ran a hand through his thick brown hair. "It must have been a beautiful day."

"It was," Schwerlieb responded, "it certainly was." He heaved a sigh as he carefully returned the photo to the box. Hurtree noted damp circles were growing under Schwerlieb's armpits.

"Would you like to tell me more about it now?" Hurtree's heart fluttered in anticipation. *Maybe this time.*

Schwerlieb stared at the floor for several seconds. He raised his head and looked Hurtree in the eye as he spoke. His voice was low, but grim with determination. "If you provide me with a pistol so that I may shoot myself, I'll tell you about the picture. And I know everything."

Hurtree refused. Getting a weapon into the prison holding the condemned prisoners was impossible. Besides, Hurtree felt the sentence was correct. He wouldn't help.

Despite this, on the following day the war criminal used poison to take his own life, only two hours before he was to be hanged. The investigation into Schwerlieb's suicide led nowhere, but Hurtree resented the lengthy interrogations; the suggestions he had provided the prisoner with poison.

After Schwerlieb's death, Hurtree tried once again to identify everyone in the photograph. He nearly succeeded. There remained only a young girl, second from the left in the group of children. Hurtree kept the photograph in his desk drawer until the day he retired nearly forty years later, when he had returned it to the son of the war criminal.

It had been a strained meeting at the son's house in Munich. They sat in the living room. Books on dental prosthetics filled the bookcases. Hurtree asked again about the children in the photograph.

The middle-aged man before him looked at the picture briefly, then pointed to the child standing to the far left. "That's me."

"And the others?" Hurtree felt hope rise again.

"The other six children were Goebbels' children," and Schwerlieb's son averted his face. He had strong, handsome features. Dark, wavy hair above a high forehead, a prominent Nordic nose and determined lips. *A copy of his father*, thought Hurtree.

"Are you sure?" Hurtree wheedled. "The Goebbels had six children alright, but Heidi wasn't even born when this was taken. The second child, the one standing next to you, must be three, four years old."

"I can't remember." Schwerlieb's son shifted his eyes away from Hurtree. "It was a long time ago."

"Yes, it was. Even for me, but I'd still like to know who she could be."

"Perhaps some things are best left forgotten." Schwerlieb's son placed the photograph on a table next to several wartime photographs of his father. "We don't always need to know the truth about everything."

"Maybe you don't. I do."

The haunting image of the second child, a thin, dark-haired girl of three, stared back at Hurtree from the photograph, and gnawed at his soul.

Part I

The Photograph

Chapter 1

Stockholm, Sweden
Summer, 1996

The doctor was an easy target. He left his suitcase in the hall near the door, took out his cell phone, and called TaxiSnabb, the company he always used when in Stockholm. His heart pounded as he listened for the diesel clatter of the taxi.

In a taxi parked near the metro station, the driver eavesdropped on a relay of the doctor's conversation with the airline and then his call to the taxi company. He put his car into motion and arrived outside the doctor's address in minutes. The doctor opened the door onto the street, dragging his suitcase behind him, wincing in pain.

The taxi driver opened the trunk. He asked if the doctor had ordered a taxi from the TaxiSnabb Company, and asked the doctor to verify his name. He explained TaxiSnabb had engaged him for this run, and put the suitcase in the trunk before the doctor could protest.

"So where we go?" asked the driver when the doctor had taken his seat in the rear. "To airport?"

"No," said the doctor. "To the Central Station. I'm taking the express train to the airport."

"Express train to airport? Oh, bad news for you. All been cancelled today. Working on tracks. I take you to airport for half price today. Girlfriend works there. I meet her later. OK?"

The driver was pulling out into traffic before the doctor could reply. They continued in silence, and the doctor turned his head several times as the taxi left the city's core and began the long, boring journey to the airport. They passed shopping centers, trees, industrial parks, and rye fields.

The taxi slowed, and the driver turned off the ignition key as they rolled down the exit off the freeway. He turned it on after several seconds to produce a loud explosion from behind them.

The doctor was startled, shaken. "What was that?" he asked.

The driver took a left instead of the normal right hand turn toward the airport, rolling the car to a stop under the viaduct.

"My car breaking down," he said. "Please to help you, I call another TaxiSnabb. They here in only minute. Many at airport. Sorry Mister, help you with your bag?"

The doctor left the taxi and gazed off into the distance toward the airport. They were surrounded by forest, and over the treetops he saw a Boeing 747 float down toward the landing strip. He wished he were at the gate waiting for it already.

The driver placed the doctor's suitcase on the ground and closed the trunk. He waited as the doctor approached the suitcase; watched as he leaned forward slightly to grasp the handle. After a quick glance in both directions, the driver took out a small .22 caliber pistol from his jacket pocket, and fired one round into the back of the doctor's head. The doctor's body fell heavily into the ditch beside the car. The driver looked around again, assured himself there were still no witnesses, and fired another round into the doctor's temple.

The driver took out the victim's wallet, gathered the money and passports he found, and stuffed them into his pocket. He found a few credit cards with the victim's name on them, and after carefully wiping them clean of his fingerprints, threw them on the ground beside the body. He heaved the suitcase back into the trunk of the taxi, and drove to a nearby lake where he cleaned up all traces of his fingerprints on the suitcase, wallet, and car. He splashed gasoline onto everything, and in seconds the car was engulfed in flames. He took a few steps and entered the car where his contact waited.

In less than five hours, the assassin was relaxing with a glass of ouzo in a bar in Athens.

*

Under a Viaduct Leading to Arlanda Airport, Stockholm, Sweden | Summer, 1996

Sven Peterson, head of Homicide at the NBI, Sweden's National Bureau of Investigation, studied his most recently appointed investigator, Sara Markham, while she took details from the caller.

The sun warmed as the day wore on, and Sara removed her police jacket, revealing a simple white shirt and a body which attracted considerable attention in the lunch lines. Few people noticed the pair of miniature handcuffs holding her brunette ponytail in place.

The man who had found the body was happy to provide her with intricate details of what he had seen. When the interview was over, Sara and Sven waited in the car for the technicians to arrive.

"What was it your judo instructor called you?" asked Sven. He leaned back in the car seat, raising his arms to stretch his back.

Sara bit down on her lower lip. Her boss had done his background work well. "Terrier," she said. "He called me the Terrier. I bit him on the arm during a training exercise."

Sara reddened as she looked at the floor of the car. She continued, "He had me in a hard choke hold from behind. I could barely breathe. I didn't bite him that hard. He was just joking when he called me that."

"Yeah." Sven glanced down at the report in his hands and took the pencil from between his teeth. "Well, live up to your name and you'll be OK in this job. Just don't bite me. I bite back."

"The patrolman said it looks like the body is fairly fresh," said Sara, "not too many flies yet, in spite of the heat. He said he saw a gunshot wound to the head."

"Uhmm." Sven kept his eyes on the draft of his budget report. He removed a calculator from the breast pocket of his shirt and punched in some numbers.

Sara had heard of Sven's dress habits. He hated shopping, and when he found a shirt he liked, he would buy seven of them, one for each day of the week. He had been wearing blue plaid shirts and blue jeans for four years now.

"A fox wouldn't start eating a body that's too far gone either," she added.

"Uhmm," he said again, and flipped to a new page.

"Strange place to find a body," Sara continued. "It doesn't look like he walked here. Maybe he was dumped. Do you know why the locals called us in instead of doing this themselves?"

Sven glanced up from the document in his hand and twisted his head around both ways as he made a mental picture of the scene. "We're under a viaduct," he said. "That would help mask the sound of a shot if the killing was done here."

Sara scribbled a few words on her notepad and got out of the car. She decided to keep her thought experiments to herself for the time being. *No reason to show Sven I don't have all the answers yet.*

She walked toward the body, careful to keep her sensible brown loafers on the asphalt. Vibrations from trucks on the E4 highway played dark drums on the viaduct overhead, and she looked for signs of footprints or tire tracks in the dust. Sara returned her gaze to the corpse, noticing the credit cards strewn next to it.

She would ask the forensics team about the position of the body: if it could tell them anything about whether the shooting had taken place here, or if it had been dumped. The viaduct she stood under was just outside the airport security perimeter. There was little chance any CCTV cameras or sensors would have picked up the event, but she would visit airport security just in case.

Sara stood still for a moment and closed her eyes, imagining she was about to shoot someone. She opened her eyes and panned her head, saw a clear view of the exit ramp and approaching traffic from all directions. The bustle of traffic toward the airport came in regular waves, about one car every other minute. *With good timing, and a little luck, a killer would be able to take a shot and never be detected.*

After another half hour, both Sven and Sara welcomed the forensics team, who cordoned off a much larger area before they carried out their work.

"You running this show?" The aging head of the forensic team motioned for Sara to get closer. "You'll want to look at these," and he handed Sara two credit cards.

"Thanks," she said. "Cause of death?"

"We'll know more when the Crime Lab in Linköping does their wizardry, but the two bullet holes in his head certainly contributed. One from behind, one in the temple. No exit wounds. Small caliber. I'd say a .22 cal."

"Wallet? Other ID?" Sara poised her pen over her notebook and waved away a persistent fly.

"Nothing, just the credit cards."

They weren't much to go on, but the credit cards helped Sara get the address of Dr. Göran Stolpe's apartment in the Old Town. She located the building superintendent while she drove from the airport. He was waiting for her on the narrow cobbled street outside when she arrived thirty minutes later.

She followed him through the thick wooden outer door and into the dark vestibule. The superintendent flipped the light switch, revealing gleaming white marble walls. Sara saw the name *G Stolpe* on the brass plaque with other residents; the only resident living on the first floor above street level.

Sara and the building superintendent ascended the circular marble staircase, their footsteps echoing off the ornate frescos decorating the wall. She motioned for the building superintendent to stand behind her on the landing and silently moved closer to Stolpe's door.

She carefully raised the bronze flap to the mail slot, put her ear next to it, and whistled. Silence inside. *Good, no dogs*. She rang the doorbell, waiting for the courtesy minute to go by before motioning for the superintendent to open the door.

He turned the key and stepped back onto the stairwell to admit her to the apartment.

"It's the police," she shouted, and entered, hands clasped around her pistol. She made a quick survey of the hall in front of her.

The tiny hall led to a cubbyhole on the left where a washing machine and dryer were stacked on top of each other. From the hall, she entered a modern kitchen, flooded by light through three *Jugend* style windows dating from the turn of the century. Still crouching, Sara turned right, where the high ceiling continued into a dining room. The hardwood floor creaked under Sara's shoes until she reached the hand-woven Persian carpet. She felt the cushioning lift even through the soles of her loafers. A walnut dining table with matching chairs stood in the center of the dining room.

She went through a portal into an elaborate sitting room. The same type of windows lit up each room, all filled with French antiques and glittering chandeliers made of crystal. *Looks like a wing of the palace in Versailles,* she thought.

Antique stuffed chairs lined the edges of the sitting room. The Tabriz silk carpet covered the entire floor, which was as large as her entire apartment. The threads of gold inlays glittered in the morning sun.

"Police," Sara shouted again before she swiveled and crouched through a right turn, continuing through an arched opening up a small flight of three steps. Off to the right another short stairway led up to a loft. She pointed her pistol toward the loft and searched for movement in the dark. Nothing. Only her breathing broke the silence.

With her pistol still in front of her, she moved straight through to a well-appointed *en suite* bathroom, and beyond that the bedroom. The luxury continued there too, with French Impressionist paintings on the wall. Sara looked into the walk-in closet. Cashmere suits hung next to full-length trench coats in various shades of leather. There was nothing to indicate another person shared Göran Stolpe's affluent way of life.

Sara returned to the short set of stairs leading up to the loft. A small window took in light from the enclosed courtyard below. The loft held a desk, a black leather chair, and a large filing cabinet. The filing cabinet was unlocked. Sara looked into it and saw it contained medical records for only one patient and international research regarding autism. Many of the documents in the filing cabinet were in German.

Penciled notes on the doctor's desk recorded flight times. Next to them, a letter-opener. Sara bent down to focus her camera on the desktop and drew back in surprise when she noted a swastika emblem on the ornate handle of the letter opener. She had managed to finish her photographs as she heard a voice from the dining room call out, "Police. We're coming in."

She held her pistol to one side, muzzle to the ceiling, raised her left hand, and shouted, "Me too. In the back."

A minute later, a man peeked his head around the corner and said, "Commissioner Lars Ekman, National Security Service. Here's my ID."

"Sara Markham," she said as she holstered her pistol and held up her ID card, "Homicide."

"You alone?" Ekman asked as he walked up the stairs to join her in the office.

"Yes, just the building superintendent outside."

"May I ask what you're doing here?" Ekman glanced at her ID and holstered his pistol.

"Investigating a murder. And you?"

"We've had this place under surveillance. We saw you enter. Is Dr. Stolpe the killer or the victim?"

"The victim. Surveillance? Why?"

"We'll get to that later. Sven's your boss, right? You two should come over to the NSS tomorrow morning. In the meantime, we're going to secure the premises."

"Can I stick around? I might find something I can use."

"No."

"Does that mean you want me to leave?" Sara asked. Her voice broke.

"Yes. See you tomorrow. Eight o'clock."

"Unbelievable," muttered Sara when she reached the street.

Chapter 2

The meeting at Homicide regarding the Stolpe case began after lunch. Sven Peterson entered the meeting as Sara went through the details they had gathered. Robert Johnson, so far her only other team member, sat doodling on a yellow pad in front of him. Only a week ago his muscular body had been browning to an attractive tan on a Mediterranean beach. His blond hair framed a face with two large brown eyes. Women loved him. Sara demanded professional competence instead.

"So this was an obvious professional hit," said Sara. "There was no other identification on the body. No wallet, no money, nothing. Just the credit cards which led us to the apartment in the Old Town."

"Which turned out to be under surveillance by the National Security Service," said Sven. "The killer could be giving us a heads-up."

"Why would someone do that?" asked Robert.

"It's a letter from the killer. We just haven't read it yet," said Sara, and she turned to Sven. "What do we tell the guys at the Security Service? They've asked for you and I to meet them in their offices tomorrow morning. Do you think they'll tell us why they were watching that apartment?"

"The NSS doesn't usually tell us anything. They ask us what we know. They usually nod and take notes. Then we go to lunch."

Sara assigned Robert to apply for access to any available CCTV video tapes in the vicinity of Stolpe's apartment. "I think there's a bank ATM close by, and you might want to ask at the shops where any security videos are focused."

Robert mumbled a sullen reply, "Right. The shops," then he gathered his notebook and left.

Sara watched his back disappear out the door and swallowed an angry thought before it became audible. *What's eating you?* Then she drove to the airport again.

The head of Airport Security was friendly, but not very helpful. "There's really nothing I can do if a murder has been committed outside the security perimeter, but I can show you the facilities available had one occurred inside my jurisdiction."

There were cameras everywhere. Sara averted her eyes when she saw a man dropping his pants before turning and sitting on the toilet in one of the men's rooms in Terminal 5. She was told there were security guards who monitored several hundred screens, watching for suspicious behavior or unattended luggage left lying about. The videos were stored on computer databases for one week, then erased.

She had better luck at the Scandinavian Airlines information desk. They gave her a list of names of passengers for the flight to Copenhagen noted on Stolpe's desk. She scanned the list, but Göran Stolpe's name was missing. At the bottom of the list she found a Wolfgang Winter listed as a no-show.

"You've got a man who didn't show up for this flight?" Sara pointed at the list.

"Yeah, that happens a lot. More than you'd expect," said the clerk, who then went back to scanning a computer monitor.

"Could I see the details for his ticket?" she asked.

"Details? For someone who didn't show up?" The clerk raised his eyes to meet Sara's.

"Can I just see the details for his ticket? Please." Sara's voice found a new firmness.

"You'll have to speak with my supervisor," said the clerk. "He might be very busy."

"So am I. You're not obstructing a police investigation, are you?"

"No, of course not." The clerk sighed, then asked her to come behind the desk where she could talk to his boss. Within minutes after asking, she was watching as payment details for Wolfgang Winter's ticket to Copenhagen flashed up on the screen with a MasterCard payment registered to a Göran Stolpe. The address matched the office in the Old Town. She looked at the photocopy of the credit cards from the forensic team. The number was identical.

I wonder what the NSS will say about that, she thought.

It was too late to drive back to her office in Stockholm after visiting the airport, so Sara parked her car behind her favorite student bar just outside Karolinska University Hospital area. She locked her police jacket in her Peugeot 210, and made her way to the bar in her field uniform: blue jeans and a white shirt.

The walls were painted black, and the place smelled of burnt sawdust and spilled beer. Empty wine bottles held candles, providing most of the illumination. The bartender, a young woman of about twenty-five, nodded in recognition. Several metal studs pierced her eyebrows and lips. When she asked Sara what she wanted, the stud in her tongue clicked on her teeth.

"A beer," said Sara.

A technician from the Medical Examiner's Office in Solna sat alone at the bar. He recognized Sara and tried his pick-up skills on her once again.

"How was your day? I got stuck with a probable suicide. An old lady who jumped in front of a train. Not too much left of her. Makes you wonder where they all come from."

Sara's beer arrived, and she started to gather her things to move to a quieter place.

"Wait," he said, "I'm sorry. I just thought we could talk outside the ME's office. I work for the ME."

Sara paid for her beer. "Yeah, I know who you are and where you work. Look, I had a tough day too. Too bad about your train-jumper, but I'm sure you'll understand if I just sit down alone over there. See you tomorrow, or maybe not. Bye."

She sat at a table where she could turn her back on the technician. "Nice." She heard a woman's voice behind her, and grinned at one of her few school friends who sat next to her.

"Sure," said Sara. "Just what I've always wanted, to share time and space with a guy who cuts up bodies for a living."

"Sounds like you've been busy," said Karin, a blond thirty-year-old with an attractive figure hidden under a yellow blouse and baggy jeans. "Were you working on the suicide he spoke of?"

"No, but I still had a crappy day today," said Sara. "We got a murder case, a guy whose body was left out in the open and a fox got to it before we did, so you can imagine. Not so pretty, you know. On top of that, my grandmother called again."

"How is she?" Karin asked over the rim of her beer glass.

"She's still having problems trying to get into a Service Center. The people who run the centers say she's not old or sick enough yet, and the Social Services people say she has too many assets, so she'll have to sell her apartment and use up all her money before they can help her. What kind of a place do we live in?"

"It's a great country if you screw up. You only have problems if you try to take care of yourself, then you're in real trouble," said Karin and shook her head.

"So from now on I should try to blow every pay check on parties, fun, and games. Do you really believe in all that?"

"Not really. But I believe in the trip to Finland. Are you still on for that?" asked Karin.

"I'll be there with bells on. What time does the ferry leave next week?"

"Friday. 5 p.m. And don't miss it."

Sara grabbed her purse and drove home.

At 5 a.m., Sara woke up and paced back and forth in her small apartment. The sun had already roasted the tiny enclosed courtyard outside for several hours, and a seagull swooped near her kitchen window, squawking demands for a free meal. She put on a gray fleece sweatsuit and orange sneakers, and left for her morning run.

After graduation from the Police Academy, Sara had moved to the tiny city of Sundbyberg, just north of Stockholm. Refusing to be a bedroom suburb to big sister Stockholm, Sundbyberg had a long tradition of luring companies to relocate workplaces to its city center, but Sara commuted into Stockholm. Sundbyberg was a vibrant place to live, but expensive, and she struggled to make the monthly payments on her modest loan.

Sara jogged down the short street where her apartment was located, and turned right on the main street, Tule Street. A few minutes later, she entered the section of the city named Duvbo, where million dollar Victorian villas butted up against simple one-family homes built by clerks or train drivers. An hour later, she was back in her apartment, and she showered. She opened a blank page in her notebook and placed it on her kitchen table while she dried off.

The scent of green tea steeping in her favorite pot reminded her she was hungry. She popped a frozen rye breakfast roll in the microwave and removed a block of sharp cheese and a cucumber from the refrigerator. When the microwave dinged, her breakfast roll was hot and ready to eat.

Sara drew a circle in the center of the page, then doodled a swastika in the middle of it. She carved off a piece of cheese, and added several slices of cucumber to the roll. She wiped off errant crumbs from the page in front of her, then made two smaller circles flanking the larger one. Sara added Stolpe's name and a small swastika in the left circle, and the word 'killer' and a question mark in the circle to the right. She bit thoughtfully into her breakfast roll, then filled the page with a flurry of swastikas and question marks.

Chapter 3

Sven accompanied Sara around the block to the National Security Service wing for their meeting. She wore dark pants to match the dark dress jacket over a light blue shirt. Sara tried to avoid the puddles left from last night's rain. Sven splashed through them. Drops of water stained his blue jeans, and he wore a freshly washed version of the blue plaid shirt.

The sun had been up since 2 a.m. and the air was chilly, freshly scrubbed. To their left, water seeped from the scarred gray granite cliff, dynamited to make way for Polhems Street, in the days of Alfred Nobel. They turned to the right off the sidewalk and strode between the bicycle racks flanking the entrance. They went through the extra security lock, entering just in time to make their meeting.

Sven rapped a polite knock on the door of the conference room and they went in. Both NSS officers stood up and asked them to sit down. One of the officers poured coffee, and hot water for Sara's tea. She opened her notepad.

"Please don't make notes here" was the response. Sara cocked an eyebrow, looked over at Sven, and put down her pen.

A few seconds later, the door opened and an officer in plain clothes entered. He was short, muscular, and well into his thirties. The man dropped a thick suspension file onto the desk with a thump. He smiled a tight-lipped smile of recognition at Sara. After the formalities of identification, NSS Police Commissioner Lars Ekman sat down.

Ekman opened the suspension file, removed a few papers at a time, and related the story of a Dr. Habermann from the perspective of the National Security Service. His voice was dry and matter-of-fact. Ekman barely looked up as he read.

"Habermann—you might know him as Stolpe—was a Nazi implant, like many who came in toward the end of the Second World War. He worked at Långbro Hospital, and from what we know he cared for only one patient: a girl named Dolfin. Her last name was never recorded. Habermann changed his name to Göran Stolpe. Someone in the Swedish Foreign Office was involved in the name change."

Ekman glanced up at Sven and Sara. "And don't ask who. All subsequent investigations were sidetracked with a reference to the sensitivity of the case because of the war. Habermann worked with a nurse, also an implant. Her name was Anna Eiderbach. The two kept to themselves. Our file ends with comments indicating nothing to suggest Habermann's or Eiderbach's activities were dangerous for Sweden, and no one has ever asked for a Dr. Göran Stolpe from Germany."

Sara shifted her gaze to her boss, her eyes opened wide in wonder. She wanted to ask Sven if this was a normal occurrence at Homicide, but said nothing. Sven slowly nodded his head in understanding.

Commissioner Ekman took out another sheet of paper from the file, and continued, "A month ago, we intercepted a message between cells of an extreme right wing organization. Habermann, Eiderbach, and the woman named Dolfin were to be assassinated in Stockholm."

Sara jerked back her head in surprise and her jaw dropped. Sven looked over at her and then smiled at Ekman, who continued, "We put Habermann's apartment under light surveillance, and mounted a Webcam across the street, covering the entrance. The woman, Anna Eiderbach, was also watched, but when nothing happened for several weeks, we removed her surveillance. The woman named Dolfin was never found. We assumed she had moved from Stockholm." Commissioner Ekman closed the file and looked at Sara.

"We'll be handling this case from now on. So what do you know?"

Sara's voice faltered. "Excuse me, Sir, this is my first time at the NSS. I had no idea I'd be involved in trying to solve a political assassination." Sara consulted her notes and steadied her voice. "We've been investigating Stolpe, uh, Habermann since his body was discovered yesterday. He was found under a viaduct near the road to Stockholm's Arlanda Airport. Shot twice in the head with a .22 caliber weapon. Forensics says he was shot there, they're certain. No shell casings. Probably a small revolver. There are no airport security cameras covering the area where the shooting took place. We have found out Habermann used an alias to book his flight to Copenhagen, so he must have been running scared. He used the name Wolfgang Winter to book his ticket to Copenhagen. We didn't know about your Webcam, of course..." Sara looked over at Commissioner Ekman, who stared back at her with no change of expression "...so we couldn't use that information to try to track Habermann's movements just before he was killed. We did call several taxi companies yesterday, and TaxiSnabb had a run to the Habermann address. The passenger never showed. They told us Habermann wanted to go to the train station only a kilometer away."

Sara flipped to a new page in her notepad. Ekman interrupted her before she could continue.

"Do you have a time for that?"

"Yes, Sir. About 8.15 in the morning."

Ekman made a notation, looked up, and said, "Please go on."

"We found two credit cards near his body. No prints, of course. No trace yet on the bullets found in his head, no fingerprints or footprints at the scene. We did get a possible tire track in some dust, but we're unsure it belongs to the vehicle which brought him to the crime scene. A vehicle was found, completely burned out, about fifteen minutes away, but there was no other indication it could have been involved, except the burned remains of a suitcase in the trunk. Oh, yes, Stolpe had a letter-opener with a swastika on it, but you guys probably knew that already. That's about it so far." Sara closed her notepad and leaned back into her chair.

"Well, there may be one other thing," said Sven. "It seems the murderer gave us a direct lead to the victim's identity. Those credit cards didn't have to be there. They led us directly to Habermann's apartment."

"And to what was in it," said the youngest NSS officer, sitting next to Ekman. "We found a filing cabinet full of documents covering the entire time he worked with the Dolfin woman. We're still reading them."

"What was the name of the first woman again?" asked Sara.

"Eiderbach, Anna Eiderbach," Ekman replied.

"And what happened to her?" asked Sara.

"Nothing, as far as we know. Like I said, we cancelled the car outside her apartment quite a while ago. Why do you ask?"

"Just a hunch. She and Habermann would be about the same age, right? Can I check this out? I mean, without getting into trouble with the NSS?" Sara smiled at Ekman, but his expression remained unchanged, and his answer was short and clipped.

"Yes. I'll send you her address this afternoon."

"And does anyone know where this Dolfin woman is now? Could I check that out too?" asked Sara.

"We don't know where she is. If you can find out anything, tell us." Ekman gathered up the suspension files in front of him. The meeting was over.

The NSS, the National Security Service, was the Swedish version of the CIA and the FBI rolled into one, with the authority to carry out operations even on Swedish citizens. With them involved, Sara could at least rely on getting more help, but she was also worried their involvement might lead to her case being closed before it was solved, and a 'Secret' stamp being placed on all the files.

Sven and Sara were walking back to their offices at Homicide.

"Is it always like this when the NSS gets involved?" asked Sara.

"I thought they gave us a lot. Usually they don't tell us anything.

At least we know what to look for as we continue. Just remember to keep what you learned under your hat. Your team can't know anything you just heard." Sven kept a brisk long-legged pace as they turned the corner onto Berg Street.

"Anything?" Sara struggled to match Sven's stride.

"OK, you can let them know about the name change. That's public knowledge, so a good investigator will find that out anyway. Just don't tell them how you know."

Sven went back to his budget, and Sara met with Robert Johnson. She carefully avoided everything from the Security Service officers, and gave only a summary, not mentioning the meeting she and Sven had just come from. She added the name Habermann, then 'aka' before 'Stolpe' and 'Winter', on the whiteboard, and asked if there was anything new about the video tapes near Habermann's apartment.

Robert began by telling her about the intricacies of Swedish bureaucracy, and she cut him short.

"I know all that. When can we access the tapes?" she asked.

"Next week at the earliest," Robert replied, "but I could re-interview people on the street outside Habermann's apartment. Maybe someone saw something they can remember better today."

"No, don't. I want you to go to the Medical Examiner in Solna and see if they had a suicide case on Tuesday. A woman who fell in front of a train. Get all the details you can and bring them in. There might be a connection to our case." Sara noticed Robert hesitate slightly, as if he wanted to say something, but he stopped himself.

"Was there something else?" Sara cocked her head to one side.

"What does one have to do to become a principal investigator?"

"What? What do you mean?" Sara frowned.

"I've been here for more than a year, and I think it is my turn to be the lead." Robert glowered.

"That's not my call."

"No, I was just asking."

"Asking what?"

"Never mind." Robert gathered up his notes and left.

Nitwit, Sara thought. *With him on the team I'll end up doing everything myself.*

Sara went to her office and closed the door. She punched in the code for 'In a meeting' on her telephone, drew the blinds, and turned the light out, sitting quietly in the darkness.

She had begun meditating while at the Police Academy on the recommendation of her Martial Arts instructor, a Buddhist monk who could kill with his bare hands if required, but who always preferred non-violence unless there was no other option. After learning how to meditate, she had added her new skills to other aspects of her life. Sara discovered that instead of the quick-draw tactics used by her colleagues, she was far more successful in solving crimes by withdrawing to a quiet place for a good think. It made her a little less social than most other policemen, but very, very efficient. Like all Terriers, she had a hard time giving up.

Sara began by imagining Habermann calling for the taxi. If he had called for one, why was he not there when it arrived? Had someone else intercepted his call and got to him before the taxi got there? Why had he gotten into the car if it wasn't a taxi? And why had he been shot outside the car, under the viaduct? Had there been a struggle in the car? The Webcam the NSS had installed in front of Habermann's apartment could reveal something. She cursed herself for not asking the officer if they could view material from it.

Then there was the alias Habermann had used to book his flight, Wolfgang Winter. He would have had to have a passport in that name to get onto the flight, and yet there were no passports or other identification documents found on his body. Why had they been removed? And why had the police been directed to his apartment? The credit cards had led them there like a homing device.

What was it in the apartment the killer wanted them to find? And why was it so important Habermann's background be revealed? Certainly the assassin would just want to kill his victim, wouldn't he? Or was it a she? Sara turned on the light again to add the questions flooding into her mind to her notebook.

*

Robert Johnson drove to the Medical Examiner's office at the County Morgue in Solna, where he asked to speak to whoever was working with the suicide case on Tuesday. He asked if anyone had claimed the body and found they were waiting for next of kin to be notified before burial could take place. If nothing happened in two weeks, the body would be cremated and her ashes spread onto an anonymous hill at a local cemetery. Robert asked for the box containing the clothes and purse of the jumper and a copy of the ME's report.

Robert waited until he was in the car before opening the box and looking through the dead woman's purse. There was a small medallion at the bottom, heavy enough to be made of gold. A swastika enclosed in a ring, attached to a gold chain. He picked up the medallion, weighed it in his hand, and gauged the consequences of taking it.

Robert's brother Thomas collected memorabilia from the Second World War. His entire apartment overflowed with military objects from the period: helmets, medals, even flags when he could get them. And they were all from the German side.

This is something for Thomas. Definitely. Robert tried to imagine if anyone would ask for it, even next of kin should they ever show up. The ME's report indicated the woman had committed suicide, so she wouldn't miss it. That much was certain. He put the medallion in his pocket and drove home to lock it in a drawer inside the closet. Robert looked at the medallion again before closing the drawer; he was certain it would be appreciated.

Guilt began to creep into his mind as he drove back to work, but he replaced the thought with a rationalization: this woman was probably a collector herself; someone who'd like to know her medallion had now find a home in the hands of another serious collector, like Thomas.

Back at headquarters, he placed the evidence box with the dress and the victim's purse on the long desk in the Habermann room. He laid the hospital report on top and went to Sara's office. He knocked at her door, and was about to leave when she opened it.

"Do you have any news from the ME?" asked Sara.

"I got the file and personal effects from a suicide victim who fell in front of a train at the Central Station. An old woman. Her purse was full of things women need, very little cash, some keys, and nothing more," said Robert.

"Good," said Sara. "Where are they?"

"In the Habermann room. Do you have any other news?"

"No. Just a lot of questions to answer."

"Then I'll get busy on those tapes again," he said.

Sara stood alone beside the long birch table in the Habermann room, glanced at the ME's report, and read the victim's name.

"Well, hello, Ms. Anna Eiderbach," she said quietly to the report form. "I hope you can tell me a little about what's going on here, because right now I really need your help."

The light cotton dress Anna Eiderbach had worn the day she died was in a plastic bag. Sara put on her rubber gloves and removed it. She grimaced as she held it up to the light. It was dark blue with white polka-dots, stained with blood and torn in several places where Anna's body had been dragged along the tracks by the train.

Sara put the dress back on the table and reread the report signed by the ME. She whispered the words at the end: "Probable suicide," then added to herself "Yeah, right."

Sara opened Anna's purse and emptied the contents into the box, spreading them out as she did. She spent several minutes probing and re-sorting the contents, and ended by turning the purse inside out, shaking it, running her hand through every pocket. She went over the hospital report again, carefully piling up the contents of the purse on the bottom of the box while she compared them item by item to the list in the report. Everything was there except a gold medallion.

Chapter 4

Summer, 1996
Philadelphia, U.S.A.

John Hurtree's eyelids fluttered open. He coughed, waiting for the water to soothe the acrid taste still in his mouth. The burning in his throat subsided. Hurtree stood in his small apartment in Philadelphia, Pennsylvania. He wondered if his recurrent memories of the unsolved mystery in Munich lay behind the reflux attacks each night at 4 a.m., but he couldn't remember if he'd been dreaming this time or not. Some nights, the memories he most wanted to forget kept him awake until he fell asleep, too exhausted to remember.

He had investigated war criminals during the Nuremberg trials, but the horrors weren't ruining his sleep. The photograph with the face of a little girl standing in a group of children with Adolf Hitler in the background kept him awake. A girl he could never find.

Readjustment to life in America was difficult. On more than one occasion, he longed for the life he had led in Germany for nearly forty years. Hurtree had become more of a European than an American. He used to joke about having his citizenship welded to his soul. Now he joked the weld had broken years ago.

He lived for his work as a CID investigator for the U.S. Army. He couldn't understand the friends he worked with who had retired to play golf in the Florida sunshine. Hurtree never had time for golf, and he had liked the temperate climate of southern Germany. The magnificent Alps were a few hours drive when he felt the need to clear his lungs. And his mind.

Hurtree woke in a sweat. The next morning's summer sun beamed through the flimsy curtains in his bedroom window. The final part of the recurring nightmare where two children ran off and taunted him was troubling, but it seemed less serious when examined in the heat of the morning, and the smell of freshly brewed coffee filled the kitchen.

He sat at his little kitchen table and glanced at the morning newspaper. He leafed through pages and pages of dread and speculation about the end of the world when the millennium ended. Computers would fail, wars would be started automatically, and mankind would go up in smoke. *Bullshit*, thought Hurtree, *mankind will just go on being mankind, mostly bad, but occasionally showing a good side or two. This is probably just a marketing gimmick to get us to buy new computers.*

Outside the apartment, life on Sixth Street near Lombard began to come alive. Hurtree threw the newspaper into the trash bin and walked to the bookcase. He surveyed a row of thumb-worn notebooks, took down the newest one, furthest to the right, and grabbed a pen from a drawer. He opened the notebook to a fresh page and began a new list.

Who was the second child in the photo?
Where is the child? Is she still alive?
What did Schwerlieb mean about knowing a lot about the photograph?
Why was the photograph so important for Schwerlieb he thought he could exchange it for a bullet?
Why did his son refuse to remember who she was?

Hurtree flipped through previous pages and shook his head. Each page bore the same list. He returned the notebook to the shelf next to the collection of identical notebooks. *Nothing has changed. I'm the last person alive who cares about this. When I'm gone, it's over.*

Sara met Karin at an Irish bar in Stockholm's Old Town. Her friend arrived late. Sara had changed into a black-and-white stripped summer dress covered by her dark jacket. She sat at a table out of the way of the television set blaring a hurling match from Kilkenny. Sara spotted Karin's floral pink dress as soon as she came in through the door. Karin sat down and ordered a glass of Pinot Grigio. They were alone except for three Irishmen who shouted occasionally, punctuating the quiet of the almost empty bar.

"Hi, I'm really glad I could make it," said Sara. "Let's help you get over whatever ordeals life has dealt you today." She held up her beer as they saluted each other: *Skol.*

Karin lowered her glass. "I just got a couple of free tickets for the ferry to Finland, and I need to know what you're going to do for Midsummer."

"I'm on duty," said Sara. "Midsummer is a good time to get killed, unfortunately. I've also been assigned as principal investigator on a really complicated case, so I'll probably still be working on it when Christmas comes. Hey, you work at a hospital. You can help me understand some information I found while working on a case. Interested?"

"Yeah, I might be able to help out with some of the medical terms, if that's what you need."

"That's some of it. The technician from the ME's Office, the one in the bar the other day, he was rambling on about a suicide victim, remember?"

"Yes." Karin rolled her eyes to the ceiling. "I never gave it another thought. That guy is just like the ones who work in the morgue—kind of, well, weird."

"I'm looking into that case. She was old, but there doesn't seem to be any reason for her to commit suicide. And there wasn't any note in her purse." The three Irishmen shouted out their enthusiasm, and Sara glanced up at the hurling match on TV, shaking her head when the camera focused on the bloody lips of a hurling player, smiling through broken teeth. She continued, "She lived in Fruängen, near where you live. She had a nurse's ID from Långbro Hospital. Is that place still active?"

"Not anymore," said Karin. "It's being turned into a housing project now. Imagine choosing to live in an insane asylum. Must be creepy. Anyway, age usually doesn't have much to do with suicide. People do away with themselves at all ages. Very depressing, really."

They finished their drinks, and Sara suggested they work their way through the better spots of the Old Town. This part of Stockholm was like a living museum from the Middle Ages. City planners had allowed no changes since the early nineteen hundreds. Although most buildings had electricity installed, many apartments only had cold running water. Some apartment owners still used outdoor toilets. Very few buildings had elevators, and narrow and winding staircases connected floors. Still it was one of the most fashionable addresses in the country; people spent millions for the chance to purchase a lease.

Sara and Karin ducked into the narrow medieval alley called *Gåsgränd.* Karin's high heels wobbled and she put out both hands on the buildings beside her to regain her balance.

"Only you would wear high heels in the Old Town," Sara chided.

"And only you would wear hiking boots to match a summer dress," Karin retorted, pointing to Sara's loafers.

Cars, mostly taxis, drove on a few special streets. And there were many, many bars and restaurants. Usually, a single door from the street led to a steep staircase down to a remodeled coal cellar or storage room. It was a city living on the edge of another time.

They climbed up and down stairs most of the evening, attracting the attention of many young men, and enjoying each other's company as they traded stories from their professional lives.

At about 2 a.m., they emerged from the Irish bar where they had begun their pub crawl and squinted into the chilly Arctic summer morning sun. Both women ambled down Västerlång Street toward a taxi stand, and Sara glanced up at the outer door leading to Habermann's apartment. She stopped in front of the door and spotted the tiny black cube hiding the Webcam mounted on the lamppost across the street. She wondered if the NSS was still monitoring the street, and made a mental note to ask them at their next meeting.

"So what made you become a cop?" asked Karin.

Sara shrugged her shoulders. "I wanted to be one when I was a kid. It was something that happened at the day care center. I guess I just wanted more control in life than I was getting. What about you? Why become a nurse and not a stockbroker?"

"Same as you, day care center. I sometimes wonder if any of us were raised by our parents."

Sara spent several hours juggling during the weekend, trying to keep a number of questions from appearing in her mind. She tried and she juggled and then she tried again. At 10 p.m. on Sunday night, she finally sat down and added several questions to a list she had in her purse.

Why did Habermann need to use an alias at the airport?
Where is the medallion mentioned in the ME's report?
Why is it missing?
Was the Eiderbach suicide really a suicide?
Why was a right wing group out after Habermann, Eiderbach, and Dolfin?
Who was Dolfin, and where is she now?

Monday morning, clear and crisp. By afternoon, clouds would fill the sky and rain would pour down, but right now the birds ate their breakfast and insects scattered in full flight. Sara woke early, and was relaxing with a crossword puzzle when her telephone rang. Her grandmother again. With a reminder her mother would be celebrating her fiftieth birthday next week, and she would need a ride to the party.

"Shit. The party," Sara said, more to herself than to her grandmother. Her grandmother chided her on her language, but Sara wasn't listening. She was already making notes about organizing her mother's birthday party.

Sara threw the newspaper into the shopping bag she always carried to work and put on her jacket. The page with her questions from the evening before was still lying on the kitchen table when she left, but it didn't matter. Her photographic memory had already done its work. She put on her shoes and jacket and locked her door as she left for work.

Sara caught Robert Johnson as soon as he entered the coffee room at headquarters.

"Robert, I looked through the effects of Nurse Eiderbach on Friday. There's mention of a medallion in the Medical Examiner's report, but I can't find it among the things you brought back." She handed him the report.

"Medallion?" He flushed red through his tan as he glanced at the report of the contents of Eiderbach's purse. He stammered as he explained he hadn't noticed this before. "I'll—I'll go to the Medical Examiner at once. Someone must have taken it."

"Good," said Sara, sipping from her tea mug as she studied his face. "While you're at it, talk to the ME. Ask him if he knows where it's gone. And what about the video tapes from the Old Town? Have they arrived yet?"

"They're supposed to come in during the day," said Robert.

"We'll look at them then. The ME's office first. I'm going to talk to people myself, and I'll see you after lunch."

Robert drove quickly back to his apartment. He put on his uniform and took the medallion from inside his closet, then drove to the Medical Examiner in Solna. He waited until he found a cleaning woman swabbing a floor near the cold room of the morgue. He watched as she methodically mopped each section of floor, carefully avoiding the feet of other employees as they passed by. When her back turned to the scrub-bucket, he let the medallion plop to the tip of his shoe. He shook off his shoe under a chair in plain view, just a few meters from where she would soon be swabbing, then backed off.

Robert watched her find the medallion, saw the furtive look on her face change to a frown when she noticed him in his uniform. She picked it up and walked to the duty office. Her glance returned to Robert one more time, then she handed over the medallion to the woman on duty, pointing in the direction of the chair.

Robert waited for the cleaning woman to disappear, then reached the woman who ran the duty office while she was sealing the medallion in an envelope marked 'Found Evidence'. He told her he was inquiring about a medallion which might have been found on the second floor.

The envelope with the medallion was on the table in the Habermann room that afternoon. Robert Johnson was relieved he could erase his mistake so easily. He was used to covering his ass and he reveled at his creativity.

Chapter 5

Sara turned her car toward Solna and the hospital. A question cropped up in her mind, and she wove through the back streets to the office of the Medical Examiner. She saw Robert's car disappear as she turned into the parking lot.

The Medical Examiner sat slumped behind his desk.

"It's about the woman who died in the Old City," Sara asked, "I was wondering if there was any evidence that might indicate something other than suicide."

"I won't be able to tell you more than what is already in the report. The woman died of a massive loss of blood. Everything points to her being run over by a train. I found no trace of drugs or alcohol, and nothing to suggest a long-term debilitating illness. She was healthy." He looked up from his notes. "I'm afraid that's all there is."

Sara glanced around the ME's office. It was drab, with light-gray paint chipped off here and there, feebly covering thirty years of attempted repairs. She tried with another question.

"Do you think there's anything to indicate a third party? Anything at all?"

"Like what, for example?"

"Any sign she was pushed?"

"That wouldn't show up in an autopsy. There was no mysterious cause of death to warrant more than a quick examination of the body and an ID check. I think we did a blood sample, and someone took her fingerprints." He paged through the file in his hands. "Yes. That's it."

"And the medallion? I'm sure my colleague already asked you about it, but there was a medallion logged in on your report and we can't find it."

"What? I'm sorry, I don't know what you're talking about. I remember the medallion. Very strange thing for an old woman to carry around in her purse. I put it in the evidence box as usual. Your colleague hasn't arrived yet."

Next on her list: Karolinska Hospital. Dr. Bergman's office was a small but pleasant enclosure, glassed in on three sides with a window overlooking a small park. The late afternoon sun lingered at the horizon in Stockholm's beautiful summer sky.

"You said you wish to speak to me about a previous employee who has had some sort of, uh, accident or trouble," he said while Sara took a seat opposite his desk. "I'll tell you what I can remember of this woman, Miss Eiderbach, but it was a long time ago. The records have all been removed to the National Archive."

Sara nodded and withdrew her notebook and pen from her purse, and began taking notes.

"Well, I came to the hospital in 1962, and Miss Eiderbach was already part of the staff. She always worked alone, and had responsibility for a single patient the whole time: a woman. I don't know what happened before I came, but that's the way it was while I was there."

"Do you remember anything about her?" Sara looked up from her notebook, her pen poised.

"Miss Eiderbach never took part in any of the courses we held, never mixed with any of the other nurses, never went to any of the parties we had. Just a loner, I guess you would call her. She was 100 percent conscientious, was never late to work that I know of, and I don't think she was ever out ill. She was one of those 'private' nurses, who took care of a private patient, you know."

"A private patient?"

"Yes, I know it sounds a bit strange for Sweden, but it happens sometimes. The care of some patients is paid for by outsiders, we never really know who or how. They just show up in an ambulance or a taxi with a letter from some high government official. Admin checks them into our system and then we take care of them like all the others, unless they have their own staff, of course."

"Was there a doctor assigned to Miss Eiderbach's patient?" Sara's hand tightened up on the pen as she waited for the answer.

"I'm sure there was. Stolpe. I think his name was Dr. Göran Stolpe. Much like Miss Eiderbach. Kept to himself. He thought we were rather primitive up here."

"Up here?"

"Yes. In spite of his name—I think he must have changed it at some point—an unmistakable German accent. Or Austrian. Somewhere down there. Miss Eiderbach was from there too."

"And the patient?" Sara's hands began to perspire, and small patches of moisture mixed with the ink on her notepad. "Can you remember her name?"

"Oh, we never know their names. They have numbers. Room numbers for us on the staff, person numbers for the administration. I never had anything to do with her so I can't even tell you which room she was in."

Dr. Bergman looked at his watch. "Are we done here? I have an important staff meeting to prepare for. Can you find your way out alone?"

Sara returned her notepad to her purse. She spun around in the doorway and tried one final question. "And if you did know what room she was in, would that help you if you wanted to know her name and what happened to her?"

Dr. Bergman was already concentrating on the fishing he was going to do in just a few hours. "I really don't know. There was a ledger: a journal where the patients' details were noted when they arrived. If you could find that, it would contain all the details of the patient: personal identification number, parents, who to call in case of an emergency. Admin always wrote the room number on this ledger once they had been assigned a room so staff could match them up if needed. It would take a while to find because it was all done manually. This was done in B.C.—you know, Before Computers. Anyway, all the records were sent to the National Archive when the hospital closed. Everything will be there, if you can find it."

Sara joined Sven back at headquarters. It was late afternoon, nearly time to end the workday. They both entered the Habermann room. Sara saw the envelope lying on the desk. She opened it, removed the medallion, and handed it to Sven as she said, "This was found in Anna Eiderbach's purse. She died in the Central Train Station last Tuesday. A probable suicide, according to the ME's Report."

Sven's eyes opened wide and his head angled backward in surprise. He took the medallion and held it close to his eyes. It was ring-shaped, about an inch in diameter with a swastika in the center. He tossed it twice in the air.

"Heavy. Feels like gold." He squinted, held the medallion up to the light and read out loud the inscription stamped on the outside edge of the ring. "*Eva und Dolfin, in Liebe Wolf*—Eva and Dolfin, with love, Wolf. So our suicide victim was from Germany. We already knew that, but who's this Eva woman?"

Sara shrugged her shoulders.

"And what were Nazis doing working at a Swedish mental hospital?" asked Sven.

Sara shook her head.

"This Dolfin person must be the same Dolfin the NSS talked about. The one on the hit list," said Sven. "But Wolf? Who's he?"

Sara wrote the text of the inscription on the outside of the envelope. "If it's the same Dolfin as the woman on the hit list, then it's no coincidence the medallion was in the purse of the woman who died. The NSS told us Eiderbach was Dolfin's nurse, and I confirmed that today. Maybe it wasn't a suicide. She was on the hit list too. Maybe someone just did a good job of getting rid of her," said Sara.

Sven joined in, "Eiderbach's first name was Anna, so we can probably assume the medallion didn't belong to her. She could have been holding it for the Dolfin woman."

"Perhaps." Sara nodded her head as thoughts tore through her mind. "Or maybe the Eiderbach woman knew a Nazi from her past life in Germany. She could have stolen it."

This time it was Sven's turn to shake his head. Sara continued, "And the name, Wolf, could this be Habermann? Let's have another chat with the NSS."

She chose to keep her question about where the medallion had been for the past few hours until she had a chance to talk to Robert. Sara placed the medallion back in the envelope. When she raised her eyes, she saw Sven's back as he left the room.

Beside the envelope holding the medallion she noticed a box with video tapes. A note from the Stockholm Regional Authority gave the police the right to look at them. The tapes could not be used as criminal evidence without the permission of every single person caught in the images. A pack of five CD's from the NSS lay behind the box. They were dated, one for each day, from the day of Habermann's killing backwards. A wry smile formed as she read a note attached reminding her the surveillance videos could not be used as evidence to convict anyone for a killing, but they might help her collect information from other sources.

Sara placed the first Webcam CD from the NSS into the player and waited impatiently for the images to appear on the widescreen monitor on the wall. She did a fast forward until she saw a taxi stop in front of Habermann's door. The license number of the car matched the burned out vehicle found near the Habermann crime scene, but the camera angle blocked any useful view of the driver of the taxi. Sara saw that the Taxi sign on the roof was removable.

This car will never show up in the register of vehicles licensed for use as taxis, she thought.

She backed the CD and leaned forward. She froze the presentation to one frame at a time when she saw Habermann exit his apartment, limping as he carried his suitcase. The driver, head down, placed the suitcase in the trunk as Habermann got in.

Sara tried one of the videos from a camera placed near an ATM one block away, but it was too grainy to provide any identifiable pictures of the taxi driver. She rolled it back to the day before.

She stared as she saw a car shoot down the pedestrian street, then observed a man limping back to enter the door to Habermann's apartment only minutes later. She returned to the NSS video files for that same day, and watched the high-resolution image of Habermann limp up the street, glancing behind him even as he unlocked the door. *He knew he was a target. I wonder where he was trying to go?*

Sara spoke with the group investigating the crazy person who had tried to run people down in the Old Town the same day Anna Eiderbach was killed. They showed her several videos of the event. She noticed Habermann swing his body up away from the speeding car, just managing to survive. Sara went into Sven's room with the tapes, and she showed him what she had found.

"There's something strange about your case," said Sven as he rewound the tape.

"Only one thing?" asked Sara.

Sven turned to her. "It looks like Habermann had two murderers, one who succeeded and one who didn't. The first assassin tried to make it appear to be an accident, but failed to kill him. The second seems to want us to find the victim of the murder and led us directly to where Habermann lived."

Sara stroked her forehead. "I wonder what happened to the driver of the car which missed Habermann." She logged onto Sven's computer and searched for the Old Town accident file.

"A witness reported that the driver was injured in the crash against the wall just after missing Habermann," she continued, "He was saved by the airbag and seat belt, so he wasn't injured too badly. The police took him to the hospital after a little first aid."

"Let's call them," said Sven.

The driver had been released from the acute center only hours after meeting with a doctor. An appointment for his return was recorded for the next day, but he never showed up.

"Are you surprised?" asked Sara. Sven shook his head and called the liaison officer at the NSS for a meeting in the afternoon of the following day. Sara phoned forensics and asked for a search of Anna Eiderbach's apartment the next morning.

She returned to her office and logged into Europol on her computer. She accessed the databases and tried several combinations of last names, looking for some kind of background information. She entered *Habermann, Habermann-Germany, Habermann-Austria, Habermann-Nazi*, all without any kind of response.

She encountered no criminal files in Sweden on Habermann. When she expanded the search to Germany, she retrieved only recent criminal records of a small-time car thief, incarcerated as an eighteen-year-old for six months and then released. The same combinations using Anna Eiderbach led to no hits at all. Anna Eiderbach was non-existent as a criminal in any country. When Sara tried to examine Stolpe's file in the enormous database covering every inhabitant in the entire country, she noticed several important fields held no data. The only birthplace noted in the database was the country, Germany. *Maybe the tax authorities weren't too careful with foreigners at the time he entered Sweden*, she thought, even though she suspected this wasn't true.

She found the same unusual pattern in the background files on Anna Eiderbach, whose person number provided only her birth date and country of birth, Germany.

Sara logged off and locked her office. On her way out she stopped in front of the Habermann room and unlocked the door. She removed the key to Anna Eiderbach's apartment from the evidence box and put it in her purse. *I'll have a look at the apartment on my way home*, she thought as she left the building.

Her Internet searches sped through cyberspace, weaving their way through the nooks and crannies of the world wide web. On a U.S. Army computer in Heidelberg, Germany, one little sniffer program patiently waited to capture Sara's queries.

Sara put on her rubber gloves before pushing the doorbell button or touching the door handle at Anna Eiderbach's apartment. She stood on the second floor of an apartment house located on Fruäng Street 1, only a short walk from the center of this suburban village. She planned a quick look to satisfy her curiosity and then go home. Sara pushed the doorbell and waited before she put the key in the lock and opened the door.

"It's the police," Sara's shout echoed in the stairwell behind her.

The apartment was quiet. A single flyer lay on the floor, advertising a sale at a local food market. Sara stepped over it carefully and walked through the hall.

The apartment belonged to a cooperative where only a minimum of capital and monthly payments was required to purchase a lease. There was only one catch. Those who wished to move out could only sell back to the cooperative, and at the same price they had paid to get in. The idea was to short-circuit the tendency for people to use their living quarters as a capital investment, and it fit well into the socialistic paradigm of Swedish wellbeing.

Signs of a single modernization told Sara that few improvements had been made since it had been built in the 1950s. The beige wallpaper with orange medallions told her it had been done some time in the seventies. *You were a very neat housekeeper, Miss Eiderbach. Much better than me. And no animals popping out looking for food.*

She always felt sorry for animals when people died. Sometimes discovery did not come until weeks had gone by and the poor creatures had either resorted to cannibalism or tearing apart cupboards in search of something to eat.

Anna Eiderbach had cleaned her kitchen before departing. A small plastic bag under the sink contained the residue of her breakfast for that day: coffee grounds, and the wrapping from a package of cheese.

Sara opened the refrigerator. Inside she found nothing out of the ordinary, and certainly nothing to make her think the Eiderbach woman had committed suicide. Sara knew many suicide victims prepared for their demise by doing a final cleaning, removing any food which might spoil. This refrigerator had several plastic boxes filled with left-over food, a carton of still drinkable milk, even a carton of eggs which wouldn't spoil for another two weeks. A bottle of German brandy was in the door, half-empty.

She continued through to the sitting room. No newspapers cluttered the coffee table, as were to be found in her own apartment. Black-and-white photographs hung on the walls: snow-covered mountains, a close-up of a rose in full bloom, and a wolf, standing proudly over a dead rabbit.

A book on German churches and a book about the Second World War caught her eye. Sara noticed a thin layer of dust covered both. There was only one window in the sitting room, and when she opened the venetian blinds, the room flooded with light and provided a view of a gourmet restaurant across the street, a building previously part of Långbro Hospital before it closed.

Sara peered into the bathroom, but saw nothing out of the ordinary: soap, shampoo, a toothbrush, and everything else a single woman would have. She began to compare it to her own apartment and noticed there were a few similarities.

Sara saw a woman who had no wish to construct a complicated, elaborate nest. She stood in the home of an inhabitant who left few clues to divulge her true personality; a woman who carried most of her secrets in her mind and heart. She found none of the untidiness she had seen where her friends lived. Those people lived their lives so intensely they had no time to pick their clothes up from the floor.

Continuing into the bedroom, Sara found the bed made, a quilted bedspread neatly folded over the corners. Anna Eiderbach's bed was narrow, with room for only one person.

Sara knelt down to open the drawer of the nightstand, and removed the only personal item seen in the apartment so far. It was an old black-and-white photograph.

There were seven children laughing into the camera, mostly girls. To the right, one of the young boys was dressed in shorts and a shirt with a swastika patch on his right arm. His jaw jutted upward, and his right arm stretched proudly to the sky in a Nazi salute. In the background, Sara noticed the unmistakable profile of Adolf Hitler gesturing to a uniformed man. The photo was in a wide, ornate silver frame, and it glistened as Sara returned it to the drawer. *Hmmm. Recently polished.*

Chapter 6

A red-blinking alarm flashed on Captain Charles Peters's computer monitor. He sat at his desk at the Heidelberg office of the U.S. Army's Criminal Investigation Command, the CID. Hurtree's sniffer program had provided Sara's Google search profiles.

At the bottom of the report, Capt. Peters noted Sara's IP address and the street address of the building where the server was located. At the same time, an email from Europol arrived with information on the databases Sara's search profile had tried to access, including the search words she'd used. It detailed her name, rank, and office, including her cell phone number. Capt. Peters reread the alarm and dialed John Hurtree's number in Philadelphia.

"Hi, John, it's Charlie in Heidelberg," he said, "how've you been?"

"As well as can be expected. What makes you call? I thought you'd gone and died after that shoot-out in Munich."

"Too ornery to die, I guess. I'm calling because I just got a mail from Europol that shows that someone in Sweden has been searching for the same names you put there before you went into retirement. She was even googling the same profile. I can't get involved in this because there never really was a case to investigate, if you know what I mean. You can't get involved either. You're a civilian now and should be chasing gray panthers instead. Still, I thought you might want to know."

"Charlie, I've never been able to drop that mystery, ever. It might be only a random search or an error, but I'll take that chance just to be able to wake up without unanswered questions one morning every week. Tell me more."

Hurtree listened as Peters read the alarm information from the sniffer report and the Europol email. He was making notes, and asked several times for certain information to be repeated.

"OK, Charlie, you got me," said Hurtree. "What happens next?"

"Sorry, John, there's nothing I can do. We're up to our butts right now. I've got six cases of suspected terrorists within the Army. If anything gets done, you'll have to do it on your own."

"Things have definitely changed since you took over." Hurtree chuckled. "You can tell the guys at Ramstein I'll be visiting them. Do you know who I should talk to?"

"You'll only have access to Ramstein Air Force Base as a civilian visitor, sorry."

"Is Horrible Helga still working at German Customs? I'll call you if she won't let me in." Peters grumbled something inaudible into the telephone, and Hurtree continued, "Retirement is killing me, Charlie. Yesterday I paid for my groceries and left them at the shopping center. This'll be like getting back to work, and that feels really good."

Hurtree began packing his suitcase as soon as the telephone hit the cradle. Before leaving for Europe, Hurtree walked to the park to watch the sun go down over the Delaware River.

He traversed the red brick middle class residences on Lombard Street and turned onto Front Street and crossed over the Expressway on Spruce Street, dodging paper and garbage blowing across the highway in the afternoon wind. He entered the park and made his way to a view of the river in time to see the sun being reflected on windows from a bank on the other side.

The bank became a bronze pillar in the afternoon sun, and beyond that lay Europe. He paced back and forth for a few minutes while the sun set. Lights began to illuminate the New Jersey side of the river. He had felt the same excitement the first time he had left for Europe, only then he was worried he might never survive.

This time, Hurtree only cared about surviving long enough to come home to burn his notebook collection. He would be satisfied with an answer to the question plaguing his mind for thirty years. He watched a 747 disappear in the distance. Mosquitoes buzzed around his head as he made his way back toward his apartment.

"Habermann, I'm finally gonna get you," he muttered, and his thoughts returned to the image of the child in the photograph. *I wonder if she's still alive.*

When Sara arrived at Police Headquarters the following day, she went to Robert's office. He hadn't come in yet, but it was still early. She examined the surface of his desk and noticed the corner of a pink requisition form peeking out from under a stack of forms. She lifted the pile of papers and saw the form for a video surveillance camera mounted close to the taxi stand down the street from Habermann's apartment. *Is this a mistake?* The mysterious disappearance of the medallion still puzzled her.

As she went back to her office, she was greeted by a dour Sven Peterson. His voice was short. "Sara, are you having trouble with Robert? He complained about you yesterday. Said you were using him to investigate suicide victims instead of concentrating on the Habermann case."

"I sent him to collect evidence on a suspected suicide, yes. That's how we found out about Anna Eiderbach's death. And the medallion. I couldn't fill him in on why it was important without revealing what the NSS had told us. He complained?"

"He said he would have done it differently," remarked Sven.

A surge of adrenaline began to flow through her veins. She narrowed her eyes. "I think he wants to be the lead investigator."

Sven shrugged.

Sara continued, "We need more background information about Anna Eiderbach. I checked the criminal records yesterday and she's not there. There's very little in the national personal database."

Sven hesitated a minute, then made Sara feel like a beginning student at the Police Academy. "There's no reason to assume Eiderbach's death was anything other than a suicide. Sure, the

NSS told us there was a death threat, but so far we haven't found anything to suggest a connection to the Habermann murder case. Keep it simple, Sara. There's no reason for you to get involved in the Eiderbach death yet."

"I think they're connected," said Sara. "It's no coincidence she dies on Tuesday and there's an attempt on Habermann's life the same day. Was her death really a suicide? The first attempt on Habermann was set up to look like an accident, you said so yourself. Anyway, it can't hurt if I just test different theories against each other. You know, trying to help Robert." Her eyes gleamed with sarcasm.

Sven was impressed by her perseverance and ability to think outside the box. He promised himself to remember this moment when it came to discussions about wages during her evaluation in a few months, then said, "OK. Have forensics check out Eiderbach's apartment, and then you can look at the records from the hospital where she worked. The NSS said both she and Habermann worked at Långbro Hospital. They closed that place years ago. I'd expect all the records to have been moved to the National Archive. So bury yourself in dust and see what you can find. Don't forget we've got a meeting with the NSS this afternoon. I think we're going to have to expand the group, if I can."

Sven waited until Sara left his office, then made a phone call to the Security Department of Stockholm Public Transport. He asked for the video tapes from T-Centralen covering the train jumper who committed suicide a few days ago. He was looking for the sequence just before Eiderbach landed in front of the train.

Sara went back down the corridor to find Robert drinking a cup of coffee and reading the news on his computer monitor. She stood next to his desk without saying anything. It took him a few seconds to react, first sitting up straight, and then standing up, almost at attention.

"Good morning," he said, his eyes darting back and forth. "I was just checking to see if there was any news about our case in the newspapers."

"I have a couple of questions, Robert." Sara's voice was slightly louder than necessary. "I want to know what happened at the ME's office. How did the medallion suddenly find its way onto the desk in the Habermann room?"

"It was in Lost Evidence." Robert looked away into the hall. "It must have fallen on the floor at some point and been picked up by one of the cleaners. Anyway, we got it back, that's the important part."

"You've made a mistake we can't make. You collected evidence material without checking off the contents of the box before leaving the ME's Office. You'll be more observant in the future." Sara waited for the words to sink in, and continued, "And I hope you clear off some of the papers on your desk. It looks to me as if one of the requisitions for the video tapes we need for the Habermann case is still on your desk."

Robert's ears flushed bright red with embarrassment. He had a hard time speaking, but managed finally to find a few words. "I—I've been really busy. That form must have been buried by all this other stuff. I'll get it off to the Regional Authority today, carry it up there myself and see if I can get the tape back with me."

Sara left him standing holding the pink form as she turned to go back to her office. "I'm planning on expanding the team. You'll meet the rest of them later," she said, speaking over her shoulder. She left for Anna Eiderbach's apartment to meet with the forensic team. She arrived just before they did and gave them the key she still had in her purse.

For Sara Markham, being a policewoman was a profession she had secretly aspired to from the early days of her childhood. It began at the day care center where her mother had left her before going to her job at the office.

One of the young childminders who worked there had assembled all the children in a ring and lit a candle as they all sat, hand-in-hand, listening to the vast void of silence. It was at the beginning of the seventies and the new-found revolution of make-it-happen pills and love-the-one-you're-with music.

The children sat silently, listening intently for the hum of the Universe. Young Sara squinted through half-open eyes and saw a little girl across the circle throw a pair of scissors she'd been holding in her hand with as much force as her five-year-old body could muster. They flew right at Sara's head and she ducked, the scissors bouncing harmlessly off the wall behind her.

"Now then, Sara," the young caretaker said, "be nice to Jasmine and she won't do it again."

Sara had done nothing to Jasmine or anyone else at the nursery. She was aware, even at that young age, that the responsibility for the attack had been shifted from the attacker to the victim. The attack shaped an early wish to be able to deal with the violence hidden under the surface of the nearly perfect environment researchers usually described when writing about Sweden in international journals.

For Sara, growing up required finding the balance of avoiding situations where human nature was sometimes given wild opportunities to express its darker side, and to find those times when she could take in the knowledge she knew was available and would need in the future.

As she grew older and began school, she observed how victims were made out to be the guilty parties. It was the victims of the bullies who were moved to another school, not the bullies. Sara always sided with those weaker students who couldn't fend for themselves. Her choice of profession became clearer and clearer.

"I'm gonna be a cop," she said when asked in the second grade. It was the last time she publicly told anyone about her plans. She was severely bullied after that; even her teacher took part.

When the videos from the train station arrived, Sven went to the reception to collect them and hurried into his office. He found the video of the platform at the time of Anna's death, and after only one sweep he noticed the man in the black baseball cap following Anna Eiderbach. He was muscular, filling out his gray sweatshirt and black pants; a well-trained young man, probably in his early thirties.

Sven's stomach tightened as he observed the man place himself just behind his target, the bill of his cap swiveling from side to side. Sven saw the man inch closer to the white haired woman in the polka dot dress as the wind from the train ruffled her hair. The train rushed into view on the left of the screen, and Sven saw the man suddenly become shorter for only a second, his knees breaking her stance, causing her to tip forward. Sven flinched as he observed the shove pushing her body in front of the train. She fell forward, arms outstretched, her purse flying against the window of the open-mouthed driver.

Sven froze the action to one frame at a time to see the man move backwards. The killer's face was still not visible to the cameras as he hurried off toward the exit, keeping his head low at all times.

"This was a professional hit," muttered Sven to himself. "What's going on here? She was over eighty years old, for Chrissake."

Sara and Sven had lunch together before their meeting with the NSS. They could choose between two main courses each day, guaranteed to be healthy, nourishing, and tasty. The police at headquarters shared the same menu as the prisoners in the holding cells. There had been newspaper articles about the cost of food for the prisoners, comparing it to the food served at the country's schools. The prisoners won. Their food cost more than ten times the average lunch for the pupils.

Sven was the first to speak as they settled into their chairs at the station restaurant. "You were right. We have two murders to deal with. The Eiderbach death was definitely a professional hit, and Habermann had two attempts on his life, one which failed and the other that worked. That should interest the boys in black."

"Yes," said Sara, trying to conceal her smile, "I wonder what they'll say when we bring up Eiderbach as a murder victim."

"They'll probably just stare us down like they usually do, as if they knew all the time, which they might have. I wonder if the NSS is involved in this in any way," said Sven.

"What, in the killings? The NSS?" Sara looked at Sven over her plate. "This is Sweden, Sven. Sure, our guys can get a little out of hand occasionally, but isn't murder off-limits? At least that's what they said at the Police Academy."

Sven dropped his glance to the tray in front of him. "They wouldn't tell us if we asked," then he looked her in the eye. "We have to make a list of the questions we have to see if they can help. They did send the CDs from the Webcam in front of Habermann's apartment, even though we can't use them for evidence. And they were helpful. The car found torched near the viaduct is the car used to pick up Habermann on the day he was shot. That's something, anyway. Did you learn anything at Eiderbach's apartment?"

"Yes, a lot." Sara went through the report she had already memorized. "She lived in a one bedroom apartment just across from the hospital park where she had worked before. A very meticulous woman, neat and tidy. No pets, no indications of other friends. No newspapers or letters. Nothing to connect her to anything except a photograph I found in her night stand. She had a picture of some kids with Hitler in the background in a silver frame. Not that strange since the NSS told us both she and Habermann were Nazi implants. Things like swastika medallions and pictures of Hitler would seem to fit. What puzzles me is the NSS said the threat came from an extreme right wing group. That part is weird for me. What do you suppose it means?"

"Let's put that question high up on our list for the meeting," said Sven. "Did you ever get anything more from your Europol search on Habermann?"

"The only hit I got was a kid who stole a car in Munich last year," said Sara. "I was hoping to see something a little older than that."

She was about to get her wish fulfilled.

Chapter 7

John Hurtree threw his hand luggage onto the back seat of the taxi and called out his destination. His wallet bulged with several packs of traveler's checks in Euros and Swedish Kroner, the withdrawal nearly wiping out his bank account. Hurtree figured this would be his last vacation; at least, the last one he would enjoy. The excitement of the trip in front of him had made it hard to sleep, and he yawned as the taxi made its way to the airport.

First he'd fly to Germany to visit with Captain Peters, then take a flight to Stockholm, arriving on Friday morning. He hoped Peters could give him some pointers on how to spend the weekend in Stockholm. While looking for his passport, he'd found a box with some mementos of his time in Europe: some faded brochures of the Bavarian Alps and several tickets to the Hofbräu Haus in Munich where the October Beer Festival ended every year. He wondered if things had changed since his retirement, and then wondered just how much. Of course things had changed. He had changed, why wouldn't the world around him change?

Hurtree was returning to where he had become a man; where he grew from being a kid with pimples to an officer in the Army. He was once someone who commanded respect, and now he could be that person again. *I've been living my life under a jar. Where have my feelings been all this time?* His life in Philadelphia was an exercise in marking time, marching in place while he waited for his life to end. Hurtree wondered why he hadn't returned years ago, and he couldn't wait to get to Stockholm. *Finally, a chance to leave something behind me. A chance to say, "I was here"*.

*

Sven and Sara walked around the block to the unassuming entrance to the National Security Service, and passed through the security gate one at a time. They were ushered into a conference room. The young officer looked at his watch and adjusted his glasses while Sara and Sven took their seats.

He spoke with the slow near-Danish drawl from Skåne, Sweden's southernmost region. "I've been told to divulge historical details about the Iron Guard. I assume you know what you learn here is not to leave this room." The officer raised his eyes, waited until both Sven and Sara nodded, and then continued, "The Swedish Iron Guard in Stockholm is one of the oldest Neo-Nazi cells existing." The officer flipped open one of the binders in front of him to a page marked with a paper clip. "The whole thing was set up by the station chief for the German Secret Police, soon after he'd opened the Stockholm office in the early fifties. He used the name of the Romanian organization, the one which had helped the Nazis exterminate Romanian Jews during the war.

"The Iron Guard worked across all existing political party lines, and survived regardless of who was in political power wherever it set up shop. There have even been some who say the Iron Guard holds the key to political power here, and that our elections are just window-dressing to maintain the appearance of democratic rule. That's bullshit, of course." The officer blushed when he realized how unprofessional his addition sounded, then he continued, "What we do know is many key political questions are discussed internally in the Iron Guard before they become labor union policy."

"Wait. How do you know that?" Sara widened her eyes, surprised that surveillance on the group was so broad. "How could such a group get that much power in Sweden?"

The officer chose to ignore her questions. "Many of the members work for security companies, and there are even those who are members of the police corps."

The NSS officer abruptly stopped his description and looked

up from his notes, waiting for a reaction, but both Sara and Sven stared at him in silence. He cleared his throat and took a sip of water from a plastic bottle beside his notes.

"In 1949 the CIA recruited the man who had started the Iron Guard in order to gain access to the so-called Gehlen Network."

Sara interrupted him before he could begin the next sentence. "Stop for a minute. This all sounds sinister, but I still don't see what this has to do with our murders. If our politicians, our labor unions, and maybe even our own corps are infiltrated, that's serious, but how did it get these two people killed? And how did you guys manage to intercept a message from a group like that?" she asked.

The officer clamped his jaws together.

"OK, wrong question." She leaned forward across the desk. "What I don't understand is why a group like the Iron Guard would want to assassinate Nazi implants. It seems so unnecessary. Why didn't it simply tell them to leave if it wanted them to stop whatever it was they were doing? And the victims were both so old. Why didn't it just wait for them to die of natural causes?"

The officer leaned back in his chair. "I read history at Lund's University. I'm an historian here at the NSS, so I don't speculate on matters like that. From what I've heard, we know very little about the three people mentioned in the message. We were hoping you could provide us with a few more details found during your investigations."

Sara summarized their findings. She reported on the video from T-Centralen, and that Eiderbach was now a murder victim. She finished by mentioning the medallion. The officer put down his pen and looked up from his notes for a moment.

"Sorry," he said, "did you say Eiderbach had a medallion? A swastika medallion?"

"Yes, quite small. Nothing special, except that it's a swastika."

"That would be very unusual. There were a few thousand of those made, but Hitler usually gave them out himself as a sort of personal reward. His own version of the Iron Cross, which is given out by the German Army. Could you fax me a copy of it?"

"Sure," said Sara, "I'll get it to you today."

Sara and Sven left the NSS wing and returned to Homicide.

"Have you ever heard of this Iron Guard?" she asked when they were inside the building.

"Not exactly," said Sven. "I knew there were groups out there, all kinds of people who like to associate with Hitler cults. Usually just young kids, skinheads. Those sort of people. But a group which could actually arrange an assassination? That's a new one. I wonder if we'll ever catch this killer. Or killers."

"Don't wonder. I'm going to do it," Sara said with decision in her voice.

"No wonder they call you the Terrier. OK, you continue with the Habermann case," said Sven, "I'll run the Eiderbach case, and we'll co-ordinate results. We have to find out if there was one killer or more. We also have to find out if they're still around. I've asked for some more help. You've got Robert, is that enough?"

"I don't think so," said Sara as she looked at the floor. "I don't really know where I have him yet. Sometimes he does good work, other times he seems to be a little sloppy. One more would help if we can get it."

Sven called everyone into his office during the afternoon coffee break. Eiderbach's name was already on the whiteboard, along with her age and occupation, and the words, 'When? Where? Who? How? Why?'

The team, including Andersson and Berg, the two new members from Violent Crimes, entered his room, still sipping coffee from their FBI mugs, gifts from the seminars hosted by the FBI to help train them in the latest techniques. They stood up in Sven's room, which was too small for so many chairs. They watched the video of Eiderbach's murder in silence. When it was over, Sven switched off the video.

"Andersson, make a copy of this video and use the techies downstairs to make blow-ups of the faces and clothes of every single individual on the platform during the murder. Visit the platform at the time of the murder every day until you have identified and talked to everyone in this video. Somebody must have seen something."

Sven gave each member of the team a task. He turned to Robert Johnson, and said, "We have a video of the killer during the murder, maybe we can find out where he went. There must be other video cameras in the area. See if he met someone else, or if he got into a car or bus or walked away. You and Berg, get over to T-Centralen and start collecting videos from the shops nearby. Identify any potential witnesses."

Sven looked over at Sara, then said, "We have a video of him doing the murder. You and Andersson can try to find out where he came from. All we see here is him standing on the platform. Maybe he got there in a car or another train. Let's try to track him back to where he lives."

"Thank you for our surveillance society, Uncle Sweden," said Sara with a low voice.

The team stood there, trying to think of something else which would make itself apparent from the brief information they had. Sven stared at them for a second, and then shouted, "So, what are we waiting for? We're already on a trail that's a week old. Report back in tomorrow morning at eight sharp." And the team left him standing alone in his office.

Everyone except Robert was waiting at 8 a.m. in Sven's office the next day. Sven's "You're late" turned to a smile and nods as Robert played back the video of the murderer leaving the station area, his back to the camera. Robert finished by reporting that the murderer just seemed to disappear without a trace once outside the station, and couldn't be found on any other tapes.

Sara and Andersson hadn't found the murderer on any tapes

prior to the murder, so her report was the shortest of all. She kept looking at Robert during her entire presentation.

"The camera covering the stairwell right beside where Eiderbach was pushed has been out of order for two weeks now. He could have come on a train from a lower level. I checked all the cameras, but he can't be found."

Andersson made a quick report about how much the techies downstairs had helped to produce the file with pictures of all the potential witnesses singled out. He said he'd begun to interview everyone he could find on the platform, and had even posted a note on the pillars of the station platform, asking anyone who was there to come forward.

When the team left his office, Sven sat down with his head in his hands, and closed his eyes. Details of the daily reports swam in front of his eyes. He heard a knock on his door, and looked up to see Sara enter.

"I forgot something," she said. "Can I sit down?"

"Sure," said Sven, "what's up?"

"You assigned me to look at the tapes leading up to the murder, so anything happening after really wasn't my job…" Her voice trailed off.

"Yes?" asked Sven, irritation mounting in his voice.

"Since I couldn't find our murderer in the time slot I was assigned to, I spent a little extra time looking at the tapes after the murder."

"Yes?" The irritation was now apparent. "You know I hate backbiting. Get to the point."

"Well," Sara began cautiously, "I saw the murderer leave the scene, just like Robert said. But I also saw him get into a cab and watched it drive away."

"What? But why didn't you say something at the meeting? Obviously this is something that affects the whole investigation."

"I—I'm sorry. I just didn't want to criticize Robert's work again, especially in front of the team. I was so surprised he didn't report what I'd seen I didn't know what to do. I mean, it wasn't my job. I didn't mean to do anything wrong."

Sven shifted his gaze beyond Sara. He'd heard only good things about Robert from other group leaders. It seemed unlike him to make such a blunder.

"Everyone can make a mistake," said Sven, then pensively, "Leave this with me, Sara. Do some background checking on our victim, Anna Eiderbach. Get as much detail as you can. We need to know who she was before we can figure out why anyone would want to kill her. Do we know anything about the other woman? The one named Dolphin?"

"I'm going to the National Archive tomorrow. If there are records there, I'll find them." Sara left his office.

Sven took the copy of the video she had given him showing the exterior of the station area. With dismay in his heart, he watched as the murderer got into a taxi which had been waiting at the curb, just outside the taxi queue. He noted the license number, the name of the taxi company, and their telephone number. He focused on the frame where the murderer stretched his hand to open the door. A poorly defined dark spot on the killer's arm caught Sven's attention. *That's a tattoo*, mused Sven. *Forensics will enhance that for me.* He rewound the video and placed it back on the pile.

"How could Robert miss that?"

Chapter 8

Hurtree showed his passport at the Customs window at Mannheim Airport. He recognized the Customs officer, who stared at him, then looked again at his picture on the passport.

"And why are you coming to Germany?" Horrible Helga asked.

"A vacation." Hurtree tried to put a tourist's smile on his face.

"And how long will that be?"

"I suppose about three weeks."

"And do you have a return ticket?"

"Yes." Hurtree withdrew his ticket from his breast pocket.

"You will show it to me." She studied Hurtree's return ticket in minute detail.

Very thorough, as usual. Hurtree turned to smile at the irritated travelers behind him.

"You may enter the EU for a period not to exceed three weeks," she said, and stamped his passport with a wallop which must have left an impression on every page, "and you may not work while you are here."

"I'm on vacation." Hurtree tried his best to sound civil.

"And you may not access the social services or hospitals during your visit," she said, withholding his passport and ticket until Hurtree looked up at her. "You will have to use your own private insurance for any medical emergencies," she continued, sliding his passport through the small opening in the glass window, staring Hurtree in the eye even after he put his hands on it.

"Yes," he said, "of course. I have my own medical insurance." *And I'll need it after I've crawled through your little window and socked you in your miserable, little bureaucratic jaw.*

"And you will need your return ticket, *natürlich*."

Hurtree bit his tongue and glared at Horrible Helga as he snatched his ticket through the tiny glass window.

Hurtree took a train to Heidelberg, and then a taxi to CID headquarters where he asked to see Captain Charles Peters at the sentry post. He was let through, and Peters met him outside in the early morning sunshine as the taxi pulled up to the building. They exchanged hearty greetings, joked about the ravaging effect of so many years, and then got down to business.

"I've pulled a little information on the person who alerted your tracer. She's an investigator at Violent Crimes, Homicide in Stockholm, a Miss Sara Markham. I suggest you make contact with her as soon as you land there. We can't tell her you're coming since you're not really on official business, but you'll find a way, I'm sure." Peters handed a single sheet of paper over to Hurtree, who put on his reading glasses.

"Shit, Charlie, I can't even shoot anymore. I have to put my glasses on to see the sight, then the target gets so fuzzy I can't aim. If I take off my glasses I can see the target, but I can barely see the end of the muzzle. By the time I pull the trigger, whoever I was trying to hit has either run away or shot me dead three times. Getting old sucks. Jesus, she's young enough to be my granddaughter, if I ever had one," he said. "Why weren't there police like that when I was working?"

"It wouldn't have done you any good anyway, Hurtree. You're too ugly to attract duck shit."

"Thanks for the compliment, Charlie. I'll remember you in my will."

"I won't have to wait too much longer for that." A wide grin spread on Peters's face.

Sara was on her way to the National Archive, and she fished up Karin's telephone number from her purse while she waited for a traffic light to change. It was Karin's day off and she had agreed to help. Sara pulled up outside her apartment in the unmarked black Volvo only fifteen minutes later.

"So tell me more about where you live, Fruängen. What's it like?" Sara asked as Karin buckled her seatbelt.

"All the streets in this area have women's names. Otherwise it's just your normal bedroom burb: lots of apartments, the occasional cellar being used for some kind of local business, a church that looks like a warehouse, a few shops and restaurants, last stop on the Line 14 Underground. That's it really."

Sara slowed down as she drove past Anna Eiderbach's apartment, and a road sign caught her eye as she turned toward the National Archive.

"Do you know anything about Långbro Hospital?"

Karin pointed out the right window. "It's just over there behind all those trees." She gestured to a line of hundred-year-old firs which hid most of the buildings. "One of Sweden's most famous, or infamous, mental hospitals, now made into apartments."

"Must have been an interesting place to work," said Sara as she turned into a small lane leading into the grounds. "I'd like to hear a little more about it. Have you ever worked here?"

"No," Karin said. "It closed a few years before I began my studies, but it's close to my apartment and I love to walk through the park." Karin began pointing out the major buildings as they slowly drove through the estate. "'The Big Women's Hall, 'The Big Men's Hall'. There's the Crematorium, almost the only way out of here when it was running," said Karin. "Most patients were just sedated to non-existence until they died. Occasionally a famous person would be treated, however, and they got special treatment."

Sara was looking from side to side, listening to the commentary as the Volvo crawled between the buildings.

Karin pointed toward a four-story building across from a small pond. "Before the Second World war started, Hitler's second in command was here to be treated for drug addiction. It didn't work very well, though. I think I read Schwerlieb was still an addict until his trial in Nuremberg."

The story of a high-ranking drug addict in the German Government coming to Sweden before the war was news to Sara. Like most Swedes, she hadn't been told very much about what went on during the Second World War, which was fine with her since she hadn't found history very interesting anyway. But a Nazi connection to Långbro Hospital might be helpful for her case, even if it was before the war, and she stored the item in her brain for later use.

"I was told the woman who committed suicide, Anna something, worked at this hospital," said Sara. "I have to gather some background on her so I'm on my way to the National Archives. It might cut some corners if you could help me instead of having to turn to our Medical Examiner every time I don't understand some of the terminology. That's why I asked you to come along."

"Sure," said Karin, "I've taken a few days off anyway, so I have time."

Sara called Sven and told him she'd be at the National Archives all day and would have to miss the morning meeting, but that she'd be available on her cell phone if necessary. She didn't mention anything about Karin accompanying her, and didn't ask anything about the rest of the team.

Sven's only comment was "Knock yourself out."

Sara and Karin arrived at the National Archive at opening time. Sara noted a white van had followed her Volvo up to the circular entry point, but had stopped just a few hundred yards away. A timely bureaucrat was just opening up, and he greeted them.

"Welcome, welcome, what can I help you with?"

Sara showed her ID, introducing herself and explaining that Karin was her medical interpreter.

The senior archivist invited them into his office. He listened carefully to their wishes while he stroked his mustache. When he nodded and looked down to make notes, a few strands of graying hair dislodged from his balding pate. He used his left hand in a familiar movement to stroke them back into place. When Sara had finished, he pushed the notepad away and began explaining in a very official voice there was no way the records they were asking for could be released without a *written* request from the Swedish police, and even then it would take days to acclimatize the documents to the warmth and humidity of the reading room.

The archivist explained in detail about the care of documents at the National Archives, how important it was they be given the correct environment so researchers in coming centuries could access them. He pointed out there were researchers today who were looking at documents nearly 500 years old. He leaned back in his chair, adjusted his Uppsala University tie, and said, "One can't treat documents like some sort of trash which ended up in the archive on a whim."

Sara was nearly falling asleep, and finally said, "OK, OK. It seems we've come to the wrong person. We're investigating a murder. I need some details on a woman who worked at Långbro Hospital. If you can't help, then I guess we can note what you've said and add it to the file. Do you have a business card?"

Karin looked at her in surprise. *Did she say, murder?*

"Yes," said the archivist, "I do have a business card," and he gave them both the embossed business cards he had worked so hard for so many years to get. He was already calculating the risk his name would be found in a negative context later on, and he didn't like the odds.

Sara and Karin were nearly at the exit when they heard someone running behind them. They turned to see the archivist catching up with them. After he had caught his breath, he said, "Umm, I think I have a solution for you. But you'll have to be prepared for a rather chilly room. If you can take that, then I can let you look at some of the documentation you're asking about while I take my coffee break. Follow me."

Most of the National Archive was under the ground, built to be secure from bombings and natural disasters. They got into the elevator, which dropped them with a near zero gravity plunge below the bottom of the lake which cut through the center of Stockholm.

Then they continued several seconds more, to feel their weight increase as the car stopped and gravity caught them again. Sara thought she could feel the weight of millions of tons of water just over their heads. She looked over at Karin, who had turned an ashen-gray color.

The archivist led them into a series of tunnels, and finally to a door which bore a sign: 'Långbro Hospital'. He opened the door to another tunnel, and they both shuddered as the temperature dropped another five degrees to just above freezing.

"I doubt you'll stay here very long," the archivist chuckled. "Now what is it exactly you want to look at?"

"We're trying to find out more about a nurse who worked at the hospital, a Miss Anna Eiderbach, and if possible the name of a patient who was in her care. Miss Eiderbach worked there until the hospital closed."

The archivist began by rolling away several document holders, complete bookshelves on wheels, to find the final year of entries. He went into the small space between holders and rummaged for a few minutes.

"Here," he said as he dropped a black ledger with red binding on the document desk. "This is a personnel file for all those working at the time of closure."

Within minutes they had located Anna Eiderbach's name, and beside it a room number, 306K. The archivist was already on the way out as Karin stopped him.

"And now we need to find the admission ledger for the patient in room 306K."

"But that information is very difficult to find," he said, rubbing his hands together. "I'll have to know what year your patient was admitted into the hospital to have a chance to find it."

"We don't know that yet." Sara was insistent. She cupped her hands and exhaled warm air on them. "We know Anna Eiderbach was German and her patient might have been admitted during the war years. Does that help?"

"It might," he said, "it just might."

Actually, he knew it would. A colleague of his had done his doctorate on the relationships between Germany and Sweden during the war years, and there was a surprising amount of contact between the two nations. His eyes seemed to curl up at the edges as if he were laughing at them.

"I assume you mean the Second World War. We have information on many wars in this archive. Let me take out the journals for those war years. She might be in there."

He returned with five leather-bound journals, and Sara opened the first book immediately. Her skin was already showing signs of exposure, and she regretted not bringing a sweater with her. In the third journal, for the year 1940, she saw something that gave her a start.

"Here," she said, "I think I've found her!"

Karin shivered, slapped her arms, and said, "I wonder if you really need me down here," then stood closer to Sara.

They both read the elegant black handwritten line of information about a girl named Dolfin, born on September 12, 1936, admitted on October 16, 1940. Sara pointed to the column for Attending Physician and noted the name Dr. Habermann.

In the column for contact or next of kin, they both read, out loud and in unison, "Hermann Schwerlieb, Reichsmarshall." Out to the left in the last column someone had penciled in the room number 306K.

"She's Schwerlieb's daughter." Sara grinned in triumph. "Now that really is something. I don't know what it explains, but at least I've heard of him, thanks to you."

"Let's get out of this freezer," said Karin, massaging her cheeks with both hands.

Sara thanked the archivist after he returned from his coffee break, and invited Karin to lunch at a restaurant near Karin's apartment in Fruängen. They arrived after only a few minutes. The white van began following them at the first intersection, and remained a discreet four car distance behind them. The two women talked about their short vacation, booked to begin the following day, and after lunch Sara dropped Karin off at her apartment.

Sara met with Sven as soon as she came into headquarters. She cleared off a space on the table in the Habermann/Eiderbach room.

"So here's what we know," she said, and began drawing little circles on a piece of paper. "Anna Eiderbach falls in front of a train, and she dies, murdered by someone who tries to make it look like suicide. She turns out to be a nurse at a hospital which no longer exists. This hospital is where a big-time Nazi, Schwerlieb, signs in the Dolphin woman as next of kin. So why kill Eiderbach? We're still stuck for a motive. This Dolfin, the woman patient, was on the hit list too. And where do we find her? Has she been killed too? And Dr. Habermann's killing, we need a motive for that also. Can we get any details from the filing cabinet from his apartment?"

"Wait," said Sven. "Let's look at this Nazi thing again. I don't understand this part at all. We were supposed to be a neutral country during the Second World War. How could there be Nazi connections to Sweden? And why would Nazis want to kill other Nazis?"

Sara looked over at him. It wasn't every day she felt she could tell her boss something he didn't already know. She felt like a newly hatched teacher with fresh knowledge to be dispersed.

"The man at the National Archive gave me a few details about that. He told me about a few articles written in the past few years. We can call him if we need his help later. He's a very knowledgeable guy."

Sven shook his head. "I don't want any more people involved in this investigation. It's running away from us already."

"OK, but we're going to have to relearn a few things about our country. Apparently, we were only neutral when it actually came to sending troops to fight for Germany. And there were even a few Swedes who did that. In lots of other ways there was support for the Nazis, and it went from allowing troops to be carried on Swedish trains up to the north of Norway and Finland where they fought, to supplying iron ore, ball-bearings, and steel. We even sold timber to German coal mines so they could keep their mine shafts propped up. Seems like Germany was an important partner even before the war. This guy Schwerlieb had even been treated at Långbro for his morphine addiction."

"Morphine?" said Sven. "Could there be a drug connection to these cases?"

"Well for Schwerlieb it would be kind of late. He was tried at the Nuremberg trails, you know, as a war criminal. I think he was executed."

"So if this was his child, Dolfin—what a name for a child, especially a girl—what was she doing in Långbro? Do we know if he even had a daughter?"

"I don't know," said Sara. "It's very strange. Långbro had one specialty and that was mental illness. Then of course, in Schwerlieb's case, drug addiction. The archivist said Schwerlieb was married to a Swede, some baroness or something, but I don't know if they had any children."

"Let's meet with the NSS again tomorrow. I want you to spend some time reading about this creep Schwerlieb. We need to know more." Sven was about to leave the evidence room when he turned around in the doorway.

"Oh, while you were at the Archives, we got some new evidence on the Habermann case. The video tape covering the taxi stand outside of Habermann's apartment gave us a really good image after enhancement. Airport Security ran it through their database for last Wednesday. We got a positive hit on a man who left for Athens on a flight just two hours after the time forensics estimated for Habermann's killing."

"That's great news. So do we know who we're looking for?" asked Sara.

"Not exactly. We know what he looks like. The name he gave, John Smith, was probably bogus. I wonder how many passports there are for men named John Smith. Anyway, I've asked the Greek police via Interpol to pinpoint him if possible and pick him up and bring him in for questioning."

On Friday morning, Sara and Sven went to the NSS wing again. Ekman listened with interest as they related the progress on the investigation and made a note there was a photograph of Habermann's killer.

"We might be able to use that picture," he told Sven. "Send me a copy."

Ekman asked Sara to summarize the details she'd found in the National Archives. When she got to the part about Schwerlieb, he stopped her.

"Wait," he said. "Schwerlieb didn't have a daughter. His only child was a son."

"Then what about the girl he brought to the hospital?" she asked. "He signed her in as next of kin."

"Schwerlieb's only *legal* child is a son," said Ekman. "Perhaps he brought a love child with him. He was pretty famous for cavorting, I've heard. At least you have a connection. I've been looking at the Habermann files, and there might be some things which can help you out."

Ekman took out the file on Dolfin found at Habermann's office and began to translate. There was a large section with entries beginning in 1940, which increased in volume in the early fifties after Dolfin had turned sixteen. Ekman's competence in German was limited to a few courses in school, but it was good enough to get the general gist of the content. Many entries in the files dealt with Habermann's fears someone wished to sterilize Dolfin at the hospital.

"Sterilize her?" Sara drew her head back and her lips curled in a grimace. "But she was mentally, well, challenged."

Ekman put down the file and looked up at Sara and Sven.

"Most people don't know it, but laws in Sweden were amended

in 1934 to follow Germany's race-biological laws from 1933, and those laws were strengthened in 1941. Sterilization was done with some mode of voluntarism, but that was just cosmetics. In reality the victims had little choice in the matter. Habermann included in his file some of the recommendations for sterilization mentioned in the law." He looked down at the file again as he read them out loud. "One: eugenic indications. That is, if the individual could transmit serious illnesses or traits to a coming generation. Two: social indications, in other words, when the person is obviously unfit to take care of a child because of mental illness or retardation, or other similar circumstances. Even the woman's social way of life played a role. Three: medicinal indications, when the person had some kind of illness which could endanger their health at childbirth."

Sara looked over at Sven. "Is this us? Sweden?"

Sven shook his head, and said, "It shouldn't have been."

Ekman took out another NSS file and read about a man known as the Professor who had been instrumental in getting the law onto the books, using his position in the Government and contacts in the Swedish Parliament. A university professor in sociology, he was also a minister in the Swedish Government. He had shown considerable interest in the child. Ekman told them there had been a serious conflict between the Professor and Habermann, and there were even surveillance notes made when Habermann had tried to enlist the help of a Doctor of Psychiatry at the Karolinska Institute. All this had happened many years ago, when the world was witnessing the results of eugenic policies turned into social engineering.

"So, someone in the Government at that time was trying to get this woman sterilized?" Sara shifted her weight on her chair. "Why? She was already in a mental hospital."

Ekman pursed his lips. "I admit, it is embarrassing," he said, "but it seems this woman was singled out. I've never heard of any other person who got the attention of a Government minister in cases like this. I wonder who she is."

"All we know is Schwerlieb signed her in as next of kin," said Sven. "What happened to him?"

"He was sentenced to death at the Nuremberg trials for crimes against humanity." Ekman closed the file in front of him, and continued, "So you won't get much help from him."

"This Dolfin woman must be around sixty today, if she's still alive," said Sara. "What makes her a target? Habermann and Eiderbach were in their eighties. Who can be so important at that age?"

"When you figure that out, you can arrest the killers," said Ekman.

Chapter 9

Sara glanced at the overnight suitcase standing next to the door. She longed for the opportunity to unplug the job from her brain. Her cell phone rang, jarring her back to reality. She answered and heard an American accent on the other end, a voice sounding like whiskey stirred into gravel. He introduced himself.

"My name is Lieutenant John Hurtree, retired from the U.S. Army, CID, and your name is Sara Markham, a Homicide Investigator for the Violent Crimes Division at the Swedish Police Board in Stockholm." Sara sat down at her desk as he continued, "We probably shouldn't talk much on the phone, but I think we can help each other. I'll explain later, but I know about your database search for Habermann," said Hurtree. "So, where can we meet?"

Sara was surprised at the directness, the no-bullshit manner, of this man—someone as straightforward as she was. She had a hard time getting her first response out.

"Habermann? I—I don't know. We might have to speak to each other, but how could you find me? Am I that visible?"

"Lady, you're sticking up like a bump on a log," said Hurtree. "Your database search set off alarms all over the place. I just got into the airport, and the taxi driver says I'll be outside your building in an hour or so. Can we meet somewhere? I might be able to help you with some background on Habermann. Will you still be at work?"

Sara picked up the ferry ticket from her desk. "No. I have plans for the weekend. But I'll be back on Monday. We can meet then if you wish."

"Miss Markham, I just flew across the Atlantic to speak to

you. I know you folks over here work a little differently than where I come from, but I'm getting old and I may not make it through the weekend."

"Like I said, I'll be back on Monday. What did you say your name was?" Sara took up a pen to make a note.

"Hurtree. John Hurtree."

"And you know something about Habermann?" Sara looked at her ferry ticket again, bit her lip, and said, "I can spare one hour. After lunch."

She gave Hurtree the address and alerted the reception, telling them they should require the visitor to provide his passport for identification. His status on the inside of the building would be 'Must be accompanied at all times', a red badge. She went into Sven's room to inform him of the visit and found things were already changing. Sven was still in charge of his team, but now he was reporting directly to Ekman at the NSS. They were collecting all information on both homicides.

Sara asked Sven if he could be at the meeting with Hurtree and he nodded, examining the register for a vacant meeting room.

"I can only take an hour with this guy if I'm going to make it out to the ferry terminal on time," she said.

"Let's see what he has to say first," said Sven. "One hour may be too long."

Hurtree went through the long, protected portion of the reception facing Berg Street, where he admired the security the police had put in place. *If our guys in Lebanon had had a system like this we probably wouldn't have lost those men in the truck bombing*, he thought, waiting for the return of his passport. He entered a security passage, and in front of him he could see another door. He walked toward it, and the doors behind him shut, making his ears pop. It was airtight. *I'll bet they could suck out the air in the passageway in ten seconds if they wanted to,* he thought, and he was right.

John Hurtree stood waiting for the airtight doors to open on the other side of the security sluice, and he saw a young woman and middle-aged man approach. The doors opened with a hiss and they all shook hands. After a quick confirmation Hurtree was who he said he was, Sven and Sara guided him toward the meeting room, using their ID badges to open doors all the way.

Hurtree followed them through the corridors. He thought it strange the Head of Homicide wore faded blue jeans and a blue plaid shirt. At home it would be a white shirt and tie. He noticed the shapely body of the young woman in front of him, and the miniature handcuffs holding her brunette hair in place.

Sara offered Hurtree coffee as they sat down. Hurtree stroked his closely cropped white hair and his eyes wandered between his two hosts.

"Thanks, don't mind if I do," said Hurtree, and poured himself a cup of coffee.

He studied the small meeting room, painted in a pleasant off-white. The oil paintings on the wall seemed to have come from an exhibition hall. He ran his hand over the surface of the table. Made of light beech, it completed the Scandinavian touch the interior decorator had endeavored to produce. In the center of the table someone had already placed a tray with a plate of cookies and candies beside the cups and two thermoses, one for coffee and one for tea.

Hurtree tried to resist taking any of the candies, but couldn't hold back. His hands, large baseball mitts with fingers, expertly chose a green tube with chocolate covered ends.

"I shouldn't, but I just love chocolate," he said and took two.

"So do I," said Sara as she took one herself. "We call them Hoovers, you know, because they look like little vacuum cleaners. Now, if you could quickly get to the point of your visit. I'm sure you'll understand we have other things to do. Tell me everything you can about Habermann."

"In just one hour?" Hurtree held his eyes level with Sara's.

"One hour," she said.

Hurtree took a sip of the coffee, strong and definitely Colombian. "Good coffee," he said. "Coffee in the States is just hot black water."

"Habermann?" Sara glanced at her watch.

"He was on Schwerlieb's staff, at least until 1940. He was a doctor. There one day, gone the next. When the war ended, my job was to interrogate Schwerlieb for the war crimes trial in Nuremberg. My assumption at the time was Habermann had become part of the Diplomatic Corps in some other part of the world to work as a spy as the war started. We tried everything to find him. We even enlisted several Israeli and Austrian organizations to help us."

Sven nodded. "We've heard of them too."

Hurtree took another sip of coffee. "The closest we ever got to him was a hint he might have gone through Stockholm to get to Montevideo around 1940. At least the Stockholm connection looked good enough for me, so I sent off a request for help from your Security Service, but there wasn't a Habermann to be found in Sweden. So it's a bit odd" Hurtree paused to focus first on Sven, then on Sara "you'd be asking about him now."

Sara's eyes met Sven's. She recalled the voice of the officer at the NSS reading from the file: "No one had ever asked for a Dr. Göran Stolpe from Germany". Her voice became softer.

"Why were you looking for Habermann?"

"And you want all that" Hurtree glanced at his watch "in less than an hour? Part of my investigation had to do with a child I was trying to identify. We were looking for a, uh—now I know this sounds crazy today, but we were looking for children who might be used as figureheads in the future. By the Nazis, of course."

"Would one of Schwerlieb's children fall into that category?" asked Sven.

"Schwerlieb?" said Hurtree. "He only had one child, a boy. We knew all about him. Strange kid. I met both him and his father. We had his mother in jail for months trying to get information out of her, but she never said a word. Neither did the boy."

"Yes, we heard about him today," said Sven. "Did you say you actually met with Schwerlieb?"

"Yes. I did," said Hurtree. "There were a lot of things happening at the end of the war and during the Nuremberg trials. It was a mess at the time. When you read about it today, it all looks so neat and orderly. At the time we hardly knew anything. Take Schwerlieb, for example. He had actually given himself up just a few days after the two Hitlers had committed suicide in Berlin. Schwerlieb had somehow managed to avoid a death squad Hitler had assigned to take him out when it became known he was on the way to Austria to give himself up. One of Hitler's last official acts had been to strike him from the Nazi party, then order his execution. We came close to missing him because we couldn't believe he really was Schwerlieb, previously second in command of the whole of Germany."

"Did you say two Hitlers?" asked Sven.

"Adolf and Eva. She was his mistress up until then. They got married just before the end and then they both committed suicide. At least that's the official story. Now it's your turn." Hurtree leaned back in his chair. "I'd still like to know a little about what made you start looking for Habermann."

Sven looked at Sara, and spoke as she was about to respond.

"We're working on a double homicide, and the details of the case have now been classified by our Security Service. I'm afraid we can't provide you any further details, Mr. Hurtree."

Hurtree could feel the disappointment, beginning somewhere in his stomach, spread up over his face. He'd been right all those years ago to look for Habermann in Sweden, that much was now clear.

"Well, shit," he said. "Two people get killed and you can't talk about it. And certainly not to me, 'cause I know something that might help you out. You guys are going to bury the truth about these cases, I know it."

"Not us," said Sara. "Like Sven said, our Security Service has classified this case. We want to know anything you can give us which will help us solve these murders, we just can't provide you with any details ourselves."

"So you guys ask the questions and I get to answer," said Hurtree.

"Yes," said Sven, "that's exactly right."

"OK. I can figure something out by what kind of questions you guys ask. Fire away."

"Have you ever heard of an organization called the Iron Guard?" Sven opened his notebook to a blank page.

"Oh yeah." Hurtree smiled. "Homicide wouldn't be new to them. They were involved in assassinations even before the war. One of those shadow groups, always working in the background. They never make public appearances, never allow anyone to divulge anything about them. A power structure you used to find in Europe only, but as far as I could find out before I retired, it's a worldwide organization now. Are those guys involved in your homicides?"

"And did you ever have contact with them during your work in Germany, Mr. Hurtree?" Sven refused to answer Hurtree's question.

"Only once. That really is a long story, but it doesn't have anything to do with Habermann. Hey, you can call me John," said Hurtree.

"Was Habermann a part of the Iron Guard?" asked Sara.

"I doubt it," responded Hurtree. "The Iron Guard as it is today, if it still exists, was set up after the war ended. Habermann disappeared at the beginning of the war, before things really got started. The Iron Guard during the war was just a bunch of Romanians trying to set up their own Nazi party."

"Then what would the connection be today?" asked Sara.

"I don't know," said Hurtree. "You guys are the ones asking the questions. What makes you think there should be a connection? If you never answer my questions, I can't give you anything more than empty answers. Sorry."

"I'm sorry, John," said Sven, "I know it must be frustrating, but this case is a little unusual. I'm sure you'd do the same in our shoes."

Sara's cell phone rang and she stared at the number before answering.

"Sara Markham. I'm in a meeting. Uh huh. OK. I'll call you back. That's great news. Thanks." Sara switched off the call, looked at Sven, and said, "That was the police in Athens. They have a name for Habermann's killer. Our 'John Smith', remember? They're staking out his place and will take him in for questioning as soon as he shows up. They want us to be there."

Sven rubbed his hands together.

Sara's cell phone bleeped a signal she had just received a text message. She looked at her watch in dismay; the ferry would be leaving the terminal soon, and Karin was wondering about Sara's whereabouts. Sara would have to dash to make it; the ferry would wait for no one, not even the blue flashing lights of a patrol car.

"Well, you have been very helpful," said Sara, "but I'm afraid it's getting late. It seems I'm in danger of missing the boat, as you would say."

Hurtree rose in tandem with Sara. "I'd sure like to give you guys some more help, if you want it. What about on Monday?"

Sara looked at Sven, who was examining his notes. He glanced at Hurtree and said, "OK. You have a great deal of first-hand knowledge of a period where we might need more background. Would you have anything against talking to our Security Service?"

"No, that'd be fine. I can ask them questions at the same time," said Hurtree.

"Bye. Have a nice weekend," said Sara as she disappeared from the meeting room with her overnight case trailing behind her. "See you on Monday then."

"I'll walk you to the reception area again," said Sven. The two men retraced their steps to the air-lock. "You might try to remember as much as you can about the Iron Guard. We think they might be important to our investigation."

"Gladly," said Hurtree. *So Habermann was murdered,* he thought.

Chapter 10

Hurtree spent several hours in the hotel bar. His attempts to find others to talk to led only to disappointment. He had never been able to get on with tourists, especially American tourists, and this hotel was full of them, mixed with local party-goers.

On Saturday he found a supermarket near the hotel and wandered through the aisles, trying to decipher the products behind the foreign names. His knowledge of German was still good enough to make the jump to Swedish. *Brot* became *bröd*, and bratwurst was just bratwurst.

In one of the aisles he found a young woman dispensing samples of curried chicken with rice, and in another aisle a man dished out samples of potato salad with Polish salami. He made several rounds at both booths and managed to eat enough to skip lunch at a restaurant.

Late Sunday night, John Hurtree raised his eyes from his Guinness to the hotel bar mirror and faced a total stranger. Everyone else in the bar was young, vibrant and in the prime of their lives. As Hurtree blinked, he realized it was his own image in front of him, and it had been a very long time since he had actually seen it.

He seldom looked into his own eyes, even while shaving in the morning. The last time he could remember had been when he was thirty. He was at a party celebrating the promotion of a friend at a beer hall in Munich. The world was still in turmoil since the end of the war. Hurtree sometimes wondered if the war had ended at all. Although the horrors revealed when the Nazis were defeated were beyond his imagination, he often recoiled at the risk of intercontinental destruction.

He had seen a vision of himself as the owner of a small hotel in the Bavarian Alps, with a blond buxom housewife catering to his every whim, happy to give them the three children playing on the cobblestones of the hotel courtyard. He would be wealthy enough to provide them with summers in the United States, and they would all learn how to ski. His wife would adore him, pampering him with her excellent cooking, and his children would all call him *vati,* and he would love them all. His life would be the antithesis of his upbringing in his family's apartment in Philadelphia, PA.

Now, as a single retired army lieutenant, with his career ended and close to the end of his life, Hurtree watched the men and women in the Stockholm hotel bar around him as they tried to grasp the slippery eels of their own days. For him it was too late. The image in the mirror of the hotel bar told him, and everyone else around him, that his future would end in a decade at most.

He felt both sad and glad. Sad because he had achieved so little of what he had planned all those years ago. Glad because what he had achieved was at this moment worth so much more. He was finally close to finishing his most important case. He glanced back at the image in the mirror, and the memory of the Munich beer hall flashed back into his mind.

Hurtree grinned at the memory, and the bartender at the hotel bar seemed to take that as his reply about one more for the road. Before he knew it, he had another dark foaming beer in front of him.

"I'm sorry, I seem to have interrupted your thoughts." The man beside him held his own Guinness toward Hurtree. "Cheers."

Hurtree grasped his glass. "Cheers," he said in return, and turned to face the stranger next to him.

"The Guinness here is quite nice. Correct, Mr. Hurtree?" The man beside him was short, his olive skin almost black in the dimly lit bar. The stranger's hair was too short to be wavy, and his nose protruded into his beer glass. He stared over its rim while he waited for Hurtree to answer.

Hurtree put his glass on the bar and took a step back. His right hand went to the spot on his waist where in previous years he had carried a .45 caliber Colt semiautomatic pistol. He scratched at his belt to mask his reaction, and asked, "How do you know my name?"

The stranger in front of him followed Hurtree's hand with his eyes, then returned his view to meet Hurtree's. He grinned as he said, "I stood beside you when you checked in."

"I don't remember that." Hurtree waved at the bartender for the check. "And I don't know your name."

"Mr. Hurtree, you should be very watchful on your journey," said the stranger beside him. "There are those in this country who do not wish for you to succeed in your task."

"What the Hell do you know about that?" Hurtree scribbled his room number on the check, then continued, "And who the Hell are you?"

"You have nothing to fear from me, Mr. Hurtree. I want you to help the police. I'm just reminding you there are those who do not."

"So you're a cop?" Hurtree drew closer to the man on the barstool and hovered over him. "I want to know who you are."

"No. I'm not a policeman. Not in this country. I was told to assist you if you need it."

"You stay away from me. Understand?"

"Perfectly, Mr. Hurtree," and as Hurtree left the man, he heard "Shalom."

Ten o'clock the next day came all too early, even without that last beer. A policeman called for Hurtree at his hotel, and he went through the security procedure again. This time Sven was accompanied by a middle-aged man, short and slightly balding, who extended his hand in a greeting.

"Lars Ekman," he said in a low voice. "I am a Commissioner

for the Swedish Security Service, the NSS. Sven seems to feel that I may be of assistance today. May I join you?"

"Sure," said Hurtree. "I hope I get the chance to ask a few questions myself at one point."

Ekman looked back at him with no emotion. They settled in the meeting room. Hurtree noticed Ekman's blue short-sleeved shirt bore his rank on the shoulder: a royal crown and two bands of oak leaves, all in gold thread.

"Sara's ferry has just disembarked and she will arrive soon. How was your hotel room?" asked Sven as they poured themselves coffee.

"The lounge area was nice," said Hurtree, "and the bar with the garden was fantastic. The room was clean, but it was kind of small. Actually I kept looking for it all night, but all I could find was the closet. And we've got to talk about leaks."

"Leaks?" Sven drew back and began a question. Before he could continue, Sara knocked on the door.

Hurtree looked at each one of them as they began. "I really want to help, but if all I get to do is to answer questions, then you might be missing a lot of information. Suppose you don't ask me the right questions?"

Sven looked over at Ekman before speaking. "OK, John. I've been authorized to give you a little background. As you know, Sara and I work at Homicide here at RPS, the National Police Board. We're working on a dual homicide with connections to Germany, and it's led to the case being taken over by our Security Service, the NSS. And that's where Commissioner Ekman comes in."

Ekman sat silently and thought about how much he would disclose to the man in front of him. "We got involved in this case some time ago." Ekman raised his eyes to meet Hurtree's.

Ekman stared.

Hurtree stared back.

Ekman continued, "We watched one of the persons recently murdered for some time. This man, you know him as Dr. Habermann, was suspected of having contacts with Neo-Nazi groups. After Dr. Habermann was murdered, we found some files in his apartment regarding his work with a patient at Långbro Hospital. He was a physician there until it was shut down a few years ago. I understand from Sven you were looking for Habermann at the time the war ended."

"Yes, sir. That's right," said Hurtree. "Who was the patient?"

"We know who the patient was. We would like to know why you searched for Habermann and more about this child you were looking for. And whatever you can tell us about the Iron Guard," said Ekman.

"We were looking for Habermann because he worked with Schwerlieb. We hoped he'd help us convict him," replied Hurtree.

"And the child you were looking for? What was the connection to Habermann?" asked Sara.

Hurtree smiled at the question, and answered, "Habermann was a pediatrician. He took care of Schwerlieb's child until he disappeared. The child I was looking for was—well, I suspected I was looking for Hitler's child."

Lars and Sven responded almost in unison, "But they never had any children."

"That's the story in the history books. I was one of the investigators looking into it. We were really interested in finding any surviving children to keep them off the market in the future, if you know what I mean."

Hurtree looked into his coffee cup for a second, grabbed another green and brown candy. "May I?" He glanced over at Sara, and continued, "Even before the war ended, there was a rumor that even though officially they had no children, they actually had a family and hid them from the public eye. They were both too afraid for the lives of their children if things started to go badly, so, just like Hitler's relationship with his mistress, they kept the children a secret from the German public."

Ekman interrupted, "Yes, that's strange. I always wondered why Hitler hadn't married his mistress. I saw a photo of her on the Internet. She wasn't that unattractive."

Hurtree warmed to the chance to give them even more information. It had been a long time since he'd had the pleasure of speaking with anyone who understood his work. "That was one of the questions I followed up. We interrogated everyone related to him and to her to find out, even the creeps in Nuremberg prison waiting to be executed. What they told us was that the higher-ups in the Nazi Party felt that public knowledge of her relationship to Hitler would have been a political threat. A lot of his support was coming from the widows of soldiers lost during the First World War, but included a bunch of single young women who could all imagine a future with Hitler as long as he wasn't married. Kind of like a rock star, I guess."

"Hitler as a rock star?" said Sara. "I can't imagine Hitler as a star at all. He was just a murdering piece of shit. Sorry."

"Yes," said Hurtree, "he was. But that's our version of the story. We wrote the history books. You have to understand, at the time he answered a lot of people's needs by providing them with jobs and food for their children. He gave them the security France and England had taken away from the German people. He was their hero."

"That's right," said Ekman. "He was a dictator, but an elected dictator."

"Oddly enough, most of them have been," said Hurtree, emptying his coffee cup with a final slurp. "Hitler had already been in jail because of his political activities before he came to power, and he didn't want to give his enemies anything they could use as ammunition against him. We assumed if there were children, they'd be kept a secret even within the Government. Our interrogations with the men in Hitler's closest circle never gave us anything to make us think differently. It only emerged when a nanny to one of the children was repatriated by the Russians.

"She'd been put in a prison camp for twenty years, and kept her mouth shut the whole time. In 1964 she was released back into Western Germany, broken, but with a huge secret. She was given a job at an engine factory in Aschaffenburg by 'The Industrial Powers', the people who fixed things in Germany after the war. She got drunk in a bar one night and her story slipped out. Several people heard it, but no one took it seriously, except me. I was there investigating illegal drug use by Army personnel stationed in Aschaffenburg. I tried to find out more from her, but she kept her mouth shut. She was run over by a bus shortly after, and the trail ended there."

Hurtree stretched his hand for another chocolate Hoover and continued between bites, "That probably would have been the end of my search, but a gunner who was in the plane Schwerlieb had used to fly the daughter and her nurse to Sweden was blubbering in a drunk-tank. He was found dead in the morning, suffocated by his own puke. I heard about it when an American prisoner who had been arrested for drug use, and had shared the cell next to the gunner, wanted to trade his story to get a better deal when he was released into military custody the next day. That's when my investigation went into high gear again." Hurtree wiped his lips and crumpled the napkin into a small ball in front of him.

"Wait a minute, Mr. Hurtree." Ekman scribbled in his notebook. "Did you say Schwerlieb flew into Sweden during the war?"

"Yes. We figured you guys knew more about it than we did. We kept it a secret because by then we were just a decade away from the Berlin crisis and people were getting shot for trying to cross the border between East and West Germany. I was at the CID in Heidelberg at the time, and I went back over our old files from Nuremberg and interviewed everyone I could again, asking specifically about the children. I had Russian spies tell me Hitler's mistress was pregnant with Hitler's child when she died, but they had destroyed the bodies, so that didn't help much. Between the nanny and the gunner, I thought I had first-hand something which seemed to prove the couple had had two children, a boy and a girl. The boy had died in 1932, even before the burning of the Reichstag and Hitler's rise to national power."

All three police sat still, listening intently as Hurtree related the details of his investigation. "The nanny's story was that when the boy died, Hitler's mistress, Eva, had become so despondent she tried to commit suicide by shooting herself in the neck. Then, in 1935, after her second attempt at suicide by an overdose of sleeping pills, she and Hitler had conceived again and a girl was born in 1936. According to the nanny's drunken story, the girl was ill, and she had been sent to a specialist for children's mental illnesses.

"Mentally ill? Did you say mentally ill?" Sara leaned forward, eyes fixed on Hurtree.

"Yes. She was supposed to have been in a day care center until just after the invasion of Poland, before the Russian front turned into a disaster for the German Army. I searched everywhere for all three of them: Dr. Habermann, the nurse, and the child. All over the world. Even enlisted the help of Wiesenthal in Vienna at one point, but they had disappeared, if they'd survived. My inquiries to the Swedish police led nowhere—sorry, Lars, but even though I had some kind of evidence the daughter was flown here during the war, they told me all the records had been destroyed regarding just that flight. The nurse and the girl had always remained nameless and no trace of them could ever be found. It was one of those cases I worked on while I was at the CID in Heidelberg until I retired. Even though it was never really a CID case, it was still an open case for me when I left. Sara, when you began to search the Internet for information on Habermann, your computer sent out search robots that triggered my alarms."

Sara, Sven, and Lars sat dumbfounded. Were they looking for Hitler's daughter? The enormity of it all hit them square in their stomachs and none of them spoke.

Finally, Ekman broke the silence and thanked Hurtree for his contribution. He looked at Hurtree, and then spoke again, smiling as he did so.

"Mr. Hurtree, you obviously have a great deal of knowledge about this, even deeper than ours. Ask us a few questions, and maybe we can help each other out."

Chapter 11

Hurtree settled back in his chair and faced the three police sitting on the other side of the table. He reverted to his professional role as investigator, and from out of nowhere an interrogation strategy formed in his head. He turned to Ekman and began.

"What brought Habermann to Sweden? What was he doing here?"

"Sara has been looking into that. Sara?" Ekman glanced in her direction.

"He was working as a doctor at a hospital," said Sara. "The only patient he had was a little girl when she arrived. When the hospital closed, she was an elderly woman."

The image of the black-and-white photograph flashed in Hurtree's mind and he tried to imagine the young child as an old woman. At the same time an identical image formed in Sara's head and she looked over at Sven, seeking help about how much she could say,

"I have a question for you, John," asked Sara, "The woman working together with Habermann was also murdered. What was the name of the nurse who was taking care of this child—Hitler's child, if that's who she is?"

"Like I said before, we never had a name for her. Just some information she existed, and that she might have traveled to Sweden. What was the name of your homicide victim?"

Both Sven and Sara looked at Ekman for guidance. They had begun to loosen up the constraints on how much to divulge, but neither of them was sure where the line was actually drawn.

"Her name was Eiderbach." Ekman splayed his elbows on the

desk, lowered his head, and said, "Anna Eiderbach. Although we know Habermann was allowed to change his name when he moved here, there is no such record for her. Our only name for her is Eiderbach."

"And the woman, Hitler's child, what's her name? Do you know that too?" Hurtree began to take short breaths, as if he was about to be the first to cross the finish line on the longest marathon in the world. He could see the string stretched in front of him, knew there were just a few more steps to go. He had waited for decades for this triumph, and his entire body tingled with excitement.

"The name used to enter the little girl into the hospital was Dolfin. We don't know if it's a last name or a first name. That's all that was given," said Ekman.

"Of course," replied Hurtree, and he gave the table a light slap. "Of course. Dolfin. A-dolf's child, a girl. Dolf-in. It's just too perfect. But how could Habermann get her into Sweden? He must have had some clout with the Government." Hurtree noticed his question had been a little too close to the mark. There was a silence before Ekman answered.

"That name proves nothing. And it wasn't Habermann who had the connections. It was Schwerlieb. He was the one who signed her in as next of kin."

Now it was Hurtree who sat silently. He hardly knew what to say. Schwerlieb, after all these years. The image of Schwerlieb as he begged for a pistol to kill himself came back to him. Hurtree wondered if anything would have been different if he had taken Schwerlieb up on his offer of providing information in exchange for a bullet.

"Did you say, 'next of kin'?" asked Hurtree finally.

"Yes, I've seen the hospital records myself," Sara responded.

"Jesus. Schwerlieb. I wonder what that means," said Hurtree, mostly to himself.

"I was hoping you could tell us. I think it rules out the woman being Hitler's daughter," said Ekman.

"Well, all I can say is Schwerlieb is the one person in the Nazi Government who could get things fixed up here. He really had good connections. So if he was involved then it would have been sanctioned from very high up in the Swedish Government. When did you say she got here?" asked Hurtree.

"I didn't say," Ekman answered, then turned to Sara, "but the records indicate, uh, what was the exact date, Sara?"

"October 16, 1940." The date on the journal flashed into her mind, and she remembered the freezing tunnel with a shudder.

"Yeah, that's when Habermann went missing alright," said Hurtree. "That's also about the time Schwerlieb was up here. He had some kind of meeting up here with a Swedish aristocrat. I can't remember his name any more, but it doesn't matter, it didn't work."

"Aristocrat?" asked Sven. "John, do you think there would be any kind of political motive for the killings? I mean, with the need for political connections to get her up here, is there any chance someone in our Government would be trying to cover this up?"

Ekman scowled and threw an angry look at Sven.

Hurtree replied, "Life has always been cheap for politicians. No, I'd say whoever was involved in bringing her up here wouldn't be in power any more. All those people would have retired or died a long time ago. Revenge? Blackmail? Maybe Habermann and Eiderbach were trying to blackmail the Government. Now that wouldn't work in the U.S.A.. The people wouldn't consider it to be a scandal compared to what the Government does today, but you guys would be able to determine if that could work here."

"I doubt it," said Ekman, "and for many of the same reasons."

Sara's brow was furrowed. "We have reason to believe there was a failed attempt on Habermann's life the day before he was murdered, set up to look like an accident. The strange thing is, the following day he was executed and his killer seemed to want us to find the body, and also to be able to identify him quickly."

"Two killers, two different motives. That's the way I'd look at it," said Hurtree. "And there's probably something you're not telling me, so I won't be able to help you figure that one out either."

"What do you mean?" asked Sven.

"I mean, you're not telling me all the details of your investigations. For example, why did you ask me about the Iron Guard?"

All three police sat silently, Sara and Sven looking intently at Ekman. Suddenly the face usually set in concrete contorted as if it were exercising the muscles around its lips. They twitched, changed direction and then twitched again. Clearly Ekman was considering releasing even more information to Hurtree, but his lips were having birth pains in making the decision. Then he blurted it out.

"The Iron Guard authorized a hit on them. We intercepted the message."

"Well now, I thank you for that little snippet," said Hurtree. "I won't ask you how you could get information like that, but in light of it, I can see there would clearly be two groups involved: the Iron Guard and their enemies."

"Their enemies?" Sara leaned forward.

Ekman understood the answer immediately, and he was nodding even before Hurtree continued, "Yeah, I know, it would seem to include just about the whole world, but there is one group that really takes an interest in making things difficult for the Iron Guard," said Hurtree. "That group has their headquarters in Tel Aviv."

Ekman's voice resonated like a bell. "The Mossad."

"Well maybe," said Hurtree, "and maybe not. That's where I'd begin to look, anyway. Or you could ask the man who spoke to me at the hotel bar last night. He knew my name and that I was meeting with you."

"What?" Sven and Sara asked together.

Ekman clenched his teeth before speaking, and the muscles on his jaw stood out. "Mr. Hurtree, it seems you have attracted attention. Now that you've provided us with this valuable information, perhaps you should consider continuing your vacation elsewhere."

Hurtree's eyes narrowed and seemed to emit blue sparks. "I'm not leaving until I figure out where she is."

The room became silent except for the quiet hum of air pushing through the ventilation system. Sara broke the frost forming among them.

"We still don't have an answer to why the Iron Guard would want to assassinate these people. What's the motive for that?" she asked.

"I'd suggest finding the killers and asking them," said Hurtree. "I don't suppose you guys have any leads on them?"

Ekman, Sven, and Sara dropped their heads to look at the table in front of them, silent for several seconds. "That's what I thought you'd say," said Hurtree, breaking the silence. "Anyway, at least you seem to have a good start. You know who was behind the killings, you know how and when, and you have at least one motive. It shouldn't be too long before I'll get to read this in the papers."

"I rather doubt it." Ekman closed the file in front of him. "Anyway, let's break for lunch. Mr. Hurtree, I would like to invite you to a prison meal, if you're up to it. It's only three courses including the dessert, but if you can manage that, it will be our treat and our way to thank you for your contribution." Ekman looked over at Sara and Sven. "You'll pay your own way, of course."

They sat in a secluded corner of the restaurant, enjoying their baked halibut in a white wine sauce and potatoes au gratin. Sara asked Hurtree if he had enjoyed history at school.

"You seem to know so much about what went on during the Second World War, you must have been reading history books when you were five."

"No, actually not," said Hurtree. "I was asleep during most of our history lessons. All we ever got to learn about was presidents and wars. The only reason I know about what went on in Europe is that I was there."

"You were making history instead of reading about it," said Sven. "Meeting with Hermann Schwerlieb must have been special. That's unique knowledge today. Was there anything you noticed in your contact with him which would point to anyone who would have an interest in harming this girl?"

"He didn't seem to be too interested in anyone except himself," said Hurtree. "Schwerlieb did everything he could to avoid being hanged and kept asking for a pistol to be able to kill himself. There was nothing in those interviews about children except his own son. Schwerlieb was a little worried about what would happen to his family, but he seemed to feel his wife would be able to manage if we left them alone."

"Suppose our murders had happened just after the end of the war," said Sara, "would you have been able to help us out then? Try to think back to then."

"I wish I could go back to then." Hurtree looked over Sara and grinned. "Life was a lot simpler for me then, believe me. I do remember we spent a lot of time talking about the fact he'd been thrown out of the Nazi Party at the end of Hitler's life. Schwerlieb was bitter about it, seemed to think he was still the leader of the entire German nation after Hitler's death."

"What about the other people on trial? Did they see him as the new leader?" she asked.

"Some did, others didn't. And in the end it didn't matter anyway. The really bad guys at the trial got hanged. Almost everybody."

Commissioner Ekman stared blankly into his empty plate, using his fork to push a fish bone back and forth. "So there could have been a schism in the Nazi party. Still, it may not mean anything." Finally, he asked, "What do you mean, almost everyone got hanged? I thought they were all executed."

"No, everyone seems to make the same mistake in believing everyone was convicted. Actually I was involved in getting one of the women on trial acquitted."

"Women?" asked Sara with surprise. "Were there women on trial too?"

"Oh yes," said Hurtree, "and some were convicted and executed. You wouldn't believe the things they did."

"My knowledge of history is so bad. I hardly knew anything except the name of the trial and that it involved the genocide of millions of Jews." Sara glanced over at Ekman, hoping her admission had not registered, then she asked Hurtree, "What about Schwerlieb's son? Did he really never say anything?"

"Nope, like I already said, we never got a word out of him at the time of the trial. I spoke to him years later, when I was about to retire and I cleaned out the case file. There was a small box of personal items which had been collected in the investigation leading up to the trial. It seemed wrong to keep it then, so I tried to take it to Schwerlieb's wife, but she had died a few years before. The only surviving relative was the son. He was unfriendly when I met with him, but what would you expect? Anyway, he seemed grateful to get back the box."

"What was in it?" The question seemed to come from all three police officers at the same time.

"Not much. Just a medallion and a few pictures of Hitler together with a lot of other people, usually Schwerlieb, except for one that was strange since Schwerlieb wasn't in it at all. All I could figure out was it must have been Schwerlieb who had taken it. It was one of the photos Schwerlieb wanted to see just before he died."

"This medallion." Sara squirmed in her seat and her voice went low, and she spoke each word with determination. "What did it look like?"

"A small swastika in a ring. About an inch across. Made of solid gold. Something you'd expect the second in command to have received from Hitler. We found out there were a few others made."

"So they came from Hitler personally?" asked Sven. "Was there any other way to get one?"

"No. I suppose you could have got one as a gift from some other person who got one. Otherwise you'd have to have received it from Hitler's hand personally. That's just the way it was."

"Was there any inscription on the one that you gave back to Schwerlieb's son?"

"I never thought to look," answered Hurtree. "What's so special about the medallion?"

"I just wanted to know if all the medallions Hitler gave out had an inscription," Sven replied.

"Sorry," said Hurtree, "I never imagined it was important. How far have you got in solving your murder cases?"

Sven answered, glancing at Ekman who nodded in support, "I can't provide any details in an open investigation, but we're pretty good at catching murderers here in Sweden. But the ones we usually catch are those who kill because they got drunk. Most of the time they give themselves up. This is different. Our evidence points in many directions. There are political implications, since Commissioner Ekman here is involved. There are many groups involved, and it means the investigation is a lot wider than it usually would be for us."

Sara asked the next question, her bright blue eyes darting back and forth. Hurtree felt a strange feeling of pride as he watched her, glad to see such a young woman asking all the right questions.

"Did the son tell you anything about any of the items you gave back to him? Comments or questions? Anything?"

"Not really. I asked him about the pictures, especially the one of the children. I wondered who was in the photo. He said it was the Goebbels kids to the right and that he was standing on the left. Either he didn't remember or he was lying, because there were six other children in that picture, and the Goebbels had five children at the time. I still have nightmares about those poor kids. Did you know that their parents killed them, before the Goebbels took their own lives? Such horrible people."

"Are there any copies of that photograph?" Sara asked carefully. The photograph she had found in Anna Eiderbach's nightstand filled her mind. She flashed a warm glance at this old man, who could have been her father.

"No. We weren't allowed to make any copies before the trial because they were evidence, and it felt wrong to make any when I was releasing them to the son. So he's got the only photograph I know of."

"I wonder if we could get a copy from him," said Sven.

"I really doubt it," said Hurtree. "He keeps to himself. He hates us—the U.S. Army, I mean—for what we did to him and his mother during the war. They sat arrested for a long time and we interrogated them almost every day. You never know, but I doubt he'd let you through the door today."

Chapter 12

When the Second World War ended in Europe, there had been a frantic attempt to move the political leadership of the Nazi party to safer ground, where it could wait for a better day. They had succeeded far better than they had hoped. For many years, the organization existed as independent Nazi cells, communicating via couriers and other secure means. Isolation of the individual cells was so successful that some were barely aware there were other cells operating in neighboring countries.

The Iron Guard had no worries about funding. A large part of the gold from the German Reichsbank had been sent out of the country. Some of it had been discovered and was taken into custody. Part of it was onboard ships and submarines which had been sunk. In spite of that, gold valued at nearly a trillion dollars formed the economic foundation for the next World Government the Nazis hoped to achieve. Most of it was now safely deposited in numbered accounts in Switzerland.

At first, there were attempts to find the Nazi leaders. Several Israeli and Austrian organizations had shown exceptional dexterity, capturing those criminals indicted in absentia at the various trials in Europe. In general, however, the Iron Guard grew stronger every year it existed. In 1996, a meeting in South America's Montevideo, Uruguay was the first phase of their new beginning.

Commissioner Ekman brought back a tray with their coffee, Sara's green tea, and their dessert: a cherries jubilee with whipped cream.

"Did you say this was prison food?" asked Hurtree. "I may just go out and break a window if I can eat like this."

"Actually there are people who do just that," said Sven.

"Mr. Hurtree, I hope you'll excuse us," said Ekman when they had finished with their coffee. "You've been extremely helpful, but we have a busy afternoon in front of us. If you remember anything you think could be useful, please call. You already have all our business cards. As I said before, it would be beneficial for you if you ended your vacation here and left Sweden."

Hurtree leveled his eyes to meet Ekman's. "You know where I'm staying. I'd be more than happy to help if I can."

"We're completely satisfied with your contribution so far." Ekman extended his hand for a handshake. Hurtree grasped Ekman's hand and answered with steel in his voice.

"You've told me enough to understand I have to stay until I'm as satisfied as you are. I don't know how I'm going to find her, but I will do it. I have to."

Sven and Sara returned to the Habermann/Eiderbach room. She found the box with the material forensics had collected from Anna Eiderbach's room in Fruängen, and took up the photograph. She passed it over to Sven, and asked, "Does this look like anything you just heard about?"

"My God," said Sven, "it looks like the photograph Hurtree described. Look, there are seven children in all. Why didn't you mention this to him? I'm sure he would have wanted to see it."

"Yes, but I didn't know if Ekman would have been too happy about that, and what difference does it make anyway?" she said. "If she really is Hitler's daughter then it would be natural for her caretaker to keep it for her. I mean, it's not something you want to have lying around in a mental hospital. But I'm not so convinced Hurtree is right about her being Hitler's daughter. Hurtree seems like a nice guy, but for me, Schwerlieb is still the prime candidate to be the daddy. Hurtree told us Schwerlieb had his own copy.

We know Eiderbach had one, but she was taking care of the woman Schwerlieb signed in as next of kin. Why make it more complicated than that?"

"You could be right. Anyway, I think we'd better keep this Hitler's daughter thing close to us. I mean, there's no reason for the rest of the team to know about this. I doubt it would help them find her, and there's a huge risk someone would call the tabloids just for the tip-off money."

"Who do you mean?" asked Sara.

"No one and everyone," said Sven. "There's a risk, that's all, and I'm going to reduce it."

Sara and Sven went through the cases again, summarizing each file individually, then tried the possibility one killer was behind the two murders. It became clearer and clearer they were looking for two separate killers, both with their own motives. It also became clear the major link between the two killings was the Dolfin woman. They simply had to find her before she too was murdered.

Sara and Sven divided their work between them. Sara began by checking out police records of murder investigations for female victims throughout the country who could fit the age description. Sven would visit the National Archive to look at the original material himself. Another set of eyes might reveal something she hadn't seen.

Sara went through the files on female murder victims. It was depressing to discover how many older women had been murdered, but none of the women listed in the time slot fit the description. If Dolfin had been murdered then her body had yet to surface.

During the search in the registers for older women, her thoughts wandered to her grandmother, who was still fighting a losing battle with various authorities to get a apartment at a Service Center. The words of her grandmother's complaints still rang in her ears. Sara felt a constant gnawing at her conscious, and needed more time to visit and help her. Her grandmother had spent the entire time at her mother's fiftieth birthday party complaining to anyone who would listen, and several who wouldn't.

A police officer drove Hurtree back to his hotel. Once there, he sat in his room, trying to piece together the information he had been able to glean in the last few days. Hurtree was completely convinced the girl in Schwerlieb's photograph was Hitler's daughter. Now he even had a name for her, Dolfin, and he was sure she'd lived most of her life in Stockholm. He noticed that even Commissioner Ekman from the Security Service found it plausible the murders were connected to her.

Commissioner Ekman had mentioned the interception of a message from the Iron Guard about a hit on Eiderbach and Habermann. The part about the medallion had been interesting for the police, and he wondered why there had been so many questions about it.

Hurtree removed his airline ticket from its hiding place in his suitcase. He stared at it, then used it to fan his face. *Still more than two weeks left*, he thought, *but how do I find her now?*

Hurtree's thoughts returned to the day of his meeting with Schwerlieb just before the execution was to take place in Nuremberg.

The photograph had arrived as part of the personal effects of the Schwerlieb family. Soldiers had not only detained his wife and son, but had emptied the entire contents of the Schwerlieb mansion onto three four by four Army trucks and moved it to a warehouse outside of Munich. They had sifted through everything, sorting out the furniture, paintings, clothing, and other items used to carry out daily life. What they were looking for were documents which might have been stashed at home for safe keeping.

Hurtree's group had received over six trunks of photographs and documents, which they catalogued or returned for storage. When they were finished, there were only a handful of secret documents left, most of them dealing with the formation of the Luftwaffe and so out of date they were of little use for the trial.

There was, however, a series of photographs which led to investigations and interviews. They had all been taken at Hitler's retreat: the Eagle's Nest, high above Berchtesgaden, well-hidden in the Austrian Alps. Most of the photos were of Hitler and Schwerlieb, smiling into the camera, usually with some other military dignitary. Mussolini was there, even some of the men known as *Gauleiter*: the Nazi governors who had been given whole countries as local fiefdoms to rule.

There was only one photo which seemed to break the pattern: the picture of seven children, all smiling into the camera. They stood on the huge terrace overlooking the valleys below. Behind them, near the entrance to the huge villa stood Adolf Hitler, smiling and gesturing with his hands about something which seemed to please a German Army General standing at attention in front of his Führer.

At first Hurtree was going to throw the picture back into the box of personal items to be stored for later use, but he had stopped himself, and as he stared at the photograph, questions formed in his mind that demanded answers: *Who are these children? Why had they been chosen to be photographed on this day? What were they doing at the Eagles' Nest?* and finally, *Who was the photographer, and what was his connection to Hitler and Schwerlieb?*

The picture had gone into the evidence box and had been the subject of interviews with everyone among the top Nazi leaders or those who stood close to them. No one at that time had ever divulged the identity of the children or even the general. The closest he came to an answer occurred the day before Schwerlieb's execution.

Hurtree had glanced at the soldier standing guard just outside the cell, and he shook his head as he replied to Schwerlieb's question.

"Mr. Schwerlieb, you should tell me about the picture because it would be right to do so, that's all. Obviously the picture has some kind of personal significance to you, and so I can promise you I'll be taking it up with your wife again. There will be no pistol. You will have to be hanged as the awful criminal you are. When you die, you can be pleased you have provided someone, somewhere with some kind of satisfaction by paying for your crimes with your life."

Hurtree had put the lid on the box and the photographs rustled inside as he rose to leave. He had looked at Schwerlieb one last time, had seen how he was broken by the ordeal in front of him. Schwerlieb had been close to tears. He had wrung his hands and pleaded, "Just let me be my own executioner."

Schwerlieb had removed a ring from his right hand: a thin gold ring with a small pyramid mounted on it. He had offered it to Hurtree, and with his fingernail released a clasp on one side of the pyramid. The pyramid on top of the ring opened like a flower to reveal four triangles on a square base, covered with strange symbols Hurtree had never seen before. It looked Egyptian, and was obviously something Schwerlieb treasured.

"No," Hurtree had said, "never," and he left without another word.

He never saw Schwerlieb after that, except in the photo taken of his dead body lying on the floor in the execution chamber. They had moved it there after he committed suicide by taking cyanide, ending his life as he had wished, being his own executioner. Hurtree was questioned during the investigation raised to find the person responsible for supplying Schwerlieb with the cyanide pill, but the source had never been established.

Hurtree always suspected the soldier standing watch outside Schwerlieb's cell door that last day. The guard had seen the ring that Schwerlieb had offered Hurtree. Could he possibly have been swayed to provide Schwerlieb with the deadly pill? The ring had disappeared, that much was certain. It was obviously absent from his right hand in the picture of Schwerlieb as he lay on the cold concrete floor.

Where had it gone? Hurtree had never followed it up. It was bad enough being a suspect himself, and he tried to forget the incident. He had succeeded until Sara Markham's Internet search robot and his own tracer file had changed his life again.

Part II

The Child

Chapter 13

The Can got his nickname from the police, a tribute to his competence in collecting empty aluminum beer cans he traded for filled beer cans. He'd been like a younger brother to Dolfin from the time they met.

Only the Can knew of Dolphin's name; Nurse Anna had revealed it one afternoon. As she grew older, Nurse Anna had come to the conclusion Dolfin might need protection at some time in the future, and from what she had seen, The Can was the kind of person who would protect her. Her perception was correct. The Can was very good at protecting others, especially those who could provide him with the opportunity to erase the enormous feelings of guilt he felt about running out on his two previous families, leaving them to fend for themselves.

He had met Anna Eiderbach several times before, and even knew of Dolfin's previous connection to the mental hospital. There were already several members of the gang who had been patients at the hospital, but none of them had recognized Dolfin. Her position as a private patient meant her treatment was always done individually.

The Can was a true alcoholic humanist, a philosopher who had never read a single book of the classics, and yet knew the names of several of them. He could quote lines of their teachings from his imagination, usually managing to convince the others in the gang he really knew what he was talking about. He knew he would never be able to live what he disdainfully called a 'Svensson' life: driving to a government job, then home to the wife and two kids in a house with the family Volvo parked outside.

A misfit, the Can appreciated the congeniality of others with the same dilemma. The Social Welfare authorities had declared him an incompetent alcoholic several years ago. He received a small check every month for his subsistence from the Social Welfare Services, who also paid his rent.

It had been several hours since the Can had last seen Dolfin. He and two others in the gang sat on one of the park benches bordering the small pond in the hospital park just outside the center of Fruängen. Seagulls and mallard ducks were dueling over property rights to the water in front of the park benches, screeching and quacking either their frustration over their loss, or boasting their victory.

The Can noticed him first. The stranger approached them, and the Can saw this was not someone who would continue strolling by. This man had an agenda, and it included him or someone else in the gang.

The Can tried to focus on how to handle the situation. The other members of the gang relied on him to do something, and although he could count on their support, he would be the one who took charge if there was a fight.

The man continued to approach with determined strides. He wore a black T-shirt, black jeans, and a dark blue baseball cap with a sports emblem on the front. He was swarthy and had the appearance of someone from southern Europe. The Can was surprised to hear nearly perfect Swedish from the stranger as he asked which one was the Can.

"That's me, I'm the Can."

"They tell me you know everyone and everything that happens in Fruängen," said the stranger.

"Who tells you?" asked the Can. He was still sitting, and tried to size up the situation. This man didn't look like a cop, or one of the staff from the Social Services. He was definitely not a new gang member, and any other option could only mean trouble. Was it someone who was going to collect a debt from one of the gang?

The Can would have to scare the stranger off if he could.

"I asked the guy at the pizza place over there." The stranger gestured to a small building just across the street. "He knew about you."

"What did you ask?" asked the Can.

"I asked him if he knew where I could find a woman who calls herself Dolfin," said the stranger.

"I never heard of anyone by that name," The Can replied.

Both of the other gang members stared at the stranger, trying to look as menacing as they could.

"Oh, that's too bad," said the stranger. "I have some money for her. A lot of money, if I can talk to her."

Both gang members on either side of the Can squirmed on the park bench, but The Can said calmly, "Sorry, never heard of her before."

"I'll find her anyway," said the stranger and turned his back on the three. The Can stood and approached him with unsteady steps.

"I hope you don't. You're just one of those guys, just one of them that..." Then the Can realized he was too drunk to continue the sentence. "You just piss me off, that's all."

A sudden flash of anger took hold of the Can. "I'll make sure you don't find her. I will," and he bent down, breaking off the neck of the bottle of beer he had been holding, changing it into a very sharp and dangerous weapon. He held the bottle neck close to the face of the stranger, who didn't flinch.

"Damn people that do these things. Damn people," said The Can. The bottle neck came closer to the stranger's face with each incoherent exclamation.

The stranger moved his arm quickly and jabbed his hand into the Can's stomach. He twisted his hand back and forth for a few seconds. Then he withdrew the knife he had concealed in his hand until the last moment. The Can groaned and fell to the grass as his lacerated liver bled out inside him.

The stranger turned without another word and left, using long strides to reach the small shopping center again, stopping only to wipe off most of the blood from his hand on the grass.

He went to a public toilet at the metro station to clean the blood from his hand, left the knife in the waste basket, and took the next train to the center of Stockholm. The stranger was a professional, but the Can's attack had surprised him and the extra killing was not part of his plan. He would have to rethink this at his hotel. As the train left the station, a gray-haired man took a seat opposite him. The stranger was not the only one interested in Dolfin.

By the time an ambulance arrived, the Can was dead. His eyes stared sightless into the sun. His companions reported the Can's killing when they felt safe enough to return to Fruängen's Center. A team of local policemen cordoned off the crime scene and reported the murder to Stockholm's Southern Police District within an hour.

The death of a drunk did not command the highest priority of police resources, but the Homicide investigators from the Stockholm Violent Crimes group went through the motions of collecting evidence and interviewing witnesses. A murder investigation was started and The Can's body was removed to the Coroner's Office in Solna for an autopsy.

After only a few stops, the Can's killer's cell phone rang. His local Iron Guard commander for the operation told him he could rely on continued support only for the next twenty-four hours. After that he would be on his own and could probably count on being discovered and apprehended. The killer ended the call by thanking the caller and began to mull over what to put in his report.

Twenty-four hours was far too little time to continue his mission. He would offer no apology for spilling unnecessary blood; apologies would call attention to his failings, and he wanted to avoid that at all costs.

He sent an SMS to the chat site serving as a bulletin board for the operation. He began preparing in his mind what he would do with his luggage when he arrived at his hotel. He'd separate his clothes into two piles: things to take with him, and things which tied him to the murder and later would be found in a dumpster near the taxi stand where he would take a cab to the airport.

The gray-haired man sitting opposite the killer had already sent a text message to his local office, asking for guidance. The woman he had been assigned to protect was safe. The killer had come close to finding her, but had been diverted.

He waited for a response to tell him how far to take the surveillance of the killer seated opposite him. The SMS came before the train had gone more than two stops.

'Use own discretion. Termination authorized.'

The gray-haired man mulled over his plans. He could choose the simple answer and see to it the killer would no longer be a danger to his charge. The old woman in Fruängen was an easy target. She could barely find her own way home. Or he could opt for the complicated solution which would leave the killer only incapacitated. Regardless of what he did, he would have to leave the map which had been discussed when the mission began. The gray-haired man watched as his target sent a message to someone on his cell phone. The train slowed for the next stop and the killer rose to leave at T-Centralen metro station.

It would be the simple answer.

Still preoccupied with his planning, the killer placed himself in front of the door. The gray-haired man followed him out of the train, removed a map from the tourist bag attached to the belt around his waist, and approached the killer from behind as they crossed to the other side of the platform.

The killer glanced nervously to his left and right as the train to Farsta rattled into the station. The gray-haired man waited for his moment, then rushed behind the killer in front of him, pushing him to meet the incoming train. Onlookers stood frozen in place, shocked and dumbfounded, wary of taking part in what might become a dangerous conflict. A young man took up his cell phone and began recording the scene.

The train screeched to a stop. The gray-haired man kept his back to the video cameras. He waved the map in his hand several times, then dropped it next to the platform. Disappearing into the crowd beginning to gather, the gray-haired man removed the gray wig and his light summer jacket and folded them into a wad. He took the steps to the next level in four long strides. Slowing to the speed of other commuters to reach the ground floor level of the train station, he left his wig and jacket in two different waste bins and began running. The doors to the express train to Arlanda airport hissed shut behind him. While he checked in for his flight to Paris, the local police were speaking to the young man with the cell phone.

Dolfin had been in her apartment during the attack. That morning The Can had seen her running toward the forest and told her it was time for her to take a shower. This happened quite often, a favor Nurse Anna had asked of him. Otherwise, Dolfin could wait weeks between showers until someone told her it was time to wash.

Dolphin's world was a disconnected volley of inputs, and she related only very few to other parts of her memory. There was no separation between mind and body, between her soul and her awareness. She was one single unit, a holistic being who could only be comprehended with her own logic; a logic so unique no one else in the world was able to decipher it. Both Nurse Anna and Dr. Habermann had tried, but were always only guessing, making logical assumptions based on their own backgrounds and intelligence. In reality, they would never be able to understand her.

To enter into Dolfin's world was to be submerged in a random flood of impressions: an intense awareness of the temperature of her skin for a few seconds, followed by the sounds of meaningless words she would echo in order to hear the sound of her own voice.

Then, a few seconds later, a black void as her mind overloaded and switched off, resulting in her snapping her head against her shoulder to regain consciousness.

In this kind of internal environment, the construction of logical thought became nearly impossible. If she felt hunger, she would begin looking for food. Nurse Anna had managed to train her to seek out the Big Dipper Restaurant near the State Liquor store, frequented by destitute seniors and drunks.

Dolfin had been on her way from the restaurant to the forest when she had been stopped by a policeman in the square. She had no concept of authority regarding the police and when her effort to circumvent the officer trying to stop her failed, she tried to knock him down. He grappled briefly with her. Dolfin exploded in rage. She was grabbed and thrown into the patrol car, kicking and screaming the whole time.

She calmed down as the car pulled away and began to concentrate on the images of streets and houses flashing by, her screams now becoming moans. She was on her way to the Psychiatric Ward where she would be admitted and put in a room for several hours as the residing doctor attended to other patients. It had been a busy afternoon and he'd already seen twenty patients since his shift began. There was no room for so many patients to be admitted, so he was forced to prioritize, keeping only the ones who were an obvious danger to others or themselves. He entered the room, looked at Dolfin, and tried to establish contact.

He noticed the key around her neck and asked the nurse if it had been logged. Dolfin wouldn't allow the nurse to remove it, but the nurse managed to observe it, and noticed a number stamped on the key. It looked like a Swedish person number. She called out the numbers to the doctor, who entered them into his computer and Dolfin's meager existence within the Swedish bureaucracy popped up on his screen.

He read the details and made a few notes in the journal.

"Why did the police bring her here?" he asked.

The nurse glanced at the rose-colored form, and replied, "The police said she might have been a witness to a killing and seemed distraught. They couldn't establish contact with her and thought we might be able to help."

"Unfortunately we won't be able to do anything for this poor woman," said the doctor. "Call the Social Welfare Service and have them take her home." He left to interview the next patient.

Chapter 14

Thomas Johnson took a chair at the end of a long mahogany table. The seven graying men in front of him were well-known icons for television viewers in Sweden. When they spoke for the good of the country, their authority was unquestioned. They ran industrial conglomerates, labor unions, national monopolies, and administered the day to day dealings at the office of the Prime Minister. The dark leather portfolio lying in front of each man bore a raised embossed symbol: three horizontal lines intersected by three vertical lines. This was the Swedish Iron Guard.

Thomas began by presenting the mission's successes so far.

"Nurse Eiderbach has been eliminated, and sources at the Coroner's office give assurance it will be considered a suicide. Regarding Habermann, the picture is a bit unclear. It seems he died as the result of a robbery in a taxi to the airport. Even if our own efforts failed, he is dead and can be stricken off the list."

The head of one of the conglomerates manufacturing paper, car parts, and laser weapons raised his eyes to view the candles in the ornate baroque chandelier above the table. "And the woman? Dolfin?"

Thomas turned to face the questioner. "I received news of her today." There were nods and affirmative murmurs around the table. "We know what part of Stockholm she lives in. The south side, Fruängen. Our current operative nearly succeeded in finding her, but I am replacing him. He killed an innocent bystander in order to maintain his cover during the operation. Aside from a few minor delays, everything is going according to plan. It will take but a few more days to find and eliminate her."

"The American? Is he still working with the police?" asked the head of a labor union.

Thomas Johnson related the latest news from his brother, Robert. "Hurtree was present at two meetings. He must have told the other investigators something because they are now using Habermann's name to define the robbery and homicide investigation."

"How much does he know about us?" the administrator for the Office of the Prime Minister asked.

"No one knows about us," replied Thomas Johnson with a quick smile.

The microphone hidden inside an electrical outlet in the meeting room fed a tiny FM transmitter which routed the entire conversation onto the 220 volt line. Every word was fed into a small black cube, about four inches on a side, housing an industrial PC fastened inside a telephone switch box several miles away. Milliseconds later, staff in a well-appointed apartment in the center of Stockholm and at an operations building near the Urim Kibbutz in the Negev desert were busy translating and analyzing the content of the meeting.

Dolfin ran as fast as her body allowed. Her long white hair flowed behind her. Her thick legs shuddered under the weight of sixty years of inactivity. She had difficulty maintaining speed above a quick waddle. Sharp pains in her knees came with every stride, but she kept on, eager for her meeting with Nurse Anna in the woods at the back of Långbro Hospital.

Dolfin had spent many years strolling with Nurse Anna in this small thicket of trees and bushes. Like all other Swedish mental patients with minor psychiatric diagnoses, she was released by the Government in 1994. Dolfin suddenly found herself locked out of the only home she had known since she was four years old, seriously incapable of managing her own life.

She lived in an apartment on Fruäng Street, close to the hospital where she had lived before it closed. Very few ex-patients adjusted as quickly as the social authorities projected. Most of them had lost the lease on their apartments after three months. Some were unable to take the papers from the social authorities to the post office to convert them into money, which could then be used to pay the rent. Some had left their envelopes on the floor in huge piles; some had thrown them out with all the other papers appearing every day through the mail slot.

For Dolfin, however, life was only marginally different after the hospital closed. Her life was still regulated by daily visits from Dr. Habermann and Nurse Anna Eiderbach. The two managed to explain to Dolfin that she was moving into another hospital room. Everything would continue as usual.

They tried, but couldn't control the degree of freedom extended to Dolfin. She discovered early on that in the new hospital the doors had handles on both sides and the locks on the doors were on the inside instead of the outside. She could come and go as she pleased.

Even after two years of living on her own, she still thrilled to see large numbers of people at the same time. The anguish of discovering she was alone, however, especially when it was dark, created demons in her mind.

She had difficulty remembering the way home to her apartment. During the daytime she had learned some beacons to look out for—the large metal statues of two women in the square in Fruängen; the signs above the shops; the church and the bookstore—when she was on the way to her own apartment. Beyond her apartment there was a road to cross, the duck pond, and then the forest in the hospital park where she met Nurse Anna Eiderbach every day, regardless of the weather. She counted them one-two-three fashion on the way to the forest, and then three-two-one on the way back. It was a simple cartography, but it worked.

As a child, Dolfin had gone through puberty with the mental age of a six-year-old. Nurse Anna had tried to inform her of the changes occurring in her body, but could do little to subdue the power of her hormones as she physically made the transition from being a child to a woman. Her developmental deficiency meant she became confused, extremely temperamental, and completely unmanageable. The same change occurred when she went through the menopause, and Nurse Anna could only try to explain the hot flushes and temper tantrums with analogies from the forest.

Before coming to Sweden, Dolfin had been raised according to the principles of the Nazi educational system. The program had included pregnant women up until they gave birth, and continued for the children through the pre-school years up to, and even after, university for those that continued. The national program had been conceived by the German Minister of Education, Dr. Bernhard Rust.

Dolfin's care assumed she, as a young girl, was inherently weak. She couldn't hope to match the achievements of her male cohorts. Her function as a woman was to lend her womb to provide the Third Reich with future supermen. There would soon be a major conflict in Europe, and the Führer would need the stuff of war.

Training began early. In the nursery, *Kindertagesstaedte*, Dolfin was assigned to a group of other tots from the time she could walk, mostly the children of high-ranking Nazi officials in the neighborhood. The children were given mental exercises every day. The exercises were impossible to solve, but allowed the nurses to explain to the boys they were superior, and that later on they would, of course, be able to solve the problems. The girls were told that because they were girls they were unable to solve such difficult problems, but that it was alright. The Führer had other more important missions for them.

When children began school they were separated into classes based on gender. There was little work based on book learning. The subjects of history and mathematics had disappeared and had been replaced by racial knowledge and tenets of the Party. Before eating lunch, they would say a prayer for Der Führer, giving thanks to God every day that Der Führer had come to guide them for the rest of their lives. Attempts had been made to begin these prayers in the nurseries, but with mixed results.

Dolfin's future as a school child was never discussed at her home. Her deficiencies became obvious to the nurses early on, and her temper tantrums and refusal to accept the iron discipline of the nursery had already resulted in several discussions with her mother. Of course, no one at the nursery knew of her heritage, or even who her mother was.

Dolfin's *Ahnenschein*, the document detailing her family lineage and proving her pure Aryan descent, was a blatant forgery and designed to minimize questions. However, it soon became clear she would have to be removed as unfit to be an active part of German society.

Dolfin spent most of her time at the nursery alone and she seldom joined in with the others in the various games the nurses started. She was moody, and her frequent temper tantrums made it difficult to communicate with her. Instead of developing a language she could use to speak to others, Dolfin had her own language, just for herself. Verbs and nouns were interchanged, using her own logic, and by the time she was three even her mother had become seriously worried.

It came to a head one Friday afternoon in 1940. A nurse took her favorite toy, a wooden block with wheels, and replaced it with a doll to teach her the future roll of maternal caring. Dolfin had ripped the doll apart while screaming guttural words no one understood. Her mother was informed by the head of Dolfin's *Kindertagesstaedte* that Dolfin would not be allowed to continue on Monday. Her mother was also told there would be actions taken, although she wasn't informed what that meant.

Now an older woman, released from Långbro Hospital, Dolfin explored the environment of Fruängen's Center, a suburban residential area with a few shops, and the last stop on the Number 14 line of the *Tunnelbana*, the local urban train. Within a short time, a gang of alcoholics and drug addicts included her in their group. They spent most of their waking days lounging outside the state liquor store. Dolfin amused them by her habit of repeating everything which had been said to her in a simultaneous fashion.

Dolfin had other mannerisms which set her apart. When she was excited she would do a little dance, quickly tapping her feet against the ground as if she were taking stairs which didn't exist, her head bobbing up and down as her dance accelerated with her excitement. Among the drunks she was known as either Hugger or Dancer.

Gang member: "Hello Hugger, how are you today?"

Dolfin: "Hello Hugger, how are you today?"

Gang member: "I'm fine, and how about you?"

Dolfin: "I'm fine, and how about you?"

Dolfin rarely spoke to people otherwise and almost never initiated comments, except when Anna Eiderbach was in her company. Anna had trained her to repeat what others said, hoping it would develop her brain, establishing the connections necessary to develop her own sense of awareness. In reality there was little else Dolfin could do. She had no other language skills, except to echo what others said to her.

The gang also liked the way she hugged trees. On some days she would run over to one of the trees in the park near the hospital buildings and hug the trunk, straddling it with her legs and gazing at the crown of the tree. She muttered unrecognizable words into the trunk and inflicted her arms and legs with red scratches as her embrace became more intense.

The Can had been responsible for bringing her into the gang. He had said it was Dolfin's way to make love.

"She loves trees more than people," he said. "It's that simple. Just accept it." The gang stopped making fun of her and even protected her from passers-by who would stop and stare. Nurse Anna was pleased that the Can had shared her responsibility for Dolfin. She could not always be there.

Långbro hospital had been built at the beginning of the nineteen hundreds, when the prevailing school of medical thought was that patients were cured not only by medicine or other treatments, but by the environment they were exposed to. Hospitals built during this period were often surrounded by huge parks of land, populated with exotic trees and shrubs from all over the world. During their daily walks, Nurse Anna had pointed out to Dolfin the names of all the trees and shrubs and imprinted the message that nature was much kinder than human beings. Dolfin could expect much more from nature than humanity.

Chapter 15

Hurtree was still lost in a daydream about Schwerlieb's suicide when the telephone in his hotel room rang, startling him back to reality. He was even more surprised to hear the voice of Sven Peterson.

"Good afternoon, John. I know Ekman tried to scare you off, but I could use some help. Can you recognize Schwerlieb's handwriting?"

"You bet." Hurtree's heart raced and his voice quivered. "I must have seen it a thousand times during the investigations."

"Would you like to have a chance to see it again?"

"I'll be down in a minute," said Hurtree, and he left in such a hurry he forgot his wallet. As he ran back to get it, he found he'd also forgotten to take his hotel key and wouldn't be able to get back in until the man at the reception desk had made him a new one. He arrived in the hotel lobby looking flustered and red-faced with excitement. The exertion of running back and forth in the corridors left small beads of sweat on his forehead.

Sven Peterson stood waiting for him, noting to himself that one day he would also be a pensioner. He quietly hoped he would be as spry as Hurtree, who barely looked to be over sixty. They got into Sven's car and began their journey to the National Archive.

Sven looked over at Hurtree as they drove toward the National Archive. "I hope you don't mind the cold. They keep the documents in the archive just a few degrees above freezing, and you only have a short-sleeved summer shirt on."

"I'll get by," said Hurtree. "I've been through a lot worse, believe me."

"I'll bet you have. Did you see any combat before the end of the war?"

"Enough to fill my quota." It was not something Hurtree liked to remember. The memories of watching a German soldier slump into death as his bullet reached its mark weren't that easy to suppress. "I read you guys haven't had a war in 200 years."

"You're right. And we lost that one. Losing a war can be a good lesson for the future."

"Yeah, well, I was in the Army, so losing wasn't an option for us. We didn't do too well on the last one, though, but that may not keep us out of the next one. Some of our presidents seem to like war a lot."

"Well, for what it's worth, I think you should know there are still some people who appreciate what the U.S. did during the Second World War. If you guys hadn't come in when you did, I'd probably be speaking German now instead of my own language." Sven stopped at a stoplight and glanced over at Hurtree.

"That was so long ago," said Hurtree. "I try to keep most of it out of my mind when I can. I lived in Germany after the war, so I can tell you there were many people there who were unhappy about us being there. They felt like they were walking around with their hands up for more than twenty years. The Nazis weren't in power all that long, but they managed to make a big impression, believe me."

Sven and Hurtree passed the Government Building on their way to the Swedish National Archive. Sven was pointing out the sights and landmarks: the Opera House, City Hall, and various church spires.

As they neared the National Archive, Hurtree leaned his head back on the headrest and asked Sven, "Did you see the tail?"

"Yeah, I did. I wonder who it is."

"Could be the guy who stalked me at the hotel bar Sunday night." Hurtree leaned his head forward to use the side mirror. "A Jewish guy. Said he was supposed to assist me if I needed it. I told him to get lost."

Sven's eyes widened. "So you've started a fan club already? Did he say anything else?"

"Just that there were people who didn't want me to work with the police, but that he was OK with it."

Sven parked the car and they walked back toward the National Archive. Sven fished up the card Sara had given him and called the archivist. "I assume we're not being listened to," Sven chuckled as he dialed the number.

"At least not by me." Hurtree gazed toward the stretch of blue water below them. Buildings clambered up steep wooded slopes to their right, and the Old Town lay in front of them. "My God, what a beautiful city this is."

"Hello." Sven spoke into his cell phone. "I don't know if you remember, but my colleague was here a few days ago. It had to do with Långbro Hospital."

"Of course I remember the visit, a Homicide Investigator. Miss Markham and her associate," said the archivist.

After a cryptic discussion with the archivist about the necessity of not using the main entrance, Sven and Hurtree took a path which included a long flight of stairs down to a park on the shores of Lake Mälaren. A few minutes later they found an unmarked gray door sunk into a scar blasted out of a granite outcropping, shuttered by birch tree overgrowth and thick green moss. Sparrows chirped and scattered as the door hinges complained. Sven and Hurtree approached the open door, and the archivist welcomed the two men into the emergency exit and quickly closed the door. They had entered the chill of the National Archive from an angle few had ever experienced.

As they were walking toward the tunnel where the Långbro documents were stored, the archivist made a left instead of a right, and they arrived at the elevator which would take them toward the surface. They entered the lobby, and in a few seconds the chill of the archive's subterranean tunnels was exchanged for the normal summer air conditioning. Sven and Hurtree followed the archivist into a conference room and he closed the door. He gestured and asked them to sit down.

The archivist's face became serious, and his voice tone matched. "I'm afraid I can't allow you to access the documents at this time. There have been, uh, complications."

Sven and Hurtree looked at each other, then back to him as he continued, "I don't know who you have been speaking to, people high up in the Government, or if you have in some way leaked to others what you have read, but for whatever reason the files from Långbro have been classified as a State Secret as of today. You'll have to petition the Swedish Government, stating your reason in great detail. After that they will make a decision regarding the possibility of accessing the documents. Personally, I've never heard of any case where the secrecy decree has been removed for any reason."

Sven answered, using Swedish to exclude Hurtree, "So what does this mean? Does it mean that the Government knows we've been here?"

"I can't answer that because I really don't know," answered the archivist quickly, also in Swedish. "It appears someone must know. These secrecy decisions are made at the very top level. Very few people have ever experienced such meetings, certainly not me. What it means is, I think you should be careful. I certainly will be doing so."

There was a short silence between the two Swedish speakers, and Hurtree took the opportunity to ask a question. "Doesn't *hemlig* mean secret in English? Have the Schwerlieb documents been classified as secret?"

Sven and the archivist nodded, and Hurtree continued, "So what does this mean for us? How long are documents secret in Sweden?"

"At least thirty years," said the archivist, "and I don't really know what this means. I was hoping you could tell me yourselves. All I can tell you is I'm not going to take any further risks for your benefit. Actually I'm going to ask you to remain silent about what you already might have seen, and then I'm politely going to ask you to leave."

"Well, we thank you for everything you did for us, and I would like to offer our assistance if you come to any harm," said Sven.

"Would it make any difference if I could get the support of the U.S. Embassy to help you?" asked Hurtree.

"The help of your embassy would generate more harm than already has been done," the archivist grumbled, turning to Hurtree. "Just leave, please. I'll show you out the way we came in." And they left via the emergency exit they had used to enter.

The archivist locked the door behind them and he watched them on the video screen until they disappeared from view. He shook his head in dismay. This was a bad development, very bad.

He was close to retirement and he hoped it wouldn't affect his old-age pension, the only thing of value he owned after nearly forty years of work. He had been born just as the Second World War began, one of many products of parents who were anxious about their own future. That was a time when Europe had held its collective breath. Some people dreamed of empowerment, others hoped for a place to hide when shove turned to shoot. Everyone was hoping for a better tomorrow in which to raise their children.

The weather had changed when Sven and Hurtree emerged from the National Archive. Sven's cell phone rang and a frown sent furrows across his brow. He told Hurtree he had to meet someone, and that it was urgent. Hurtree withdrew a city map from his pocket, and after Sven had pointed out where they stood, Hurtree said he'd be able to find his own way home. It would be an enjoyable, chilly summer walk.

Sven returned to the call from the Stockholm Violent Crimes Division. "OK, shoot," said Sven.

"We're investigating a murder in Fruängen. The Coroner says it looks like the work of a professional. There is something strange with the case. Alcoholics usually don't get killed by hitmen. Can you take over?"

Sven called Robert Johnson immediately.

"Robert, how are you coming along with the tapes?" asked Sven.

"Not too bad," said Robert. "I'm almost finished with the search perimeter of one kilometer. Still no results, sorry."

"I need you on another case. I want you to drop what you're doing with the team and do a quick investigation of a killing in southern Stockholm, Fruängen. A drunk was killed, and it could be a professional hit. This takes priority over what you've been doing so far."

"OK," said Robert, and a gush of pride filled his lungs. *Finally*, he thought. "I'll inform the team on the way out."

"No, I'll inform the team when I get back from the National Archive. Here's the location of the killing and names of the police who started the investigation. Get moving."

Thank God for small murders, Sven thought. This solved his problem with Nurse Anna's investigation, which was becoming more and more complex with Robert's obvious mistake of not observing the murderer leave the train station.

Robert walked around the block to meet with the homicide investigator at Stockholm's City Police. The investigation would have been classified as a simple homicide arising from a conflict among drunks, but the Coroner's report had changed that. Someone had sliced the Can's liver with a single stab from a knife.

"As professional as they come," said the homicide investigator to Robert, and they reviewed the few details that had been found at the crime scene in Fruängen.

The Can's companions had already been interviewed and released. One of the investigators had looked for witnesses in the small square and in the shops surrounding it. She reported that there had been no one operating the ticket booth at the entrance to the train, so little could be learned there. She had also collected witness interviews made by the officers who were first to arrive on the scene.

Robert looked first at the blond investigator, then at the pile of binders.

"We interviewed everyone they saw, including people in the shops. There are about 200 pages of testimony to sift through," she informed Robert.

Robert groaned at the thought of several days of reading police reports.

"Is there anything out of the ordinary here?" Robert tapped the pile of binders. "Something that caught your attention?"

"No. No one saw anything, except two of his gang who left a good description of the killer. The drunk who got killed was well-known. Normally kept out of trouble. Hard to understand why anyone would want him dead." She glanced at Robert, then down at her watch. "The strangest thing that day was the bag lady they drove to the Psychiatric Ward. A real nutcase."

"I assume it's in one of the reports," said Robert.

"Not much," said the blond officer. "They tried to talk to her, but she was incoherent. Then she began to attack them, so they bundled her into a patrol car and drove her to the shrinks. They figured that maybe the doctors could figure out if she saw anything."

"What's her name?" asked Robert.

"No idea. Like I said, incoherent. No ID, no money, nothing. They reported she had a key on a chain around her neck, otherwise I'd suspect her to be one of the homeless." The blond officer shrugged her shoulders.

Robert cast an admiring glance at the young woman. "Can we meet over a beer after we're done here?"

The wind came in from the north, whipping up the lake next to the path leading toward Rålambshovsparken. Brave sunbathers had positioned their bodies to maximize the sun's rays, and Hurtree glanced over at a young woman who grimaced as the sharp north wind raised goosebumps on her skin. Seagulls screeched to each other, swooping lower and lower to get a better view of her topless body.

With less than two weeks left in Stockholm, Hurtree began summarizing for himself what he had learned so far as he walked back from the National Archives. What had happened during these last few days was more than had happened in his life in Philadelphia during the past year.

The Swedish investigators seemed interested in what he had told them about the photograph and the medallion. What were they not telling him? And then there was the secrecy issue. Why had the Långbro hospital documents been classified after Sara's visit?

Chapter 16

The General Director of the NSS coughed once, cleared his throat, then coughed again, this time louder. When that didn't succeed, he scraped the floor with his chair as if he were leaving.

The Prime Minister woke immediately. "General Director, what more do you have to add? I noticed nothing especially important this morning. The usual report, I suppose you'd say."

"Not exactly, Prime Minister." The PM was adamant all employees use his full title when addressing him. The General Director chose his words carefully. "Uhm, there may have been a point where I expressed myself in unclear terms about one of the details," he said. "A minor point, perhaps, but we may be exposing the Party to a certain amount of negative press in the future if this case is allowed to develop."

"Of course," said the PM. "Please expand on that point a little more," and the General Director began his entire presentation again. This time the PM managed to stay awake the whole time.

There had been several meetings within the National Security Service regarding what had become known as the German Case as it was transmitted to those higher up. The NSS was organized with a clear division of power. Information filtered up through the NSS on a regular basis and finally ended up on the desk of the General Director, who was always appointed by the Prime Minister. The most important criteria was possession of the correct political membership card. The PM was updated on the status of important or sensitive case files every Tuesday morning. Today's meeting was now over.

*

At 12.15 p.m., the PM's secretary had called the other eighteen ministers in the Government to the emergency meeting, an unusual event. It brought the Cabinet ministers to the rose-colored Government Building in the center of Stockholm during lunch, and they complained to each other as they met in the elevator and in the hall outside the Cabinet meeting room.

The secretary who usually recorded the minutes of each meeting was asked to leave after a roll call. There would be no notes recorded of the content of this meeting. There was much grumbling as they seated themselves around the long table, quickly silenced by the PM.

"It has become clear the dealings of some previous governments are at risk. There is every possibility a journalist may get hold of some of this story, and if that happens it might blow up in our faces," and the PM rotated his head to meet the eyes of each Cabinet minister. "In fact, this might mean the end of our Party. It's that's serious."

The PM briefed his ministers on the situation and threw the floor open for discussion. He would make the final decision, but he always enjoyed more input. Even though he had assembled one of the most incompetent collection of ministers in Swedish history, most of them could be relied upon to protect the Party, their most important asset.

The PM showed little concern about their gross ignorance on the subject matter of their portfolios. They had been appointed with the express purpose of never questioning the wisdom of the PM, and never, ever to suggest anything in public he would later have to recant. It was better for the ministers to do nothing than to make the error of doing something he did not agree with. This led to serious problems with the advice he received during his Cabinet meetings. He only heard what he liked to hear.

The discussion became a race for silence. No one spoke at all at first. There were several ministers who had actually met members of the original Second World War Government, and had even spoken with the Professor or his wife before they had passed away. Those ministers knew there might be issues there, but few knew if the current PM was really aware of the scope of the involvement they would be trying to cover up.

When the silence became too much to bear, the Minister of Justice was the first to speak. She had been in the Party for many years and wielded much more authority than the younger ministers, attractive young women recruited when the Party had been advised this would attract several percent of new voters in coming elections.

"I assume we can rely on the NSS in this case," said the Justice Minister. "There have been times in the past when their loyalties have been questioned, especially when exposing our weaknesses."

The PM smiled. "You're right," he said, "but I'm afraid the facts are just too clear in this case. We definitely have a problem with history, and it will be hard to avoid."

"I think we should do as we always do: deny, deny, deny. It's always worked before," said the Minister of Defense, affectionately known as the Teddy Bear. "If we get caught out in a lie we can always manufacture a new truth to counter it."

Following that comment there were a few remarks about the quality of the bakery which had delivered the pastries and whether or not the coffee came from a country exhibiting the proper social care for its people. The meeting broke up as it had begun, with little advice to the PM.

After the meeting, the Prime Minister sat with his Political Secretary, watching a news report on the status of the world in general. There were reports from Colombia about the terrorist group FARC.

"We'll soon be asked to try to keep FARC off the terrorist list in the EU," said the Secretary after watching the news blurb. "I doubt we'll be able to do it."

"It doesn't matter if we're successful, we need only make an effort to keep that group happy," replied the PM. "They muster a lot of votes out west of the city, you know."

The PM straightened his back and threw his stomach out, a sign the Secretary knew was the beginning of a new policy. "I have the answer," exclaimed the PM. "Odd it should always be me who has to supply the answers to all the real problems confronting us, but then again, it's not so strange. I mean, who is the leader around here anyway? Here's what we'll do," he continued. "Next week we'll begin a government program which exposes all the atrocities carried out by the Nazis during the war. I'll fly to Israel and pose before the Wailing Wall. After that no one will be able to question the sincerity of the Party or our efforts to take the side of truth and justice."

The Secretary paused before making his own suggestion. "Yes, that sounds great. Perhaps we could even create a museum dedicated to the Holocaust. That might give us a little pressure on the Israelis and the United States when we have to ask for their support in the U.N. on other issues."

"Perfect," said the PM. "Let's do it."

"I'll contact the appropriate ministers tomorrow morning. What do we do about the NSS?" asked the Secretary.

"Nothing," replied the PM. "Let them play their spy games until they get tired of it. They should be smart enough to figure out we want a lid kept on this. Their files will be marked 'Top Secret' by this afternoon. If anything else comes up we'll refer to what we just created."

Hurtree left the grass and shivering sunbathers, and turned right onto a paved walkway beside the busy traffic on Norrmalmstrand. He entered an outdoor lakefront restaurant built on pontoons, and was shown to a table where he admired the beauty of glittering blue water contrasted by forests, buildings, trees, and bridges. Sails popped in the brisk wind as sailboats changed their course only 100 yards from Hurtree's table. He ordered lunch by pointing to the menu and waited for his order to arrive.

So the files are 'Top Secret' now, he thought. *Someone is covering up. She must be out there. But where?*

Hurtree's Guinness arrived and he tapped on the glass, coaxing the bubbles to rise. He glanced up to see a man take the table next to him, and recognized the man from the bar the night before.

Hurtree narrowed his eyes and raised his glass to the newcomer. "Shalom, asshole."

The man smiled and nodded his head. "Mr. Hurtree. I hope you are enjoying your vacation."

"I told you to leave me alone," growled Hurtree.

"I am making sure people do just that," said the man.

"I don't need your help."

"You won't know until you need it."

"Still don't need it," retorted Hurtree.

"You're still alive. Rejoice," said the man at the table beside him. He waved off the waiter who arrived to take his order and rose to leave. "Shalom," he said over his shoulder.

"Fuck you," Hurtree replied to the man's receding back. "No, not you," said Hurtree to the frowning waiter as his lunch arrived.

Chapter 17

Sara sat in the Eiderbach/Habermann room. Open binders lay in front of her, and she held her head with both hands in deep concentration. Sven entered the room without knocking.

"I just got the enhancement of Eiderbach's killer from forensics."

The video monitor flickered to life as the CD spun up to the scene. "There he is," said Sara. "Clear as can be. We can use that photo when we interview witnesses. Has anyone talked to the driver of the taxi he's getting into?"

"I just got this. But there's more. Look at this." Sven clicked on the arm of Eiderbach's killer to enlarge the image. The smudge on the killer's arm changed to a fuzzy image, but clear enough to discern the tattoo: three horizontal lines intersected by three vertical lines.

"What's that?" asked Sven. "I've never seen a tattoo like that before."

"Me neither," said Sara. "Let's put it through TIS, the Tattoo Information System that compares tattoos instead of fingerprints, like in AFIS."

Sven nodded and turned to place the enhanced photo of Eiderbach's killer and his tattoo on the whiteboard. Sara's fingers clicked a quick rhythm as she opened the newly implemented database to assist criminal investigators. She smiled to herself and thought, *Finally, a database that actually works.* She concentrated on setting up the appropriate filters to view tattoos.

Robert's cheery greeting filled the room as he returned from his lunch with the blond investigator at Stockholm's Homicide.

"I'm back. Sven, the murder out in Fruängen was not the result of drunks brawling. It bears the mark of a professional killer. Very nasty knife work according to the Coroner's report. Not too much to go on though, lots of people who didn't see anything."

Sara's computer completed its search of graphical images resembling the tattoo on Eiderbach's killer's arm.

"Sven, I've found something. Two hits. Look at this."

Sven and Robert closed in to view the first image from the database search: a black-and-white drawing from a witness's statement.

"That's not really like what we have on the whiteboard," said Sven. "Looks more like a tattoo of tic-tac-toe. Two lines intersecting each other. Eiderbach's killer had a tattoo where three lines crossed."

Robert went to the other side of the room to look more closely at the enhanced photo of the tattoo pinned to the whiteboard. Sara clicked on the murder reference number to get more details from the database.

"Robert, was the murder you worked on today committed in Fruängen two days ago?"

Robert returned to stand behind Sara. His answer came slow, unsure. "Yes," and then, "it was."

"The drawing of the tattoo was made by a witness. It's what he remembered."

"I haven't read the case files yet," said Robert, "there are more than 200 pages. But I agree with Sven. It's close, but there are two more lines missing."

Sara shook her head slowly. She returned to the filtered search profile and clicked on the second instance. This time a pale white arm flashed on the screen. There were scratch marks, and at the bottom of the image the bone was exposed where the arm had been severed. A blue tattoo on the inside of the lower arm was positioned just above a wristwatch—three lines intersecting three other lines.

"This looks more like it," Sara said, and printed out the image. She clicked on the reference number for more information, and checked the time of death.

Robert took the printout and carried it to the photo on the whiteboard. "They look similar," he said, beginning to believe his own words. "Even the watch looks similar."

Sara was checking the time it took for a train to arrive at T-Centralen from Fruängen. "Robert, there was enough time for your murderer to take the train to T-Centralen and get pushed onto the tracks. Does he fit the description of your killer in Fruängen?"

"I haven't had time to read the files yet, but the investigator at Stockholm's Homicide, Hanna, said they got very little from their witnesses. She didn't mention the tattoo."

Sara returned to the database regarding the murder of the man pushed onto the tracks. "The face of the victim is banged up pretty bad. But the investigator from Stockholm's police made a paper copy from the train station video of both the victim and the killer. The victim's face looks like what we've got on the whiteboard for Eiderbach's killer. We should get a look at that video," said Sara.

"I think you're right," said Sven, "and the sooner the better. What else do we know about the victim?"

Sara clicked again to get all the details. "No ID, no money, just what could be a hotel keycard in his pocket and a cell phone that got squashed by the wheel as the train ran over him. We can try to find a number registered on the radio base station located in the metro station. That might give us something if we get lucky."

"I wouldn't count on it," said Sven. "There must have been hundreds of phones active in the station at that time. Are you sure he didn't have anything else on his body? Any ID at all?"

"Forensics is working to get prints and other identifiers. We can ask them to do a DNA sample. He might be in CODIS, you never know. You saw the body. It was pretty much chewed up by the train, but I think we can get a composite drawing of his face from the artist by tomorrow," replied Sara.

Sara put the video showing the murder of Anna Eiderbach into the machine. She and Sven recognized the similarity between the killer and the new victim.

Robert took a chair at the end of the long table and stared at the whiteboard. He turned to Sven and asked, "If this is the killer from the murder in Fruängen, why knock him off? Was this revenge?"

"I think we'd better get some background on this victim. Find out who he was, where he lived, and what made him worth killing. I'd like to add this to the Eiderbach case," said Sara.

Sven focused on the computer monitor where the image of the tattoo still stood out in the upper right hand corner. "Good idea, Sara. That tattoo on his arm may help. By the way, I just found out the Långbro files have been stamped 'Secret'," said Sven.

"Christ," said Sara, "just what we need, to start stumbling over our own feet."

Sven gazed at the ceiling as he spoke. "What do you think about this guy, Hurtree? Can we trust him? He came to us offering us help, and now we've got a new murder victim. Could he be involved in some way? Suppose he's a mole collecting information for people that are trying to clean up?"

"It happens," said Sara, "but isn't it usually the killer himself that tries to do a friendly deed by helping the police in order to get more information about what's happening in the investigation?"

"Nothing is usual about this case," said Sven, and he printed out another copy of the tattoo on the victim's arm.

Commissioner Ekman reached the last page of the Habermann files, and the final sentences sent a shiver of fear up his spine.

> They can do what they want, even sterilize her now. With the new technology called cloning and developments in the future we will soon be able to recreate Der Führer anyway. For this reason we must keep her alive at all costs.

Ekman's hand hovered over his phone, but before he could pick it up, it rang.

Sven asked if they could meet at the NSS. "I've got something you have to see," said Sven.

Ekman responded, "Same here."

Ten minutes later, Ekman and Sven grabbed coffees and continued to Ekman's room. "Is there any mention of the Iron Guard in anything you've read?" asked Sven, and sat in the chair opposite Ekman.

"No, it's strange. I was expecting to find at least some mention of them, but there's nothing. Most of the files contain medical notes on autism and various attempts to help their patient."

"So she's autistic," said Sven. "Does that help us find her?"

"Not really. They let people with those symptoms go when the Government started cutting costs for health care. There are notes about her from after she left the hospital, but no record which tells us where she is. She's been hidden somewhere."

Sven laid a video film on Ekman's desk. "Here's a video where Anna Eiderbach gets murdered. There's evidence that indicates her murderer was killed himself two days ago."

"What?" asked Ekman, surprised. "Can we identify his killer?

"Sara is working on it. The victim had an Iron Guard tattoo on his arm." Sven dropped the printout of the tattoo on top of the CD video.

Ekman held his coffee cup with both hands. He squinted toward the window and took careful sips of the steaming liquid. "Looks like Hurtree was right. This involves both the Iron Guard and the Mossad. Has the Terrier figured it out yet?"

"She was the one who noticed the tattoo. It won't take her long to figure it out. I just found out the Långbro hospital files in the National Archive have been classified as top secret. Did you do that?" asked Sven.

"No," said Ekman, "I didn't know about it myself until a few minutes ago. The cover-up is in progress. You'd better find this Dolfin woman before the lid gets jammed on."

"I think we can assume she was still alive at the time Habermann was killed. Neither the nurse nor the doctor seemed fit enough to travel long distances. My guess is she lives somewhere close to either Fruängen or the Old Town."

Ekman folded the pile of notes back into the file. "If we don't find her soon, she'll be dead. What about the American? Hurtree?" Ekman stood to place the file in the cabinet. "He may be able to provide more information about the Iron Guard. At least he knew what it was. My gut feeling is we can probably trust him, but we've got to be careful. He shows up offering us help and suddenly someone else gets killed."

"My thoughts exactly," said Sven. "We should continue to question him, but he gets no new information. The Mossad might be behind both the Habermann killing and this latest victim. How do we investigate that?"

"My own contacts with the Mossad are, let's say, informal. But I know someone who knows someone. I'm sure they won't admit to anything, but we can always ask. Why don't you talk to Hurtree again? Perhaps he can help us find the Dolfin woman. Hurtree thinks she might be Hitler's daughter. He might remember something which will get us closer." Ekman slammed the cabinet door shut. "You've got two days."

Chapter 18

Hurtree strode through the revolving door at his hotel. Sven and Sara rose as he waved at the concierge.

"We'd like to ask you one or two more questions, if we may?" said Sven as he approached.

"Sure," said Hurtree, "but it's one question for one this time."

"One for, let's say, three?" said Sven, and he motioned Hurtree into a more secluded part of the lobby. The hotel PA system played a recording of Vivaldi's *Summer* and brightened the mood. "Can I order something for you?"

"Sure. I'll have the Filet Mignon. Your famous hot dogs are giving me indigestion. As for the questions, it's still one for one," said Hurtree.

"OK. I'll see what I can do about your meal in a minute. Here's what's bothering me. You're convinced this Dolfin woman is Hitler's daughter. Would there be any reason for the Iron Guard to want to kill Hitler's daughter?"

"They're some pretty spooky folks," said Hurtree. "Who knows? Pissed off? I don't know. What makes you think they really wanted to off her anyway?"

"We won't go into detail. Can you just answer the question?" insisted Sven.

"Well, it sounds weird to me. When I was active they were sometimes used as professional assassins, but I never heard of them doing one of their own, unless…" Hurtree paused for a long five seconds, "unless there was something else going on. It could be there are changes taking place in the Iron Guard. Maybe that's what it's about."

"Like a *coup d'etat?*" asked Sara.

"It happens all the time in established government. Why can't it happen in underground organizations?" Hurtree sat down on one of the over-stuffed leather chairs in the hotel lounge. "I can't see any other reason for it to happen. Can I ask a question now?"

Sven nodded.

"I've heard a lot about your Swedish person number ID system. Being able to follow people from the cradle to the grave. Why don't you just punch in this Dolfin woman's number into a computer and get her last known address?"

Sara began, "John, we would have tried that, but there are some technical difficulties in this case. She wasn't born in Sweden so we need a way to find a record of her person number from another source than the database file used for the entire country. She might be in it, probably is, but without knowing the number it's like looking for a green pea in a dump truck full of yellow peas. We need a link between her name and her number. So far…" and she paused as Sven sent a sharp message across the table, a clearing of his throat telling her Hurtree shouldn't get more information, "…so far we just don't know. Do you know anything about her identity to help us find her?"

"Me?" asked Hurtree. "How would I know what to look for? Maybe she has a mustache like her father."

The efforts of the Iron Guard to find Dolfin had been severely hampered. Habermann had managed to provide Dolfin with a personal identification number, the fundamental requirement for living in Sweden, and at the same time made sure it would be exceedingly difficult to successfully search for her in the database.

Since the hotly contested meeting of the Iron Guard in Tarragona, Spain, where the decision to terminate Dolfin had been taken, nearly half a million dollars had been spent on the mission. The reports coming in from Sweden indicated both successes and failures.

The steering committee fretted over the cost and the results.

The head of the German branch had proposed and pushed through the decision, in spite of opposition from the Americans. Now it seemed the Swedes had only managed to take out one target, and the hitman for that mission had himself been killed. The mission would have to be finished, and soon. The mission's goal, to reduce exposure of their organization, was now in danger of backfiring.

Hurtree looked over at Sara and tried another question. "Right. Why are the files at the National Archive suddenly off-limits? We heard today even the police cannot access them."

"It doesn't serve the greater good for us to know what's in those files," said Sven, and his voice took on a colder tone. "I think we're wasting our time here. You don't know anything more that will help us find the Dolfin woman. Take Ekman's advice and leave Sweden."

"Am I in trouble here?" asked Hurtree.

"I wouldn't say trouble, but you are becoming an inconvenience," said Sven. "It's best to let sleeping bears lie."

"Bears?" asked Hurtree. "Do you mean I was right all those years ago? That Hitler really did have a child that survived?"

"I doubt you'll ever find anyone to confirm that over here. At least not publicly. If the question ever arises it will be answered by some kind of government commission in perhaps thirty years. We call it the Swedish Way. And for us it's bears, not dogs," said Sven.

"Well I call it crap, dog, bear, or otherwise," said Hurtree. "What's the point of knowing all this stuff if everyone's too afraid to talk about it? I don't get it." Hurtree shook his head.

Sven's face took on a very serious expression. "It's part of the job description."

"Fuck," said Hurtree. "Bureaucrats." Hurtree felt his stomach twist in complete frustration. "I hate this," he said. "I'm so close to being able to close this case after all these years, and now I just have to turn my back on it?"

"John, we have to find the Dolfin woman. Her life is in danger," said Sara.

Hurtree nodded. "What can I do?"

"Any little detail might help."

"I saw a photograph once, but she'd be a lot older today."

A question flitted across Sara's mind. "Who took the photograph? Did you ever discover that?" asked Sara.

"No, in the beginning we just assumed it was Schwerlieb. He had a copy, and his son was in it. After his death, one of our team noticed the photograph was probably made by what he called f/64 group technology. I didn't understand much of it, but he said you could see it from the fact that what was in the foreground where the kids stood was in focus, and the background, where Hitler stood about thirty meters away, was also in sharp focus. To me it was just a picture, and all the theories never helped us figure out who took it."

"Were the Goebbels in the photograph?" asked Sara.

"Not the parents. Just the kids. You're right, maybe it was one of the Goebbels who took the picture and they just gave one to Schwerlieb because his son was there too."

"But it would be interesting to know who took it," said Sara.

"There is one part to the story you haven't heard. The connection between Schwerlieb and the Masons."

"Masons? Do you mean Freemasons? In this context? You have to be kidding," said Sven.

"No, I'm not," said Hurtree. "Schwerlieb wore a weird ring during the trial. I saw it myself when I interviewed him, and even when I went to see him the day before he died. It disappeared mysteriously after his death. It was a gold ring with a pyramid on top that could be opened and that contained all sorts of little symbols on the inside. It wasn't on his finger when they photographed his body on the prison floor. I never did find out what happened to that ring, and I never put it into my report. It was enough being suspected of helping him commit suicide."

"What? Were you involved in his suicide? How did that happen?" asked Sven.

Hurtree told Sven of the day that he had been called by the

commander of the prison in Nuremberg to meet with Schwerlieb on the day before he was to be hanged. When he had finished, there was a polite silence.

"John, what you said about the ring doesn't establish a Masonic connection for me. How did you put that together?" asked Sara.

"I asked a jeweler in Munich to help me out," said Hurtree. "I made a sketch of the ring and he told me that only high-ranking Freemasons would ever be able to own such a ring. Of course that didn't prove that Schwerlieb was a Mason. He could have stolen it from one of the Mason's condemned to die for some other reason. What we did find out was that Hitler was interested in the Masonic movement because it was a secret organization with very stern discipline. Hitler even wanted to model his SS after them because he thought it would increase their status. Some people would want to get in because of all the secrecy and mysticism, others would fear them for the same reasons."

"What's that supposed to tell us?" asked Sven.

Hurtree responded quickly, "Maybe there's a Masonic connection to your murders and to Dolfin. If this were my investigation, I'd look for any kind of local connections between the Masons and the Iron Guard. Both groups have influential people in their leadership, and both are addicted to secrecy."

Sven made it clear he did not believe what he had just heard. "Sorry. This sounds like a lot of pseudo-secret mumbo-jumbo." He stood up, and they shook hands before he left. "Mr. Hurtree, this case is closed. I expect you to leave this alone from now on. Your help has been appreciated, but this is our problem, and we'll solve it on our own. Sara, are you coming?"

"No, I'll take the bus home," she said. "See you tomorrow, Sven."

Chapter 19

Sara waited until Sven disappeared through the revolving door, then turned to Hurtree. "I want to thank you personally for your help in these cases. I don't think we'd have come as far as we have without your help."

"I'm just glad I could help." Hurtree cocked his head to one side. "It still pisses me off I have to quit, but if I don't I'll end up on the wrong end of your Swedish justice. I got real close to finding out what happened here, but I never got the chance to talk to this Dolfin woman. I wanted at least to do that."

"Why would that make any difference?" asked Sara.

"It doesn't. Makes no difference at all. I just wanted to do it, that's all. Like looking at a river and wanting to swim across it. You ever feel that?"

"I don't swim very well," said Sara. "Never really learned how. My background was, uh—they didn't have time to teach us how to swim where I grew up, and I was always afraid of the water as a kid." Sara's eyes wandered as she reminisced. "When I took the swimming test to join the force, they thought I was really good during the test called 'Dive and Retrieve a Body' because I could hold my breath longer than anyone else. What they didn't know was that I almost drowned during that test. I wasn't doing it on purpose, I just couldn't get back to the surface any faster."

Sara looked away and she shivered at the memory, "Let's drop the subject of water. You might help me with one further question. I saw a strange tattoo today. On a body. Up here most criminals are tattooed, but I've never seen one like this. It was on the inside of his lower left arm. It looked like this." Sara took a napkin and drew three vertical lines intersected by three horizontal lines. "Is this something Masonic?"

"No." Hurtree watched Sara finish the drawing. He coughed into his hand, then said in a low voice, "Definitely not. That's the symbol of the Iron Guard. That means the body you saw belonged to someone with real conviction when he lived. Sounds like you have a problem. Does this have anything to do with the Dolfin case?"

An inner struggle broke out in Sara's mind. How much could she reveal? She had been told not to tell Hurtree more about matters relating to the Dolfin case.

Hurtree saw the struggle, and he continued, "Well if I were going to try to figure this one out without your help, I'd say someone from the Mossad put down a member of the Iron Guard. There's probably a reason for that. Could your Nurse Anna Eiderbach have been a Mossad undercover agent and they're just doing tit for tat?"

Sara refused to answer.

Hurtree squinted and kept talking. "But it's probably not going to help much, unless you have some kind of a working relationship with someone who knows someone in the Mossad. Anyway, you certainly can't expect them to admit to murder if they did it, can you?"

Sara sat still and shifted her gaze beyond Hurtree, and finally answered, "But if they were responsible, how can we get them?"

"You'll never be able to," said Hurtree. "When the Mossad is involved there usually isn't very much evidence, unless they want you to find something. So if they left anything behind, it was for a reason."

Sara blinked and saw in her mind a picture of the murderer waving the map up to the video camera and then dropping it on the platform. She blinked again and saw the body of Habermann with credit cards strewn on top of it.

"So they are telling us they did something, but not why. Why would they do that?" asked Sara.

"Whatever the reason, you can be sure it serves their purpose. Those guys don't usually make mistakes, and even accidents are few and far between. It sounds to me like you haven't run into this kind of case too often. That right?" Sara nodded, and Hurtree continued, "Reminds me of myself when I started out. I was such a greenhorn they painted my boots green when I got my first case."

"This is the first case I've run on my own, and now it turns out our security police get involved and I can barely move. Did you ever run into something like that?"

Hurtree didn't have to think too hard. "Oh yeah, big time. There were times when the Federal Narcotics Bureau got involved and we all had to back down. It was the shits because there were times when we thought they were the bad guys. Really bizarre. Are they reliable at your Security Service? Are they run by the politicians, or can they run their own show?"

"Generally they work independently," said Sara. "There was a time when the Government didn't trust the Security Service, so they formed a unit that reported only to them, a sort of political police formed with people from military intelligence. I think they called it the Information Bureau, the IB. There was a scandal years ago, and a couple of journalists ended up in jail because they revealed the existence of the Bureau. After that it's been quiet. I think they were disbanded," said Sara. "It doesn't matter anyway. It seems politicians get to do just about anything they want to, regardless of what country they're in."

"Well you're right there, Sara," said Hurtree. "I heard Sven refer to you as the Terrier."

Sara looked away in embarrassment. "Yes. They call me the Terrier at work."

"I won't even ask why," chuckled Hurtree. "Do you like the job?"

"Yes, I do. It's fun to be the problem-solver who puts criminals in jail. I really like that part of it. But I still have some problems with all the violence, it gets to me sometimes. That's the part I didn't know about when I was just a kid. And there's a sort of rage inside of me sometimes. I'd like to do a lot more than just put the crooks in jail, if you know what I mean. Some of these people seem to belong to another species. They don't seem to be human."

"I used to have the same problem. I avoided getting into fights with the bad guys, because, well, there were times I didn't know when to quit. Sometimes I did a little too much to keep the criminals from running away. There was this ex-soldier, a drug-dealing Neo-Nazi who was part of the Iron Guard after he left the military. He had connections making it impossible for me to catch him." Hurtree smiled and nodded his head at the recollection of their last encounter. "I put the bastard in a wheelchair."

Hurtree did a quick scan of the hotel lobby where they sat. Two middle-aged women had emerged from the bar and sat with their drinks several tables away. "Let's continue this conversation somewhere not quite so public. Is there anywhere we could get a bite to eat and talk at the same time?"

"Not this evening. I have to leave now. Suppose we do find this woman, Dolfin, before you leave. I mean, if we could find her then at least we'd have the chance to talk to her. What can that hurt? I sure wouldn't tell anyone. Without your help I don't think we would ever have begun to crack this case. I'll talk to Sven tomorrow morning and see if we can do it in two days. If we can't find her in that time then it's bye-bye, and we call it off. Sound OK?"

"No," responded Hurtree, "it's not OK, but it'll have to do under the circumstances. You can call me if you get a chance to talk to her. You know where I live." Hurtree waved his hand to include the hotel lobby. "And I guess I don't get the Filet Mignon?"

"No," said Sara, "you'll have to make do with the standard Swedish police menu of the day, *grillad med bröd*."

"Well I can't speak Swedish, but that sounds like a hot dog on a bun to me."

"You learn quickly," said Sara as she left. She flashed a wink at Hurtree, telling him he had at least qualified as a surrogate relative. He watched her leave and was pleased with the assignment.

*

Ekman used three keys to unlock the door to his apartment. His girlfriend was busy with dinner in the kitchen. She looked up as he put his brown leather briefcase on the hall floor. He approached and gave her a long, warm kiss. She stroked his chin.

"So how was your day?"

"Normal, I'd say. And yours?" asked Ekman.

"Bushed. I spent all day walking around Stockholm. That American walks everywhere. Moshe was very stupid. Got made at a restaurant..."

"Rachel, I don't want to hear details, you know that," said Ekman.

She handed him a glass of wine. "I've made us lamb racks. I had time to buy a gorgeous pair at the shop while, um, someone was in the restaurant."

"Hurtree should be leaving Sweden soon. Our PM made the case top secret this afternoon." Ekman swirled the wine in his glass. "By the time Homicide gets to work tomorrow they'll be off the case."

They had been together for nearly a year. Rachel Goldsten was assigned to Stockholm as a Mossad liaison officer. She and Lars Ekman first met at the NSS where they exchanged information regarding a mutual problem: a Palestinian terrorist group in northwestern Stockholm which trained bomb makers. The pair connected immediately. Rachel was short, dark, her well-shaped body honed as a weapon. She was friendly, intelligent, and Ekman began meeting her outside work, first at the Flying Scotsman Pub on Fleming Street later at her apartment.

One morning she caught one of her co-workers sitting in the stairwell outside her apartment as Ekman left in the morning.

"You have no right to stalk me!" Rachel had pummeled her co-worker as Ekman stood behind her, fascinated by her strength.

"You know...we have to...watch your back" came the reply between blows.

Ekman had given her a key to his apartment following the

incident, and now they met there instead. Their relationship was known to both agencies, and tolerated because of the mutual benefit to both sides.

While Ekman and Rachel Goldsten explored the depths of their passion, a museum in Argentina with an obscure collection of Nazi memorabilia was broken into. The thieves took only two items, which caused a certain amount of mirth at the police station where the theft was reported.

"They stole hairbrushes. Can you imagine? And they left a solid gold letter-opener with a swastika on it. Are thieves getting stupider today?" The investigating officer shook his head as he continued, "At least we can assume the thief is not bald. Is that not true, Pedro?" and the rest of the men at the information meeting laughed, making even more ribald comments about the robbery. Pedro, the bald member of the group, tried to join in the fun, but found it hard to laugh.

Chapter 20

Adolf Hitler's mistress had contacted a friend from the time before the Nazis had come to power. She knew who to trust, and to avoid those who would gladly use the explosive information she was about to divulge to further their own aims.

It was natural to ask Hermann Schwerlieb to meet her in a private place, and she made sure Adolf knew of the meeting, well aware that everyone in the Government was watched by the Gestapo. Schwerlieb had known Eva since the time of the trial for the burning of the Reichstag, but until that Saturday he knew nothing of the child.

He was delighted to hear that the Führer had secured the succession of leadership for the future. As second in command, Reichsmarshall Schwerlieb was happy to be able to function as a stand-in for Hitler. He was certain any future Hitler, regardless of gender, would be a natural born leader just like their father. It was when Eva told him about the event at the kindergarten he became disturbed.

"Eva," he said, searching carefully among his words, "I'm no expert on children. I only recently became a father myself, but it seems to me what's going on at the present time may be a bit dangerous for your child, Dolfin. And such an appropriate name. I dare not ask which one of you thought of it."

Eva blushed and smiled as she turned her face to Schwerlieb.

He cut a late blooming rose and offered it to her as he continued, "As I said, things are dangerous right now. We are preparing certain measures to remove, well, undesirable elements from our society. There are plans to evacuate them to Poland—for betterment, of course—but I'm sure your child wouldn't respond well to the, um, treatment. We can't allow this to happen to Dolfin."

Hitler's mistress held up the rose to savor the sweet scent. "What do you mean, treatment?"

"Treatment or betterment. It's all the same. But under the present circumstances it will be difficult to exclude her without exposing who you two are, and you do remember the agreement?" Schwerlieb had been like a grandfather at that moment, and his concern for Eva and Dolfin was genuine.

"Yes," she said, "I remember the agreement."

They both were referring to a silent understanding between her and Adolf that she would remain in the background until such time Adolf's role as Führer had been completed. It had been decided at several top Party meetings that Adolf's popularity with the millions of German widows from the First World War, and with the younger women of Germany, couldn't be put at risk by his getting married at present.

Schwerlieb and Eva made their way through the secluded garden in the center of Munich. Their footsteps crunched on the gravel pathway, and Eva's voice became determined. "No. We cannot allow her to be removed to Poland, under any circumstances. There must be an exception made for her." Her voice was strained now, and she went on, "Adolf doesn't know what happened at the nursery yet. I'm afraid of how he might react. He has his moments sometimes, as you know. But there must be something I can do. Is there any way you can help me?"

Schwerlieb was already linking this news to a plan he had recently made to visit Sweden, where he still had many friends in both government and industry. "Yes," he said, "I'm certain there is something I can do. And quickly."

Chapter 21

October 15, 1940

Schwerlieb's own twin-engine Messerschmitt Bf-110 flew north toward the Baltic Sea, leaving the German coast at Greifswald as soon as it became dark. The trip to Sweden was organized as a diplomatic mission.

Schwerlieb loved to fly, and he took every opportunity to pilot the speedy fighter-bomber converted to be his own luxury taxi. He kept the plane low, raking the Baltic Sea several kilometers off Sweden's east coast. Just south of Stockholm he steered in over land, flying low, shaking the snow off treetops and shocking the occasional farmer eating the evening meal.

He had flown a similar route as a commercial pilot only a few years before he moved back to Germany, so finding Bromma Airport was easy, even in the dark. A faint glow on the horizon told him they were approaching their destination. He flashed a light back in the cabin, alerting Dr. Habermann and Nurse Eiderbach it would only be a few more minutes before they landed.

The nurse was relieved to see the signal. She had never flown before. The vibrating fuselage, the deafening, roaring drone of the twin engines, and the sudden lurches caused by Schwerlieb adjusting their course had been too much for her. She had asked Dr. Habermann to sedate Dolfin before they had arrived at the airport, afraid she would be frightened by the changes. Now she wished she had asked Habermann to sedate her too.

Schwerlieb was cleared for landing at Bromma via his contact at the Swedish Foreign Department. The nosey bureaucrats at his own embassy remained unaware of his presence. The Bf-110 flew in over a few small Stockholm islands from the southeast, and he landed the plane. He taxied over to a small hut and parked his Messerschmitt next to a black U.S. Army DC-3 with a small white star on the fuselage.

His opponents had already arrived for the meeting. Next to the airport hut, two cars waited for Schwerlieb's party. Schwerlieb made the introductions to one of the drivers, and Dr. Habermann, the nurse, and a still sleeping Dolfin were put into one of the cars and driven away. Schwerlieb would join them in the morning when their residence in Sweden would become official. For the moment he had other matters to tend to, like his attempt to keep the Americans out of the war which would soon involve most of the world.

The meeting at the Swiss Ambassador's residence in Danderyd just north of Stockholm ended early in the morning. The air was crisp with the smell of the new snow and wisps of smoke from coal-fired furnaces as the men emerged from the mansion. Everyone wore the face of defeat.

It was clear neither side would give in to the demands of the other. It seemed as if the decision to go to war formed as a rational conclusion to a mathematical argument, and no amount of human emotion could break the deadlock at the time. In the end Schwerlieb had to admit the opposing side had a valid point: they simply refused to negotiate with the number two man in the Government. He would have to become number one before any meaningful continuation could commence, and it was something he hoped for.

He drove to the apartment he still owned in the center of Stockholm. While he freshened up he wondered if his country would survive what threatened to be a conflagration. His own knowledge of the capabilities of the opposing forces wasn't tainted by the propaganda of Joseph Goebbels, who had managed to convince Hitler that Germany's troops were invincible. Schwerlieb was a soldier, and he knew the powers surrounding them would only become more formidable as the war developed. It would be a miracle if Germany survived.

His car drove to Långbro Hospital, south of the city. He had spent several months there on two occasions almost ten years earlier. He knew several members of the staff, and the possibility to harbor Dolfin there for her private care had been easy to provide. The head of Sweden's Foreign Department left guarantees to the head of the hospital the child's care would not in any way be a burden for the hospital; she would be provided with her own doctor and nurse.

Putting her into a mental hospital was a way to keep prying eyes from getting too close, and although children were definitely not common at the hospital, exceptions could be made when enough money was used.

Schwerlieb registered as next of kin for Dolfin, signing his name, and then in a moment of grandeur added his newly acquired title, *Reichsmarshall.* The administrator read the signature and stiffened to attention, clearly impressed as the man in the white suit before him put down the pen.

Schwerlieb had decided not to wear his general's uniform to the hospital; the newly tailored powder-blue uniform with gold braiding. He had felt a surge of power through his body when he used that uniform for the meeting with the men in the DC-3. He knew that even other German generals were jealous of his capacity to invent his own uniform instead of wearing what others had worn before him. At the hospital the uniform would have meant introducing a risk to his mission. The embassy would have no trouble in identifying him if the gossipers got wind of it.

The nurse would spend the night in Dolfin's room to ease the transition until she became used to the new surroundings. The room was in a separate wing of the women's building on the third floor. Dr. Habermann would be living in a villa rented by a German shipping company to house their sea captains needing a place to stay on land while their ships were refitted. It was within walking distance of the hospital and provided him with a way to minimize his interaction with Swedish society.

Schwerlieb left the hospital and returned to his aircraft. The weather was holding, but he noticed a storm was on its way from the British Isles. *It's no wonder the British are so difficult to beat,* he thought. *With their weather they look forward to warring in foreign countries.*

He noticed the opponents' DC-3 was already gone. His own gunner had been up the entire night guarding the Messerschmitt. The Swedish Foreign Minister waited for him in the hut.

"I hear the meeting was not successful," the minister said.

"No. It seems the war has to continue." Schwerlieb rubbed his hands together in the chill of the morning. "This idiot Churchill sent a bomber flight over Munich and dropped a bomb on the street where we have our apartment. Can you imagine? He actually killed my son's nanny. He will soon see London burn."

"Do you think you will win?" asked the Minister.

"We will have to, and quickly," said Schwerlieb. "We are expanding the Reich at such a rate we will have difficulty running the whole thing even after we have won. There are simply no options for not winning."

"I suppose you know we will always support the winning side," said the minister. "For us there are also no other options."

Schwerlieb nodded. "Please do me a favor. See to it the child is cared for, for as long as possible. I consider her important for the future of my country." And with that he shook hands with the Minister and clambered into the Messerschmitt. *Time to get home,* he thought, *I need to do some fishing.*

Chapter 22

It was 5 a.m. when the hotel phone next to Hurtree's bed rang.

"Good morning, Hurtree. It's Captain Peters in Heidelberg."

"Good morning, Charlie. Don't you ever go to sleep? Did you say Captain Peters? Why do I sense some kind of official business coming at me?"

"We only get to sleep when the bad guys do, and that's not very often. John, you screwed up. I don't know what you did, but the Chief of Staff himself has signed an order asking about you. You know what that means, and you know what it means if you continue putting your nose where it doesn't belong. Get your ass home buddy and spend some time fishing."

Within hours after learning about Hurtree's involvement in the Eiderbach case, several meetings had been arranged in Stockholm. A few days later a teleconference meeting included the U.S. Army's Chief of Staff at the Pentagon. After the meeting, orders were relayed quickly through Army headquarters, and Capt. Charles Peters in Heidelberg soon found a dispatch on his desk which had been shot-gunned to every base in Europe, asking for information regarding a certain ex-Lt. John Hurtree, currently visiting in Sweden.

"Charlie, I've found her. Hitler's daughter. This is the biggest case I ever worked on, and I've solved it. She's alive, Charlie, I know it, and it won't take me long to get this out into the open."

"Get your ass home, buddy," said Peters. "If you continue you're gonna get yourself into some real trouble. No one wants this out in the open, regardless of who she is, alive or not. As of now you've been shut down here. Follow my advice, John, I don't want to have to take the next step."

Hurtree heard in Peters's voice that the warning was more than just a friendly one. He knew if he continued he could become a target. His own Government would try to stop him. He was upsetting the international apple cart. No one wanted history rewritten. Clearly he would have to make a decision involving the rest of his life. He had been told very simply—do not continue, or risk getting arrested, or worse.

He thought about the difference between speech and action, talking and doing. Did he have the courage to risk his life just to reveal a truth no one wanted to hear? If he quit now he might live another fifteen years before the bell tolled for him because of natural causes, if he was lucky. *Fifteen years. Not too bad. That's more than 5,400 days and nights to experience the boring wonders of retirement.*

"I haven't made up my mind yet," he replied to Capt. Peters. "I'll let you know."

"No, John, if you continue, we'll let you know," and the line went ominously silent at the other end.

The local train was nearly empty when Sara boarded at the Central Station. Minutes later, low rays of the sun blinded her for a moment when she exited the train at Sundbyberg. It would be hours more before sunset, and she looked forward to the warm walk home to her apartment.

She bounded down the stairs to reach the tunnel which would take her to the streets upstairs. She noticed a boy in a hoodie painting graffiti on the tunnel walls. Sara slowed to a walk. The graffiti caught her eye: three horizontal parallel lines intersected by three vertical lines. The symbol of the Iron Guard shone black on the blue walls. She stopped behind the boy, who was already stowing a paint can in his rucksack.

"Stop," shouted Sara, and held her metal badge in front of her, "I'm from the police."

The boy hid his face in his hoodie. "It's not me," he said, "I didn't do that."

"Really? Should I call for forensics to test your fingers for paint?"

He bit his lip. "Are you really a cop?"

"Yes."

"Should I wash off the tag?"

"Yes," said Sara. "What does it mean, your tag?"

The boy hesitated. "I don't know," he said.

"Then why were you using it as a tag?" asked Sara. She took up her cell phone from her purse and took a photo of the boy with the Iron Guard symbol behind him.

"It was cool, that's all. I'll wash it off. I promise."

"Where did you see it?"

The boy stared at his shoes and his voice went low as he answered, "At home. My uncle has it tattooed on his arm."

She poured a cup of green tea and settled into the easy chair. Her investigations into the killing of Habermann and Eiderbach were obviously linked to the Iron Guard. The NSS historian's words echoed in her mind: "*The Swedish Iron Guard in Stockholm is one of the oldest Neo-Nazi cells existing.*"

How have I managed to miss them? she thought. *The Iron Guard is everywhere. Kids are even using their symbol as graffiti tags.* Sara pulled up her cell phone and viewed the image of the boy and the Iron Guard symbol.

Tomorrow she would start collecting background data on the uncle with the tattoo, Bengt Ohlsson. Her mind was already looking for connections between Eiderbach, Habermann, and the dead man with the Iron Guard tattoo on his arm. She was certain tattoo-man had killed the drunk in Fruängen. He also bore an uncanny resemblance to Eiderbach's killer. Four murders, all connected, and yet somehow the final image of the puzzle she was trying to solve evaded her.

Eiderbach and Habermann were on the Iron Guard hit list, now both dead. But Habermann's killer did not fit the pattern. Hurtree had suggested the Mossad could be involved. Why would they do that? How could she catch an assassin?

Then there was the drunk in Fruängen. Who was he? Sara made a note to ask the Coroner if he had an Iron Guard tattoo like his killer. If Hurtree was right then it could be the Mossad who had taken out Eiderbach's killer too. Maybe he wasn't a drunk at all. Could he have been an agent for the Mossad? Was that the reason he had been killed? Was this about revenge? She needed more information on tattoo-man. Where did he live? Did he have a job?

The guy with the tattoo had a hotel keycard. I'll start looking for that hotel tomorrow.

Sara wondered if Hurtree had used the methods she used in her investigations, and she made a note to ask him the next time they met. She hoped there would be a next time. He was obstinate, but she felt a sort of kinship with this old man. He was obviously obsessed, but it was an obsession she could understand.

Sara shared Hurtree's need to get to the bottom of an investigation. She had a hard time giving up herself. Sara had trouble believing his conviction Hitler's child could be living anywhere in Sweden, but there were many parts of his story which fit the complicated nature of her investigation.

One thing was clear. Fruängen was a focal point for many of the events in her investigation. And where was Dolfin, the woman who had spent so many years living as a patient at Långbro Hospital, just outside Fruängen's Center?

Sara had searched all the databases she could access, and they had led nowhere. Dolfin as a first or last name came up empty. There were over 275 people born in Sweden on the day she had found in the records at the National Archive, and they lived all over Sweden. Sara was uncertain Dolfin even had a person number, but she knew that in order to find her she would need a more precise person number. She also knew who to ask for help.

*

It was late when Sven arrived at the station. He had several boring pages of budget figures to revise before the final meeting at the end of the month. His bureaucratic soul was underdeveloped. He longed for the tingle of being the lead on an investigation. He put the budget to one side and chose to review the files Robert had left regarding the murder of the drunk in Fruängen.

Clearly this was a case of self-defense. The gang had witnessed that The Can had attacked a man who had protected himself. The killer's manner of protecting himself had drawn the attention of the Coroner. The killer had been a professional. And now he was dead.

Sven noticed there was a witness who had not left a statement, but had been driven to the psychiatric ward, a nameless elderly woman who had seemed confused and disoriented. The report mentioned she wore a key around her neck and was presumed not to be homeless.

He was glad he had assigned Robert to the investigation. Robert had handled it thoroughly, and it relieved him from current suspicions regarding his conduct on the Nurse Eiderbach case. Sven read the police report about the deranged woman again. She seemed somehow to fit into a pattern he could not immediately recognize, and he jotted down a note for Robert to try to find her at the psychiatric ward. He wouldn't be able to send Sara; that would look too much like giving her the job of checking up on Robert. He might have to have her moved to another group, but it was too sensitive to do while she was still working on the homicide of Anna Eiderbach. He wouldn't have to wait long for that. Ekman's words came back to him: "*You have two days.*"

Chapter 23

Sara began her hunt for the hotel where Anna Eiderbach's killer had been staying. Visits to the three hotels near Fruängen led nowhere, and she expanded her search.

She had skipped lunch. Hungry and tired from boring and fruitless interviews with hotel receptionists, Sara walked into the Hotel Three Corners, a hotel newly constructed from what previously had been the archive for the National Institute for the Development of Workers' Leisure Time Activities. The reception was little more than a hole in the wall, positioned to give the single staff member a clear view of those entering through a glass door.

The receptionist's head popped up behind the hole as soon as Sara entered. "Sorry, we're booked full today" was her cheery greeting.

"I'm not looking for a room. I'm from the police," Sara replied, holding up her ID card. "May I ask you a few questions about a hotel keycard?" Sara held up the hotel keycard found in the pocket of tattoo-man.

"That could be one of ours," said the receptionist. "Let me see if it comes up on our system." She took the keycard Sara had put on the counter and placed it into the card reader.

"I don't really know very much about our guests," said the receptionist. "I only work here after I finish my classes at university."

"Cool," said Sara. "What are you studying?" She had already learned how important it was to be kind to hotel receptionists if you wanted information from them. Otherwise they refused and the whole procedure went into bureaucratic gridlock.

"I'm studying biochemistry. I want to work for a pharmaceutical company when I'm done," said the receptionist. "Here we go. Is there anything in particular you're interested in?"

A wide grin filled Sara's face. *Gotcha,* she thought, and told the receptionist, "I'm interested in the guest who was staying in the room this keycard opens. He probably hasn't been around for about four days."

"Yes. That sounds like the man staying in Room 18. He checked in several weeks ago. He was interested in hospitals. About four or five days ago he stopped sleeping in the room, but all his stuff is still there."

Sara felt the surge of success. "Do you have his name? How did he pay for his room?"

"His name is Zoran Slatocravic. I only spoke English to him the few times I saw him. From Bosnia, I think. I'll have to check on payment, just a minute." The receptionist began to check the computer for payment details. Sara felt a thrill go through her entire body.

"Yes, here we are. Paid in cash every week. The next time will be on Thursday. And what's this? The reservation was made using a credit card as a guarantee. Just a minute."

A computer printer whirred behind the receptionist. "Here's the number," she said.

Sara read the name beside the credit card number and was transported suddenly into a different world. It was very clear: *Visa CC Nr 2300135888775314, exp 01 /02, Robert Johnson.* The name of her colleague at the NBI.

She asked for a printout of all the details regarding Room 18, and sat down in the single chair in the small hall which formed the lobby for the hotel as she waited. Her mind raced leaps at a time. She tried to put together the puzzle these pieces implied, and she clutched the armrest to steady herself. Could it be that Robert Johnson was the one who had reserved the hotel room for the hitman? Was Robert more than just a fumbling jerk? Could he have been involved in the murders in some way? Johnson was a common name. Perhaps it was another Robert Johnson, and just a coincidence.

Sara accepted the copies of the printouts and went out to the squad car to sit while she waited for the other two uniformed policemen to arrive after their own interviews. Evidence might be found in the hotel room, and she called forensics to arrange a search.

She would have to think of how to handle this, and fast. This dealt with a colleague, and she knew how the group would form itself into a protective shield for any one of them if threatened from the outside. She would keep this to herself until she had a chance to talk to Sven.

Sven closed the door to his office as soon as Sara had entered.

"You weren't very clear about why you wanted to see me," said Sven, "but you were all too clear about us meeting in private. Should I be booking a hotel room for us?"

Sara skipped the sexual innuendo. She had become used to it since her first day at work, and found the best way to respond was to ignore it altogether. "I think I've found the hotel where the murderer who killed both the nurse and the drunk in Fruängen stayed."

Sven focused on her. "And you can't tell anyone else on the team about this?" he asked. "Does the whole team have to wait for the news until I've heard it?"

Sara pushed the page containing the details for Room 18 over to Sven. His mouth opened sharply and he drew in a breath which seemed to create a vacuum in the room.

"My God," he whispered in a low voice, "My God." He looked up at Sara and saw she was waiting for him to continue. He felt an empty spot in his brain begin to spread out to cover his entire being. "I don't think you should let anyone else in the team know about this," he said. "I'll let you know later what this might mean. It might mean nothing at all." Then, as Sara rose to leave, "And thank you. Good work."

*

Sven sat for a few minutes trying to take in what he had just learned, especially in light of the other questions this raised. He made a few notes and then made his way to the Internal Affairs Department, his heart heavy as he realized the current investigations had just become very complicated.

He entered the separate wing to the IAD, signed in with the receptionist, and asked to see an investigator. He was shown into an interrogation room and began to feel the nervousness he'd seen in many of the suspects he'd interviewed.

In a few minutes the door opened and he looked up to see a young plain-clothes officer enter. After the basic formalities, the young man asked the obvious question.

"And so tell me, what are you doing here?"

"I have to report a policeman, Robert Johnson."

"What's the charge?"

"It's a long story."

"They always are," said the officer. "What happened?"

"I'm running a homicide investigation. The man I have to report missed an obvious suspect in a CCTV tape that another officer found easily. I initially assumed it was a simple error. Even the officer who located the suspect on the tape just assumed it was a mistake. Taken by itself, it would probably have been just another little mistake that everyone can make."

"So you think he was covering up in some way?"

"It could be. I'm still not sure," said Sven.

"What makes you unsure?"

"Well he's a popular guy, to begin with. He's been doing really good work up to this point."

"And so why are you here?" asked the officer.

"We traced the identity of the murder suspect today, the one he missed on the tape. We found out where he was staying, and we also found out that Robert Johnson guaranteed his hotel room with his credit card."

The officer stopped taking notes and looked up, his eyes narrowing. "Are you sure of this?"

Sven pushed the printout from the hotel toward him. "The name fits. I talked to the bank and they confirmed the account number belongs to Johnson. See for yourself. This should be looked into."

The officer scribbled a few notes on his notepad, then wrote a number on the printout, pushed it back to Sven and asking him to initial it. Sven heard a deep sigh and was surprised to discover it came from himself.

"Is there anything else?" asked the officer.

"There was also a piece of evidence that disappeared, and only showed up after he was confronted with the loss. That's all I know today. What should I do now?"

"Who else knows about this?"

"The investigating officer who found the credit card information at the hotel. She discovered the mistake with the tape and the lost evidence. Other than that, no one."

"Leave her name on the notepad, please. You do nothing right now. You leave this to us and we do the rest. Easy, right?" The smile on the officer's face didn't seem genuine, and quickly disappeared.

Sven left the room and almost bumped into the janitor who had suddenly turned on the floor polisher just outside, an Arabic-looking man with long, dark hair and a distinct body-odor emanating from his khaki shirt. Sven apologized and the janitor mumbled something inaudible and looked intently at the floor.

From this point on Robert Johnson would be watched very closely. His files at work would disappear after he left the office and be replaced after they had been copied. His telephone at home would be bugged. A GPS tracking device would be attached to his car which would also deliver sound and cell phone traffic, including text messages. His jacket would be sprayed with an invisible substance making it easy for CCTV surveillance cameras equipped with special filters to pick him out of a crowd, day or night.

The IAD would soon know everything there was to know about Robert Johnson: his habits, his shoe size, how often he brushed his teeth, and the groans and sighs he emitted as he tried to sleep after each long day's work. They would follow him just long enough to gather the evidence that would either incriminate him or free him from suspicion. He would be called in for an interview ending with him crying like a baby.

Chapter 24

At the S-Office, section leader Olov Björnsson reviewed some of the information collated by the Professor, now dead for more than fifteen years. He noticed several entries indicating animosity between the NSS and the IB, the group two journalists had exposed years ago. He thought to himself that little had changed.

Today, instead of being a left wing-right wing conflict between the agencies, the conflict was colored by the new threats of terrorism. The NSS had deepened their relationship with the FBI and MI6. They knew terrorist groups existed in Sweden, but were hampered by Swedish law.

The S-Office had another agenda. To them the first item of business was to insure that the Party would remain in power for ever. In order to achieve that, various relationships could be forged to further their cause. The S-Office still had their contacts to the Israeli Mossad, the CIA, and when necessary even the successor to the KGB. There was no formal alliance between Björnsson's group and the foreign agencies, just a working relationship of back-scratching when it was needed. It appeared several backs were itching to be scratched again.

Björnsson polished his brief for the meeting with the woman responsible for running the S-Office. She had been a Cabinet minister and was used to making decisions affecting the nation. Section leader Björnsson knew it was important to keep his brief to less than two pages; she refused to read long reports. It had to be to the point, with no references to other documents or reports, and it had to contain a simple one sentence conclusion with a suggestion which could be answered with a simple yes or no.

The ex-Cabinet minister had been expecting Björnsson's memo to detail recent scandals involving the political opposition. She settled into her chair in the conference room at the S-Office, anticipating tales of sex or greed. He handed her two sheets of paper, and she read:

> There is currently a situation where some of our mistakes made during the early phase of the Second World War have returned to plague us. A child from one of the leaders of the German Nazi Party has been living in Stockholm since she was four years old. She is now sixty-nine. She is mentally deficient, and has been cared for by a doctor and a nurse, paid for via a secret transaction fund. She was brought here by Hermann Schwerlieb and could be his daughter, but we're unsure at present since officially he had only one child, a son.
>
> Both the nurse and doctor who cared for this woman were recently murdered. We're sure the nurse was pushed into an oncoming train by a member of the Iron Guard, a Neo-Nazi group that has been very quiet here in Sweden. The murderer seems to have come from Bosnia. The doctor's murderer is a little more unclear. Although we know who he is, and that he is in Athens at present, we don't really know who he is working for.
>
> We have followed members who work for Homicide at the National Police Board. A policewoman in charge of the nurse's murder investigation has been in contact with a previous member of the U.S. Army's CID. We're not sure how much the American knows, but he seems to be co-operating with the police. The NSS began to be involved when the doctor was killed since they've had him under surveillance for years. They have had a meeting with the PM, who is aware something has happened, but is only thinking of how to make political currency for his own benefit.
>
> There will be efforts to disarm any knowledge of the situation if it becomes public, but any competent journalist will be able

to deduce that the Party was involved in this via the Professor (a friend of your father), and it won't be pretty.

We know nothing about the woman being sought, except her name: Dolfin. We don't know where she lives, or even if she is still alive. There is every reason to believe she is also a target. What is unusual is the involvement of the Iron Guard. We would have expected them to protect her and anyone caring for her.

The situation is already beyond our control and it will be difficult for us to pre-empt any actions taken by others. We could, however, reduce the possibility of the murderers being caught and being put on trial.

I suggest we inform the Mossad about the situation and ask them to neutralize both operatives for us.

The head of the S-Office looked up from the last page. She swallowed hard several times.

"Wait a minute. I have to read this again."

After she'd read the brief again, she placed it on the desk and tapped it with her index finger. Red nail polish flashed above the report. She glared at Björnsson.

"You're asking me to kill people?"

"Not exactly, Minister." Björnsson still used her previous title when addressing her. "I wrote neutralize. We can let the Mossad decide what that means to them. Who knows, they may transport them to some place in Africa."

"It means killing, and you know it," she snapped.

"They're murderers, Minister, professional assassins," Björnsson said.

"Do we really know that? Are you sure this isn't just speculation on the part of some sleepy-eyed field agent?"

"We know it. They did it. We just don't know why."

"It means we will have to pay the Mossad back with something. Have you thought about that?"

"Yes," Björnsson flashed a grin, "I have. We can give them two of the Hamas bomb-makers who came here when things got too hot in the Gaza strip. The Mossad should like that."

The Minister tried to stare a hole in the table. Her voice went low and hard. "I can't make that decision today. I have to think about this."

"Don't think too long," said Björnsson. "We have located one of them. He may move at any time."

"I'll let you know by tomorrow morning," said the Minister. She placed the document into the shredder, making sure that it had been destroyed before leaving for the most sleepless night of her life since the incident that had left her tearfully resigning her post as Minister in front of the entire nation.

At 5.30 a.m. she called Björnsson using her encrypted cell phone and spoke quietly to keep from waking her husband as he snored in the next room.

"Björnsson, I've thought about what we spoke about yesterday afternoon. Call the agency you mentioned. Tell them the details they wish to hear. Tell them also we demand no lives be lost in the operation. I repeat, no loss of life. Do you understand?"

"Yes," answered Björnsson, rubbing sleep from his eyes, "I understand. I just hope the agency understands."

"Make it clear we won't consider it negotiable unless all the terms are met."

"Yes, Minister, I'll tell them," and he was speed-dialing his contact with the news as soon as she had dropped the connection. A few hours later, in a lavishly furnished apartment on the other side of Stockholm, a small meeting dealt with the request.

"Can you imagine, they have asked us to do what we were going to do anyway. They want us to take out the assassin from Hezbollah, the Lebanese we hired in Athens." The Secretary for the Mossad chuckled while he gathered up the reports to be burned in the fireplace.

"Do you think the Lebanese ever suspected Habermann was

not Jewish?" The Station Chief leaned back in his armchair as he watched the documents reduce to ash.

"I doubt it. He followed his instructions to the letter. Even left Habermann's credit cards at the scene and torched the car. He could have been one of our own."

"Are the Swedes offering anything in return?" asked the Section Chief.

"They're going to give us details about two Hamas bombers. They said we couldn't kill the man in Athens. It was definite," said the Secretary.

"*We* won't kill him," said the Section Chief. "I think he might drink too much. Such behavior could lead to an accident."

The Secretary looked over at the Section Chief standing close to the fireplace. "Where are we on the man from the Iron Guard? Have they been able to track the Dolfin woman's location?"

The Section Chief knelt to stir the ashes to dust, then closed the glass door to the fireplace.

"No, he seems to have been close to finding her after he killed the nurse, but he got into a fight and killed an innocent bystander to get himself out of it. Our operative asked for advice and I gave him the choice of discretion. He threw him under a train and left a pointer for the police. It may take them a while to figure it out, but the police will soon know Anna Eiderbach's killer is no more."

The Station Chief nodded in agreement. "Then there will be no further action unless the Iron Guard manages to locate their target. Remember, keep her alive as if she were one of our own until we release the entire story to the press. After that it doesn't matter. The whole world will soon know Hitler's own child has a genetic defect. That should put a stop to all this Aryan superman nonsense once and for all. This is all going much better than we had planned."

"And the American? Mr. Hurtree?" asked the Secretary.

"He should be leaving soon," said Section Chief Rachel Goldsten as she replaced the fireplace poker into its caddy.

Chapter 25

9 a.m. Saturday morning

The sun had been up for seven hours when Sara knocked on Karin's door.

"I need your help again," said Sara, her face flushed red with excitement.

"Fantastic." Karin blinked, squinted, and blinked again, and let Sara through the door. "You wake me at nine in the morning for this? I got off shift an hour ago. Did you bring your own coffee?"

"I'm looking for someone who probably has a personal ID number, but no one knows it. You told me once you learned how to construct a person number simply by knowing the date of birth and birthplace."

The coffee machine gurgled a happy morning song while the two women went over their last weekend in Finland again. Sara told Karin there were few developments regarding the identity of the woman called Dolfin, but they were still searching for her in the databases.

"There doesn't seem to be any connection to her name and any existing person number," said Sara. "It's very strange. We can usually search for practically any part of a name, address, or other detail and we get hundreds of subjects. She doesn't seem to surface no matter how we structure the search."

"If you don't have the person number it can be hard to find someone." The aroma of coffee filled the kitchen and Karin took down two mugs. "But she would have a person number if the State were to be involved at any stage, like her being registered as an inhabitant in an apartment."

"That's what I'm hoping. If we can find out her person number then I could look her up in one of the public databases and get a last known address."

Karin closed her eyes for a minute. "It wasn't on any of the documents we saw at the National Archive, but it may have been too early at that stage. I don't know when they started giving out personal ID numbers to foreigners."

"So if you could construct this number we might be able to find her with it," said Sara. "I'll pour you another cup and watch you do the math."

"And I'll try to wake up." Karin got up to retrieve a book on statistical theory. "This is how it works. We know the date she was born, and that she is a foreigner. In theory that's all we need to know to construct her person number. If she has one."

"How long will it take?" asked Sara.

"About two minutes," said Karin. "Watch."

She wrote the date they had seen at the National Archive as a Swedish birthday, thirty-six for the year, followed by four digits that gave the month and day Dolfin had been born. She then added a nine, meaning she was a foreigner, then a four, indicating she had been born in Germany, and finally a two, indicating she was a female.

"Now we only need to construct the control digit," she said, and put the sum of the numbers into a formula that produced an eight. "That's it, 360912-9428. That's her person number, if she has one at all."

Sara used Karin's computer to log into her account at work, chose the Personal Records choice from the menu, and seconds later they watched as Dolfin's existence in the Swedish bureaucracy popped up on the screen.

Sara's eyes widened, her jaw dropped. "Fruäng Street 3. I've been right next door to that address," she said, "and not too long ago."

*

In Athens, Habermann's killer sat admiring the short summer skirts of the women who passed the outdoor café where he usually sat in the afternoon. He could always count on making contact with some tourist who had flown to Greece to enjoy the anonymity of a foreign vacation, and the contact usually resulted in some no-holds-barred sex at her hotel. His profession made girlfriends impossible. The fringe benefit of well-paid contracts made up for it.

His eyes fell on the attractive redhead who sat down next to his own table. She ordered Ouzo using a typical American accent, even though she had high cheekbones that whispered Slavic ancestry. He smiled, and her eyes told him it was OK if he moved his drink over to her table.

Within minutes they were discussing Grecian history compared to America's lack thereof. Habermann's killer could already imagine her arms around his neck. He licked his lips, anticipating the long, sweaty evening. She accepted his invitation to have dinner with him.

"I have to change clothes before dinner. Would you like to join me?" she asked. "My apartment is only a few blocks away."

He followed her up the narrow flight of stairs leading to her apartment, drawn by her scent and sneaking peeks up her skirt to see if she was wearing underwear. She let him in, poured them both fruit drinks, and went to the bedroom to change. When she heard his glass hit the floor, she came back into the room. He sat immobilized on the sofa, his eyes staring blankly, his mouth hanging slightly open.

The redhead called a number, spoke a few words of Hebrew, and within minutes two men arrived to carry Habermann's killer out of her apartment and into the waiting car. The next day a harbor guard found the Lebanese assassin floating face down in the Piraeus yacht harbor.

Horst, the current leader of the German Iron Guard, sat behind a desk in an abandoned bread factory in southern Munich. Light filtering through a dusty window revealed a Nazi flag behind him and a large photograph of Adolf Hitler on the wall beside his desk. In front of Horst sat Frank Nord, a middle-aged man in a wheelchair.

"The group in Stockholm has told me the police are speaking with someone you know. A man named Hurtree. Do you remember him, Frank?" asked Horst, and he stroked his shortly cropped blond hair.

The man in the wheelchair gripped the rims of both wheels as he answered. "That bastard put me in this chair. I'll never forget him."

"Stockholm seem to be having trouble finishing their task. Would you like to help them out?" Horst twirled a letter-opener with a swastika at the end.

"Do I get to kill Hurtree too? He owes me," asked Frank.

"That's not why I'm sending you there. I want you to make sure Stockholm gets their act together. They used people from Bosnia to take care of the mess up there, and they've screwed it up. Talk to a man called Thomas when you get there. Tell him you know about the decision from Tarragona. Here's his number. Find the woman. Kill her."

Frank Nord leaned forward to take the paper with the telephone number. "No problem," he said. "Do we know where Hurtree is staying in Stockholm?"

"Ask your contact in Stockholm. Name is Thomas. His brother is a policeman. He's got it covered."

In Germany, the Iron Guard had been rebuilt after the end of the war when the occupying powers allowed the Germans to construct their own Government. Before 1949 it would have been impossible for the organization to exist because officers like John Hurtree would have been on to them immediately. After the German Government was reconstructed, they had their own secret police, formed using many previous Gestapo operatives. This provided the Iron Guard with a comfortable margin of warning if the occupying forces managed to discover some way to reveal their network.

Horst spent most of his youth as a misfit. He sought out

political extremist groups to the left and right, but had difficulty finding appreciation for his simplistic ideology. For Horst, issues others debated were easily solved. He was always right, regardless. The Iron Guard took him in after his first meeting, and within a year he led the organization in Germany.

Horst had recruited Frank Nord when he was still an enlisted man living in Aschaffenburg. They had much in common. Nord helped the Iron Guard steal weapons and ammunition by revealing the days when military exercises would occur, making it easy for the Iron Guard to rob whatever they wished from the arms depots hidden in the Bavarian forests. In exchange, Nord was afforded protection from the local police, and his narcotics business thrived. He continued to live in Germany after his discharge, and Hurtree had tracked him down when he began selling drugs to U.S. Army soldiers.

Just before retirement, Hurtree tried to arrest Nord one evening outside a pizzeria across the street from one of the men's barracks in Aschaffenburg. It was dark, and sleet made the sidewalk slippery. Nord was no longer in the Army, and Hurtree had to wait for the German police to arrive to make the arrest. In the scuffle, when Nord tried to escape, Hurtree had slammed the butt of his .45 into Nord's spine, crushing a vertebra and paralyzing Nord from the hips down. Hurtree was disappointed when his narcotics case against Nord was dropped by the German authorities. As a final insult, Hurtree was reprimanded for violence to an American citizen.

Hurtree returned from a bus trip to the giant IKEA store in Kungens Kurva, just south of Stockholm. A blue plastic shopping bag contained his purchases: a pair of glass candle holders for Sara and some items from a local supermarket. When he passed the hotel reception, a young woman with Asian features called out his name.

"Mr. Hurtree. Hello. You have a message." She waved a piece of paper toward Hurtree.

He read the message, then asked the receptionist, "Who left this? Do you remember what the person looked like?"

"There were two men. The one who gave me the message was helping the other man. The one in the wheelchair."

Hurtree stared at the message again as he sat on the bed in his hotel room.

I know details about the woman you seek. Meet me at the Nordic Museum tonight at 2200 hrs.

Hurtree was certain this was a set-up. *They know where I live. I had better change hotels.*

Hurtree had no intention of wandering outside a deserted museum at 10 p.m., waiting to be attacked. He consulted his map of Stockholm, found a hotel nearby, and arranged a room he could move into that same evening. He checked out and walked a few blocks to the new hotel. His new room was cheaper, but the TV worked and he selected a program airing news from the United States. After half an hour he chose a film and dozed off in the middle of it.

At 9.15 p.m. he woke, checked his watch, and studied the map of Stockholm. The sun was still hanging on the horizon. If he took the tram, he could reach the museum well before ten o'clock. After a moment's indecision, he gave in to his desire to finish his quest. *I'll just see what's happening,* he thought.

The tram from the central train station stopped in front of the Nordic Museum and Hurtree scrunched down, still the only passenger. He rode to the next stop. The streets and the parking lots were deserted. He got off at Skansen, the outdoor museum and zoo built to highlight Nordic culture.

A pair of young lovers glanced at Hurtree, kissed, and continued on their way to Gröna Lund, the amusement park across the street. The never-ending sunset left long shadows on the sidewalk. Hurtree made his way back to the huge gray stone building which housed the Nordic Museum. He concealed himself behind tree trunks and bushes until he came to the wall surrounding a cemetery. Lilacs and elderberry bushes afforded Hurtree cover until he could duck into a low wooden bell tower. He kept his eyes focused on the Museum, watching for signs of movement. It was quiet except for the occasional volley of screams from the amusement park behind him.

Some people have to pay to get scared, thought Hurtree.

He squatted in the bell tower. Mosquitoes buzzed around his head, and he managed to quietly slap a few as he waited. Twenty minutes past ten he saw movement near the end of the ivy-clad south wing of the museum. He raised a pair of binoculars to his eyes and focused on the ground under a group of tall trees near the entrance reserved for taxis or vehicles carrying the handicapped. A taxi arrived, and the driver opened the doors to the van. Hurtree saw the man in the wheelchair being loaded into the van, and a second man opened the passenger door and got in. Hurtree was certain. It was Frank Nord from Germany.

The taxi disappeared toward the city, but Hurtree waited another five minutes before emerging from the cemetery. The sun still hovered near the horizon, and a blazing crimson sunset filled the sky. He walked back to his new hotel, moving into a niche doorway each time a car approached in the dusk. He was now being hunted. Hurtree bit his lip as he felt his choices being reduced to one. He would leave Sweden tomorrow.

Hurtree took the stairs to his room at the new hotel. He took off his shoes and eased himself onto the bed, nursing the aches of too much exercise and excitement. He ran over his options again, too few for his liking.

He could continue his search for Dolfin on his own, with no resources and no back-up, and almost certainly die in the process. Or, he could quit and go home, keep quiet, and continue drawing his pension checks every month until he died of boredom.

Hurtree fell asleep trying to find a third option, dreaming of the hotel in the Bavarian Alps and the wife and children he had never experienced, waking in a sweat as the sun rose on his face at 2 a.m., seagulls screaming for an early breakfast outside his hotel window. He dressed, still groggy but unable to continue sleeping, and left the hotel.

There seemed to be no options at all when he looked at the street outside in the stillness of the bright, chilly summer sun. *I'm going to die sooner or later*, he thought. *The only difference will be the quality of life I get to live until the weight of my conscience drives me into the ground like a fencepost, or the certain knowledge someone else is going to choose the manner and time of my death.*

As a soldier it seemed easier to accept his own death at the beginning of the battle. Now he could choose to go to battle or not. Hurtree's promenade had taken him to the Old Town. He paid 100 Kronor for entry to the Jazz Club, Stampen.

The music was of world class quality. Hurtree ordered a Guinness and sat at a table to enjoy his last night in Stockholm. A Brazilian trio played set after set, and a young Swede asked to sit in. To the crowd's surprise, the young man was a musical genius, and the applause became higher after each new song. Hurtree made notes on the napkin and tried to summarize what he thought could be proven if someone actually tried.

He knew most members of the press wouldn't have the courage to drag this out into the open; they were too dependent upon the bits and pieces of news fed to them every day by the same forces trying to cover this up. He could take his chances with the gutter press, hoping someone would find the story interesting enough to look deeper. He also knew making the story public would have profound effects on the rest of Dolfin's life, wherever she was.

Hurtree tried to convince himself she didn't have much of a life anyway, but was unsuccessful. She was a defenseless old woman who had never harmed anyone in her life, he was certain of that. She couldn't help the details of her heritage, and it felt like he would be kicking her in the teeth by making her story known to everyone. *Hell, she probably doesn't even know who she is.* He turned off his thoughts for a moment and let the music flood his mind.

A final stubborn thought forced its way through. *Who am I to try to right all the wrongs of the world? Would there even be any justice served in the end?*

Hurtree crumpled the napkin with the few notes he'd made, paid his bill, and made his way to the street, where he took a taxi to the hotel. He was sure he had solved his last open case, and began to feel satisfaction before his trip home. It was over.

Unfortunately for Dolfin, it was just beginning.

Chapter 26

Hurtree called Sara from his new hotel and she answered after only two rings.

"Where are you? They told me you had checked out of your hotel when I tried to call you this morning," said Sara. "I thought you left already."

"I switched hotels because I think someone is after me. Sara, I'm leaving Sweden soon, but I wanted to see you before I do. I have a present for you."

"That's a nice thought, John. I may have a present for you too. We have found her, Dolfin. I think we did it without making too many waves. Too bad you can't be there. I know you wanted to talk to her."

"Do you think that's wise? I think you should do what I was told to do yesterday. Stop before this old woman gets killed, for example."

"I'd like to protect her instead," said Sara. "A friend of mine has already accessed a database. We've got an address. We know where she lives and we're on our way there. Are you sure you don't want to meet us?"

Hurtree stared at his plane ticket. "I still have another day before I have to leave. If you give me an address I can give to the taxi driver, I'll leave immediately. You tell me where to stand and I'll be there."

Sara gave Hurtree the address of a hot dog stand in Fruängen where he could meet her. "See you there," she said. Hurtree grabbed the white box with the blue ribbon he had prepared the day before.

*

They met at Bigges Grill Kiosk. The smell of hamburgers, hot dogs, and French fries filled the air, and Hurtree regretted he hadn't had time to visit the shopping center near his hotel where the supermarket was still offering free samples of food to shoppers.

Hurtree's stomach growled as he saw Sara and another woman walk toward him. All three walked from the kiosk to where Dolfin's apartment house was located. They passed a few shops in the cellars of three storied buildings. After less than five minutes they were there.

"So what's the plan?" asked Hurtree. "Who says what?" He felt the adrenaline surge in his veins: the exhilaration of seeing that last slalom gate just before the finish line comes into view exhausted from the effort to keep his skis on course, but enthralled by the sight of the goal.

"I'll try to talk to her," said Karin. "I've had some experience with mentally challenged patients. You two wait outside."

On the panel showing the inhabitants of the apartments, Karin read, Third floor, D.O. Lphin. She rang the buzzer outside the apartments several times. There was no answer. She pushed several buttons on the panel outside the door, and was finally admitted after telling a man on the intercom she had forgotten the keys to her apartment.

Karin peeked through the mail slot to see if there were any lights or sounds which might indicate Dolfin was at home, but the apartment was dark and silent.

She called through the mail slot, "Dolfin, are you at home?"

Her voice was immediately echoed. "*Dolfin, are you at home?*" It was a woman's voice, weak, but not frightened.

"Dolfin, my name is Karin, can I talk to you?"

"*My name is Karin, can talk to you?*"

"Can you open the door?"

"*You open the door.*"

There was a fumbling noise as Dolfin opened the latches on the door, and Karin entered, slightly crouched in anticipation of some unknown danger. The apartment was dark, contrasting with the bright sunlight outside. It took Karin's eyes a few seconds to find Dolfin, hunched on the floor next to a chair in the hall.

Karin sat on the floor next to her, waiting to speak. Several minutes passed in silence before Karin said, "Dolfin help."

Dolfin started to hum and she mumbled a few syllables. At the end of each syllable her head snapped down to meet her shoulder, and then, "Dolfin."

"Dolfin help," said Karin, and they repeated the conversation in this fashion for several minutes until Dolfin broke the rhythm by saying "Park" and standing up.

Karin finally saw Dolfin's full body: a heavyset woman nearing seventy. Her hair was long and white, tangled in knots in several places. She was dressed in a dark skirt and a winter sweater in spite of the heat of the summer, and wore sneakers derived from two separate sets of shoes. There was a stale smell of rotten food inside the apartment, and another indefinable odor suggesting Dolfin hadn't been very hygienic lately.

Dolfin walked by Karin and opened the apartment door. She began to close the door, and Karin hurried to exit before she got locked in. The two women walked down the three flights of stairs and exited onto the sidewalk.

Sara and Hurtree sat on a park bench as they waited.

"This must be as exciting for you as it is for me," said Sara.

"My heart is going to explode," replied Hurtree.

"I was going to ask you for a few pointers on crime solving before you leave."

"Make it quick. I'm leaving soon."

"It seems almost silly now, but we use graphical tools to create connections between events. Did you ever use those?"

"Like on a computer?" asked Hurtree.

"Yes."

"No. I used to write things down on yellow sticky notes and fix them to the wall of my room. They looked like random leaves for everyone but me. I saw patterns between the notes. Is that what you mean?"

"More or less," said Sara. They both went silent as Karin and Dolfin walked by them, moving toward the park on the other side of the street. Dolfin led the way. They took up a safe distance behind the two, following them into the park when they veered off onto a small path leading left through some brush and dense woods.

Dolfin stopped when she was standing close to a large fir tree, looking up at the dense green crown of branches and needles. She stepped closer, straddled the tree, and then embraced it, mumbling all the time. Then she faced Karin and said, "Dolfin help."

"Dolfin help," answered Karin. "Dolfin help."

Dolfin straightened in fear when she saw Sara and Hurtree. They had stopped and observed the strange scene, and remained several yards away, afraid they would scare Dolfin.

"I'd sure like to talk to her," said Hurtree.

"I'm not so sure you'd get anything out of it," said Sara. "From what I can see the woman has some serious mental problems."

"I'd still like to try."

They stood still as Dolfin and Karin went by them toward the street, Karin trying to establish contact by talking about trees and bushes.

"Hello," said Hurtree as they passed.

Dolfin paid no attention to him at all, didn't react when Hurtree captured her face on a digital camera as she passed by. They made their way back toward the apartment, first Dolfin and Karin, then Sara and Hurtree.

No one noticed the man sitting on the bench feeding the pigeons and ducks. He walked to the fir tree Dolfin had been hugging. He scraped off bits of bark into a plastic container, making sure it held bits smudged with small spots of blood where Dolfin had scratched her skin.

He returned to the rental car and drove to the laboratory on the north side of Stockholm. He was from Minnesota, but although his Swedish accent was from 100 years ago, he could still make himself understood. One of the many front groups of the U.S. Iron Guard had recruited him when he was in high school. This was a task from out of the blue, obviously because of his participation in the weekly rituals secretly held in the woods outside of Minnetonka. His contact at the airport had given him very clear instructions. Following Karin and Sara to the park had been easy. Now all he had to do was to leave the plastic cup at the laboratory.

The young man was excited. This was exactly what he had thought would happen when he joined the Americans for Racial Purity. He had no idea what he was doing, but he understood it was important. Still young and lacking training, he didn't see the car trailing him from three cars behind. Rachel Goldsten of the Mossad drove. She had been watching him since his arrival.

Karin and Dolfin came to Mickelsbergs Way between the park and Dolfin's apartment. Sara and Hurtree followed behind them, and saw how Dolfin raised her hand to join with Karin's before they crossed the street.

"Do you think she knows who she is?" asked Hurtree, and he slowed his pace to keep the two women in front of them at a safe distance.

"I doubt it," said Sara. "We'll have to ask Karin, but from what she told me about this kind of patient, there is little hope of establishing contact at all, although it seems she's managed to make progress anyway."

Hurtree held Sara back as a car narrowly missed her attempt to walk out onto the pedestrian crosswalk. "I hope my guys aren't watching in some way. We might have to duck a missile attack any minute now if they are."

"I won't comment on what's going on from our side. So it's over. Now we just have to keep her safe. Are you happy now, John?" asked Sara.

"I'm not sure. I'm glad I could be here when you found her. It feels good to have finally solved this mystery. Happy? Now that I've seen her I'm more sad than happy. Someone cared enough to keep her alive all these years. But someone is worried enough to try to kill her."

"What do you think will happen to her?" Sara nodded toward the two women in front of them as they entered the apartment house.

"Well if I had my way I'd get this into the papers, if for nothing more than to prove to myself that I finally solved this case. But if I do that I'll have the Army all over my ass in two minutes. It might be worth it though. Hell, at my age what have I got to lose?"

"What about her?" Sara motioned toward Dolfin's apartment house. "What would happen to her if you made the story public?"

"See, that's the thing. If this gets out, it would hurt her. Who knows what that would do to her? And then there's the Israelis. They'd probably just whack her and be done with it."

"Sounds to me like she gets into trouble regardless of how this gets out," said Sara.

"Yeah, poor woman. I really feel sorry for her, and that's something I never thought I'd experience for any of those people," answered Hurtree.

"Well, she couldn't help being born. You don't choose your parents, you know," said Sara.

"Now that would be a step forward for science, wouldn't it?" asked Hurtree. A cool breeze rustled in the birch trees above their heads as they sat outside the apartment building waiting for Karin to return.

"Hurtree, when I work on murder cases, I feel something for the victims. Did you?" asked Sara.

"No," said Hurtree, "I just hate killers. There are all kinds of criminals in the world, most want to take something away from others. Robbers take valuables. Killers take lives. The most valued of valuables. The mass killers are the worst of all, the ones who do it in volume. Those creeps don't do it for money. They can do it for a philosophical reason."

Sara shook her head. "I know what they feel. I know what it's like to die. I almost did during that swim test. I felt the victim's panic when I saw the surface of the water still so far away and my lungs were screaming for air. I knew it was over. I was going to die. No flashback of my life in a second. Not like that. Just the sure knowledge that it was over, and way too soon. I really wanted to stay alive and I was so angry that they made me do the swim test. I wanted to kill them for killing me. Victims feel that. I know they do. Anyway, I got this peaceful feeling as I gave in to it. Then my face hit the surface and I gasped for breath."

"I never thought about it that way. I'm glad you didn't die," said Hurtree, turning to view the apartment house again. "Your friend Karin has been in there for more than half an hour. Should we be worried?"

"I think Karin can handle herself. You should see the way she drives."

Hurtree looked up to see Karin emerge from the vestibule of the apartment building, alone.

"She's OK now, I think," said Karin. "There's no doubt about her identification, she's Dolfin alright. But if you searched for that in any of the databases you'd never find her. Someone registered her as D.O. Lphin. The only way to find her is if you know her person number, and that hasn't been connected to any other data, so she's been kept a secret so far."

"What's she like?" asked Hurtree. "Does she know who she is? Did she tell you anything about her background? Her parents? How she got here?"

Karin gave a little laugh, and replied, "Mr. Hurtree, do you have any experience of autism?"

"No," said Hurtree with a pensive look on his face.

"I didn't think so," Karin said. "There aren't too many people who have had direct contact with a patient with an extreme case of autism. And in this case it was barely treated, at least not with the treatments we have today. She's living almost completely inside her own head with very few ways for us to contact her. I don't know if we'll ever really know what she knows and doesn't."

"Autistic or not, she's gotta be Hitler's daughter. She's just gotta be," said Hurtree.

"Where's the proof of it?" said Sara. "You've got a lot of circumstantial evidence, but no real solid proof."

Hurtree stared at the gravel in front of him and scraped his foot. "Screw the evidence. I know she's their daughter."

"There's no proof," Sara's voice hardened, "just a lot of links and possibilities, but no proof. It'd be like proving something the way tabloid journalists usually do, association and conjecture. Modern witch-hunting."

Hurtree replied in a low voice, "I still think she's Hitler's child." He groaned as he stood up. "Well, ladies, I've got a trip to take tomorrow evening and I'm pooped already. I need a nap just to take a nap."

He handed the white package tied with a blue ribbon to Sara. "Here, Terrier. This is for you."

Sara flashed a quizzical smile as she accepted the gift. "May I open it now?"

Hurtree was already on his way. "I hope you're hungry," he shouted over his shoulder.

Sara untied the ribbon and opened the box. She took out the candleholders first, then laughed as she removed the dog biscuit with a blue ribbon tied to it. *Thanks, Terrier. Remember me, H* was the inscription on the card. She waved the dog biscuit in front of Karin's nose.

"What's that tied to the biscuit?" asked Karin.

Sara shook her head and chuckled. "A sprig of rosemary. I guess he wanted to make sure I eat my veggies."

Chapter 27

John Hurtree grew up in the years between the two wars during times when everyone could rejoice because the forces of evil had been eradicated by the forces of good. Churches spread the gospel of peace; bars spread the gospel of hedonistic rejuvenation through alcohol. Hurtree had experienced both by the time it became apparent that Germany was being ruled by a new force, the NSDAP—the German Nazi Party.

Growing up in Philadelphia gave him the advantage of being companion to several other boys who had recently come to the United States with their parents to test their luck in the non-European part of the world where anything could happen. In his street gang on Sixth Street there were those who spoke French, Italian, Spanish, Dutch, and even some who, like him, could speak German.

This would become key to his advancement in the U.S. Army. It would also prove to be the basis for his contact with Wilhelm Schwerlieb's father, and the obsession that drove him for nearly forty years. Hurtree could speak and understand German, and spoke it with his mother's Bavarian accent, just like Schwerlieb.

Schwerlieb's mission was complete. Dolfin was now in Stockholm. As he sat at the stick of the Messerschmitt Bf-110 flying back to Germany, he tried to imagine how the impending war would be fought. His efforts to put a stop to it had failed. His countrymen would have to prove to the rest of the world that they actually were the superior beings that they never grew tired of proclaiming themselves to be. The perfection of their culture would be severely tested, he was sure of that. He was a little less certain about the outcome. He knew that so far the planes designed and manufactured in Augsburg struck fear into pilots who had to fly battle missions against them. For the time being. They were state of the art at the time, something he had been reassured of during the several visits he made to the aircraft manufacturers as the war began.

But now it was 1940 and Schwerlieb should have had all the machinery in place to wipe out any army standing in the way of the advancing ground troops Hitler's other generals had massed. For various reasons this hadn't happened. The aircraft on the designers' drawing tables had been huge disappointments when they reached the prototype stage, and he was left trying to win the air war with aging weapons platforms that allied factories were busy using as benchmarks to exceed.

Schwerlieb had recently scrapped the once proud achievement of German aeronautical science, the zeppelins. They were easy to disable and contained tons of the precious aluminum needed to build the fighters yet to be manufactured. Spies had already provided information about the developments made to bring the newest versions of the British Spitfire and the American Mustang fighter aircraft out of the allied factories.

Schwerlieb had a military background much more heroic than Hitler's. The stint of flying an Albatross biplane in combat during the First World War made him the logical choice to head his country's first air force, and Hitler had named him Field Air Marshall, the first ever in Germany.

He knew Hitler had placed all his faith in the invincibility of the German Luftwaffe. The air war over Britain had to be won, and quickly. He also knew unless there was a miracle, it could not be done.

Schwerlieb listened to the drone of both motors as he flew back from his visit in Stockholm. His plane skimmed the Baltic Sea barely above white cap level, avoiding detection. The setting sun reminded him of the day his son had stood in the sunshine with all the other children on the huge terrace overlooking the Alps. He hoped his son Wilhelm would be able to grow up in a country with no need of war to maintain its right to exist. Hopefully their enemies would come to their senses and Germany would achieve victory soon. He would be able to spend time teaching his son how to hunt wild boar and deer on his newly built property. His wife could resume her career at the opera, and he would have time to devote to his own art collection.

When the various cultural anomalies were finally solved, German society would become the Empire which would stand for 1,000 years. Schwerlieb felt certain he would be remembered for all time as one of its founders. His son would be proud of his heritage. He was sure the world would look upon him with gratitude for removing elements plaguing the development of European society for many hundreds of years. He would become like a God.

Schwerlieb reflected on the day in the Alps when he stood beside the photographer, watching her coach the children to smile into the camera. They were all disciplined children except one, the little girl who stood next to his son. When he saw the child being drugged for the long flight to Sweden, he found comfort his own child had developed in a normal way. It would have sapped his strength to have to raise a child like Dolfin, and he thought about the strength of motherly love.

Perhaps this is the root of the evil we are trying to eradicate, he mused as his plane flashed across the Baltic toward Germany. *If we can inhibit motherly love or strong family ties, parents will be more inclined to give up their children to the Party for the greater good of the Fatherland.*

Schwerlieb found the idea interesting, and he scribbled a few key words onto his flight plan. He would take it up with Hitler at their next meeting.

Schwerlieb wondered how the negotiations had gone with Franco in Spain, and if the French Government had fallen to its knees as expected. If not, then he knew all would be lost for the Germans in a few short months. They would never be able to fight a two front war, and the resistance expected from the Russian allies, soon to be enemies, would be fierce, he was certain of that.

He woke his gunner and broke radio silence as he approached the German coastline and continued on toward Berlin. The airport he had built at Tegel was already considered to be the most modern in the world, and he always enjoyed landing there. The interior decorations included walls paneled with mahogany imported from Brazil, a country he and Hitler considered to be the new frontier for their movement.

Hurtree would be one of the first American soldiers to view the passenger hall at Tegel after the end of the war while he worked with his Soviet counterparts trying to round up the remains of the Nazi Government. He always found Tegel Airport depressing, dark, and heavy. The mahogany-lined walls seemed to have absorbed the sweat of frightened people, afraid of being stopped by the Gestapo before they succeeded in fleeing. The odor remained many years after the war ended and the East German STASI took their place.

John Hurtree's introduction to the coming war began as an early spring trip in 1936 when he went to Asbury Park with his family. His father had been fascinated by flying machines as soon as the Wright Flyer left the ground only a few decades earlier.

A mechanic by trade, Hurtree's father was sure he could make a contribution to the coming field of aeronautics, and he hoped his sixteen-year-old son would share his own interest in anything that flew. He had missed his chance a year earlier in 1936 when the giant zeppelin from Germany, the *von Hindenburg,* had docked in Lakehurst, only an hour away from Asbury Park. This year they would be there to witness the landing.

He and his son left his wife and sister at the boardwalk in Asbury Park, and then traveled the final few miles by bus to the airfield in Lakehurst. They waited and waited, and the small crowd gathered to watch the landing became disgruntled and dwindled by the hour in the chilly fog. John Hurtree and his father remained.

It was becoming dark, twelve hours after it was scheduled to land. They saw the huge dirigible appear as a gray cigar on the horizon, glinting in the final rays of the afternoon sun. John Hurtree saw the dirigible grow quickly, approaching at over 100 miles an hour, the droning of the diesel engines propelling it as it broke through the gusts of chilling wind.

Hundreds of linemen ran out onto the field to take hold of the lines soon to be dropped, and Hurtree and his father watched as the zeppelin prepared to be drawn like a silver air-borne whale toward the ground and the mooring mast.

The passengers had been ferried across the entire Atlantic Ocean, enjoying the same luxury as found on an ocean liner, but the trip went much, much faster. This was the technology of the future, and it was clearly German technology. The tail had been painted with the huge emblem of the Third Reich, a black swastika in a white circular field on a red flag as a background.

Suddenly, without warning the entire frame of the dirigible exploded in flames. They heard the piercing shrill sound of burning hydrogen, the screech of metal on metal as the frame collapsed, and the screams of passengers, crew, and linemen as everyone tried to save their lives.

It was a horrific catastrophe. Hurtree and his father did what they could to help extinguish the clothes of those survivors who ran in full panic as far away as they could from the smoking ruin of the *von Hindenburg*. It was a deciding moment for John Hurtree.

The accident provided him with clear evidence that flying could be dangerous, something he and his father had argued about several times. It also made him highly skeptical about the truth of the propaganda being spread about the wonderful successes of the totalitarian Government which had turned around an entire country. He had seen with his own eyes the destruction of Germany's largest flagship.

As a young man just out of high school he was approached by U.S. Army recruiters, and had begun to consider a military career. One of the sergeants told him he could be sure of getting free training, and that the risk of getting shot at was practically nonexistent. Since the end of the Great War there had been few military shoot-outs for the U.S. Army. He would learn how to shoot and ride a horse, but probably forget how to load his rifle before he actually had to use it. Good marketing, but a very long way from the truth.

Hurtree began looking for a job instead.

Chapter 28

Before enlisting in the Army, Hurtree had begun training as an apprentice mechanic at the same shop where his father worked. He started with the honing of intake and exhaust valves to the rough tolerances required for the A-Fords which kept the nation running. He loved the flatulent metallic sound of the four-cylinder motor in the Model A when it was running, and had learned to hand-crank it to ignition after only one muscular swing.

His life was uncomplicated, allowing him enough money to pay his parents part of what he cost at home and giving him some practice in the complicated process of growing up. He spent most of his spare time studying issues of *Popular Mechanics* and in discussions with his father about developments in aircraft. They never tired of discussing what they had seen during the disaster in Lakehurst, and they tried theory after theory in an effort to explain why the explosion had occurred.

One day just after lunch the owner of the garage came in with an afternoon tabloid with a headline about the new war in Europe. Everyone in the shop read the headline, and then the discussions began. Some felt it would be OK as long as the rest of the world stayed out of it, the German nation would have nothing to play with. Others had the view that if it started in Europe it would soon spread to the United States, and no one wanted to have to shoot German soldiers in their own back yard.

For Hurtree the matter was quickly settled. He had followed the developments in Germany since the *Hindenburg* disaster only a few years before. His individualistic spirit demanded freedom, and he understood the threat of dictatorship, even if it occurred on the other side of the Atlantic.

Hurtree enlisted as one of the many after the Japanese attacked the Seventh Fleet in Hawaii. He fully expected to become a cavalry horseman who could shoot a Winchester 30-30 at full gallop. It was a teenage expectation he would laugh about for the rest of his life.

The first few days of Hurtree's military training actually did bring him into direct contact with cavalry horses. He was assigned to rake the manure from the stalls as soon as he woke up in the chill of the morning. He and the rest of his platoon had to run to the stables in their long-john underwear, rake out the steaming manure, fill the troughs with water, and mount a full nosebag on the muzzle of each horse.

His drill sergeant assembled them, making them stand at attention as horseflies buzzed around their heads, drawn to the smell of sweat and manure. If they finished early they had to wait until the last member of the platoon had arrived. The drill sergeant knew their own discomfort while standing at attention, waiting for the last man to finish his chores, would produce group pressure his shouts could never achieve. Within a week everyone finished at the same time and they were dismissed to their barracks to wash themselves and their underwear. After that they dressed and went to morning assembly to watch the flag being raised before eating breakfast.

Hurtree never imagined horses could be so large. It took him several days to get the hang of throwing his saddle up and onto the back of his steed. His mount had experienced several riders, and was wise enough to know a saddle meant work. Hurtree tied his horse to the corral, doing exactly as he had seen the horse trainer do. At the start his horse stood perpendicular to the fence, gently chewing on a piece of grass that he had managed to find on the way to the corral. Every time Hurtree tried to throw the saddle up on the horse's back, he moved his hind quarters one or two steps to the left, pushing Hurtree one step closer to the fence. After the third try Hurtree was pinned to the fence by nearly 1,000 pounds of horse flesh that squeezed the air out of his lungs, making it difficult to call out for help.

This same horse had become an expert in determining the exact height of branches that hung over the trails where they practiced riding every day. On more than one occasion Hurtree's horse had suddenly disobeyed him and had run under a branch, scraping him off the saddle. He was left draped over the branch, swearing and trying not to hear the laughter of his fellow soldiers. His horse always seemed to smile at him on these occasions.

After six months of training he learned how to ride and how to shoot. He also learned how to run for nearly an entire day, leading his horse through terrain too tough to ride through. He and his platoon were now ready for war.

His platoon was to receive their own mounts at the end of the month, turning over their training mounts to the next group of unsuspecting recruits. Hurtree began to wonder where he would be stationed and how his new horse and rifle would stand up to the coming conflict. What he had read about the fate of the Polish cavalry left him with a great deal of doubt.

When the end of the month arrived, his unit assembled in front of the stables, fully expecting to acquaint themselves with their new steeds. Instead of receiving new horses, they were sent to a newly formed unit. They would use air transport to achieve quick deployment on the battlefield, and they shipped off to Britain. When they arrived in England they were billeted in the countryside, preparing for the coming invasion.

They would be using trucks and jeeps for transport, and Hurtree's background as a mechanic helped him several times during the campaign.

Hurtree had been involved in several battles by the time the war was ending, and he had used his rifle too many times for his own taste, earning a battlefield commission of Second Lieutenant because of his leadership in the line of duty.

The pace of the war quickened as the German Army faltered and the Allied troops pushed deep into the territory of the crumbling Empire. Hurtree's multilingual ability was discovered, and he was attached to a unit assigned to interview prisoners of war at one of the collection points in Bavaria: the city of Augsburg just outside Munich. The city dated from the Roman era and was the last Roman city before the frontier with the heathens to the north.

Caesar Augustus had the city built to honor his name and to provide proof that the Roman Empire extended well beyond the northern bounds of the Alps. The city had been bitterly defended by the German Army, and why didn't become apparent until American troops came to a small village only miles outside of town. There, in the low buildings of a converted chicken farm, they found the prototype for the factories of death built in Poland and Czechoslovakia. This was the so-called work camp in the village of Dachau, with its grim promise, fashioned in wrought iron fastened above the gate, made to anyone crossing through: *Arbeit Macht Frei*—Work Makes You Free.

Hurtree was not part of the liberation of the prison, but he spoke to those who were there. It was a frightening, horrendous experience. The soldiers who had first entered the prison were shocked for days.

It was proof for Hurtree that humans can fail to keep the thin veneer of culture wrapped around their thoughts and actions. Hurtree had seen killing in the war, it was part of the job. A tour of the camp in Dachau convinced him the men who devised this place had not only lost part of their humanity, but had substituted it with a new kind of bestiality. This was murder on an industrial scale, using the most modern and cost-effective tools available at the time. Dachau was an invention sponsored by the devil.

Chapter 29

As the war ended and hostilities wound to a standstill, Hurtree's new assignment went into high gear. He would soon meet several high-ranking members of the Nazi Government who had given up or been captured.

Hurtree was billeted in Luxembourg, near the village where his father had been raised. One afternoon a tiny Piper Cub flew in from Salzburg carrying Schwerlieb, next in line after Hitler. The prisoner saluted everyone in the beginning, careful not to use the Nazi straight-arm salute. Schwerlieb was convinced he could negotiate a high-ranking position in the coming government needed to rebuild the German nation. He kept asking to speak to General Eisenhower, but after several days in confinement, he began to understand his situation.

Hurtree entered the interview room where Schwerlieb was sitting. Schwerlieb noticed Hurtree's low rank, and surmised there was no reason for him to acknowledge his presence. He cast a furtive glance out the window at the green meadow outside as Hurtree sat down across the table from him.

Hurtree introduced himself, and explained he was now Schwerlieb's personal assistant. Schwerlieb could consider Hurtree to be his own adjutant, and although he could not offer any kind of secrecy with regard to what would be said between them, he could use Hurtree as a means to put forward his wishes in the coming months.

It was a lie, but if it worked the Army could use the information gathered to build evidence against Schwerlieb and other high-ranking prisoners. It had seemed like a good idea to Hurtree and he had no qualms about the way the investigation was conducted.

The two men started out by discussing the *Hindenburg* disaster. Schwerlieb was genuinely enthused to discover Hurtree had actually witnessed the explosion, and they spent hours discussing the event, with Hurtree retelling the story only to be faced with new questions from Schwerlieb.

"Are you sure that there were no lightning bolts from the clouds to cause the explosion?" asked Schwerlieb.

"No," said Hurtree, "I didn't hear any thunder at all."

"We were told at first that the explosion was caused by lightning. Later we heard there must have been a spark from some kind of static electricity built up when the Hindenburg passed through some clouds earlier." A grim smile formed on Schwerlieb's face. "I always thought it was a plot, a deliberate Jewish attack to bring down the finest example of German engineering we had at the time."

"I didn't see any lightning," said Hurtree, "and as I remember it, the lines had barely reached the ground when it exploded. I always thought it must have been some kind of internal explosion, a fuel tank or something."

On other occasions, they spoke of horses. Schwerlieb told Hurtree of his love for racing horses, and Hurtree amused him with the story of his short career as a cavalryman.

With the ice broken, Schwerlieb began to reveal the location of materials and documents which would later provide the evidence to convict him of the war crimes he had not yet been accused of. Truckload after truckload of evidence was deposited at the interrogation center in Luxembourg, and not only from Schwerlieb's home. In other buildings several future defendants were being questioned in the same way, with the interrogators comparing notes at the end of each day.

One day, Hurtree entered the interrogation room with a box full of photographs collected from Schwerlieb's own living quarters.

Schwerlieb refused to discuss the photographs at first, explaining they had no military significance.

"These are my own private photographs," he blurted out. "They contain no military secrets, and I have no wish for them to be in your custody. You must return them to my house at once."

Hurtree raised his eyes to look Schwerlieb in the face. He was surprised to see such a strong emotion. Schwerlieb had been congenial up to this point, even when revealing some of the innermost secrets of the Third Reich.

"OK, I will return them," said Hurtree, knowing the return would take years to achieve, "but only if you help me go through the material. We really have to be sure of the content of the photographs."

Schwerlieb agreed, and the two men spent several days verifying the box of photographs, identifying each location and person in every one of the several hundred pictures.

Hurtree took copious notes. Most of the material was completely useless for the purposes of the coming trial. No one really cared if Schwerlieb had been photographed in front of a tank as he commissioned the tank division which bore his name.

Hurtree remembered what a teacher had once said about a picture being worth more than 1,000 words. He sensed the massive weight of all those thousands of words, and a cramp in his hand began to throb as he continued. Only one photograph broke the pattern. It seemed to be a truly personal photograph, and as Hurtree handed it over he wondered if Schwerlieb would continue to reveal the location and names as he had done so far. Suddenly, Schwerlieb sat back in his chair.

"And where did you get this photograph?" asked Schwerlieb, sharply. "This is a personal photograph. It has nothing to do with what we have been discussing," and he handed the photograph back to Hurtree.

"And the children?" asked Hurtree. "Who are they?"

"Some children. You can see Der Führer in the background.

That's all I remember about this picture."

Hurtree brought back the box of pictures the next day, but he noticed Schwerlieb was on his guard. The confidence Hurtree had managed to build up during their discussions about horses and the *Hindenburg* disaster was damaged. Schwerlieb stopped revealing even the most obvious secrets, and Hurtree wondered why the photograph of the children had been so important.

Stockholm, 1996

Hurtree packed his suitcase for the journey to Germany, then home to Philadelphia. Several sampler bottles of shampoo, soap, and hair conditioner lay in one of the compartments.

I'll never have to buy soap again, and I have enough shampoo to last me until I go bald, thought Hurtree.

He took up the dog-eared notebook with the same questions on every page and flipped to the last page.

Who was the second child in the photo?

Hurtree took the hotel pen and wrote an answer on the next page.

She's Dolfin. Hitler's daughter.
Where is the child? Is she still alive?
Went to Sweden for health reasons. She lives in Stockholm.
What did Schwerlieb mean about knowing a lot about the photograph?
Schwerlieb must have flown Dolfin, the nurse, and Habermann up to Sweden in 1940. He knew everything.

Another question began forming as a nebulous cloud somewhere in Hurtree's mind, but he went on to the next question in the notebook.

Why was the photograph so important for Schwerlieb he thought he could exchange it for a bullet? Hurtree finally understood that Schwerlieb had been offering him the possibility to find out about Hitler's daughter. He also understood the importance of refusing the exchange.

Why did his son refuse to remember? Now that's a good question. Hurtree scratched his forehead with the pen. *It must mean Schwerlieb's son knew something himself. Dolfin was standing right next to him. He must have known who she was.*

Hurtree took up his plane ticket and looked at the first destination: Mannheim, Germany. *Too bad Schwerlieb's son lives in Munich,* he thought.

Hurtree read the first question again. *Who was the second child in the photo?*

Now, half a lifetime later, Hurtree was sure he knew the identity of each person in the photograph. He understood why Schwerlieb had been so secretive at the time, and why he had tried to bargain with it at the end of his life.

At least I got that question answered, he thought. *I even got a chance to get my own photograph of her.* Hurtree opened his digital camera and looked once again at the image of Dolfin.

Hurtree sat for several minutes staring at the image, and the evasive question finally formed as words in his mind.

Who took the photograph of the children in Germany?

Part III

The Photographer

Chapter 30

Sara shut the door to her office. The excitement of tracking down and then seeing Dolfin lingered, and she compared it to the time she had solved her first criminal case, a robbery, several years ago. She sat at her desk, but could not sit still, so she stood up and walked back and forth several times, a cat in a cage. Sara drew deep breaths to calm her nerves.

Questions formed about how she would protect Dolfin, the only person remaining alive from those on the hit list. Sara had to assume Dolfin's life was still in danger. But for how long? Perhaps Ekman at the NSS could help with that. Could she arrange a new identity for Dolfin? If she did, she would also have to arrange a way for Dolfin to live in some kind of protective custody. Could Sara do that? Did Dolfin have a trustee appointed? Sara would have to ask the social services in Fruängen tomorrow. Sven could help her with the other questions. And he didn't even know that Sara had found Dolfin.

How will he react to that? thought Sara as she left her room for the Eiderbach/Habermann room. She flipped the light switch and walked to the whiteboard. The photograph of the children from Eiderbach's bedroom was fixed there with a magnet. She took down the photo and sat with it in her hands.

That must be her, thought Sara. *The second child from the left. She was so young then, it's hard to see the resemblance today. The eyes maybe. Yes, the eyes.*

She rose and fixed the photo to the whiteboard next to the plastic bag holding the medallion. She took the medallion to the computer and Googled the words *Hitler-Wolf.*

Several pages told her of Hitler's love of code names. She put the medallion back into the plastic bag and returned it to the whiteboard. Before turning out the light she gazed at the photograph again. *I wonder who took it?* she thought.

When she got back to her room, Sara considered contacting Sven. She had to tell him about finding Dolfin. Or should she tell Ekman? There was a moment's indecision as she pondered what Ekman would do with the knowledge. Would he protect Dolfin? She wasn't sure.

Sara called Sven, and he answered, "Sven Peterson."

"Sven, it's Sara. We have to talk. Now."

A researcher at the Stockholm Institute for Genetic Research hesitated before walking into his professor's office for a review of the work on his thesis. He knew the results already. His work was clearly inadequate, and it would be a miracle if he managed to keep from failing.

He tried to hide his surprise when his professor commended him on his work and gave him the possibility to earn several hundred dollars to carry out a set of simple DNA tests on some material which could solve a family's dispute over a question of heredity.

The Institute had been told to be discrete. The first test was to gather material from a pair of hairbrushes. The researcher could expect the other samples for comparison in a few days.

As he examined the hairbrushes, the researcher found they were almost devoid of hair or cells, and the few he could collect had been deposited many, many years ago. He recognized his future depended on how well he could perform this task. His fear quickly translated into perseverance.

Working meticulously, he managed to collect two separate sets of cells for testing. One came from someone with dark hair, very straight and oily. The other set came from someone with long blond wispy hair that had broken off in the brush.

The preparations for testing required several days, and extreme cleanliness. He worked well into the night before he could actually view the first results producing enough samples for his comparison later on. He put the vials into the refrigerator, saved the background data on his hard disk, and went home too tired to write the report. The boring part would have to wait.

The researcher felt a sense of pride as he boarded the bus that would take him home, satisfied his work had improved so much he had been merited with work otherwise destined for the professor's own son-in-law. He had concentrated hard on this task, more than he had ever done before, and during the testing had discovered many points mentioned in theory he had never understood before.

The U.S. Iron Guard had contacts all over Europe, but the Swedish contacts had been formed only recently, in spite of it being one of the oldest cells.

As the war trials ended, and those found responsible were imprisoned or executed, public interest in capturing ageing war criminals was replaced by capturing much younger war criminals from more recent wars.

The average age of the Iron Guard members dropped as the older members were buried, one after another. Then, about fifty years after the war's end, several of the national committees noticed the democracies they were trying to eradicate were close to the point of crisis predicted by the Führer. Their day had arrived, and it was time to begin consolidating their efforts. They would change their stance from defense and survival to one which demanded respect and was on the offensive. To do this they would have to have an authority who could co-ordinate activities, a leader, but not a person who would be easy to target.

They chose the form of a steering committee, and named it *The Committee for Future Victories*, meeting in rotation among the various countries which hosted existing cells, among them Argentina, Greece, Spain, Brazil, the United States, Sweden, and Germany. Germany was chosen to be the country for the final meeting. At that meeting the Iron Guard would become public and be able to participate openly in political life again. For the present, however, they had not come that far. It was too risky to meet in Germany for the time being.

The third meeting was held in Spain. In order to disguise their activities, meetings were designated as golf tournaments for members only. It was during the commissioning of a new golf course outside Tarragona that the steering committee members were first informed of Dolfin's existence.

The organization's accountant had discovered regular payments made into Sweden, bypassing the Swedish committee and suggesting corruption within their own organization. During the heated discussion which followed, the senior member from Argentina took the floor to read the Final Wishes of Klas Belgrado, a close friend of Bordmann, Hitler's own personal secretary. There was a hush as the old man broke the seal with the Nazi emblem protecting the envelope. He read the terse message in a loud voice.

> Members of the steering committee, I'm dying and I wish to convey to you a secret told to me by a member of the original Government, one who was close to the Führer, and someone we can trust. This will come as a shock, and I am sorry I have not been able to reveal this secret until now, but it's important the secret is passed on. Our Führer had a child who survived the war. Her name is Dolfin and she has been living as a patient at a hospital in Stockholm, Sweden. She has serious mental deficiencies. During her entire life she has been cared for by one of our own, a doctor, Dr. Habermann. He was assisted by a nurse, also one of our own, Anna Eiderbach. I have not been told of any strategy for what we should do with this knowledge, just that it is important for us to know about the event.

The room went completely silent for several seconds after the reader sat down. No one dared to speak; the news overwhelmed the entire meeting. A direct heir to the Führer. This would require a complete rethink of their entire political strategy.

The first to react was the representative from the Swedish cell.

The steering committee stared at him as he raised himself out of his chair.

"But why were we not informed? We could have done so much. This is as much good news as bad."

The discussion which followed went on all night as the Iron Guard experienced its first real leadership crisis. Up to this point, their meetings had been cordial backslapping events, deepening the bond between them. From now on there would be a rift of dissension between them, and it would change the lives of a great many people, including a retired U.S. Army CID Lieutenant.

The Steering Committee for the Iron Guard continued their meeting into the early Spanish morning light. The old Roman aqueduct on the outskirts of Tarragona gleamed in a yellow hue against the dusty background of country backwoods. It would soon be hot, and flies were already at work looking for a place to lay their eggs.

The members of the Iron Guard stayed in a country house renovated during the Franco era on the outskirts of the city. A large circular courtyard had been sunk several yards into the red clay soil, surrounded by stone walls. The circle was intersected in the center by a huge letter, an A forming bridges where torches were mounted during the midnight rituals. A flagpole stood in the middle of the circle, in the center of the bridge forming the cross-member of the A. A guard went quickly to the flagpole to lower the huge red flag with the white circle encompassing the black swastika. It was still too risky to fly the flag for more than a few hours during the day.

In the conference room the dispute continued.

"We must find her. We have a duty to the Führer. She is the child. We can use her eggs to produce another Führer. Can you not imagine the possibilities?" Wolfgang from Argentina seemed sure of the future.

There were others not quite so sure.

"She is mentally deficient." Horst was the Germany representative. His words carried twice the weight of other speakers', Horst being geographically closer to the original Government. "We shall deal with her as we would have done then. I'm sure the Führer would have agreed." He slapped the table for emphasis. "Also, she is much too old to be bred. She will have no eggs at her age. We are so close now, we have had several Members of Parliament elected here in Europe. I think this poses a threat to our" his voice became exuberant as he pronounced the last two words "future victory."

"But what about cloning?" The representative from the United States was always slightly ahead on technology issues. He could be relied on to confuse everyone with long dissertations about what could be done if only they wanted to. "I suggest we use her cells to produce a clone, and then mate her *in vitro* with a suitable Aryan specimen. This could give us the Führer in just a few short years. It must be our responsibility to complete the work he started." The American turned to the Brazilian for support.

Horst stood up and closed the discussion with a comment which made even these hardened men become quiet with respect. "We have made huge gains in the past few decades. Imagine the risk to our success if news of this is made public. She is a remnant of the old order, but a defect. She must be terminated. And with her, Doctor Habermann and the nurse Anna Eiderbach. This must be stopped now. The Swedish committee will be empowered with the cleaning up of this matter. Switzerland will take care of the economic issues if they arise. Italy and Bosnia will help Sweden with manpower questions. It is time for us to move on."

The meeting ended. No one had the stamina to do eighteen holes of golf that morning. Bengt Ohlsson, the head of the Swedish committee, was already packing and on his way to the airport in Barcelona before breakfast. There was much to be done, and quickly. Ohlsson had to call in the members of the Swedish committee to a meeting as soon as he arrived.

Chapter 31

The Swedish Iron Guard was typical of what could be found in most countries: a very homogenous group comprised of members from all political parties in the country. Members worked together—social democrats, greens, far-rights, moderates—representing the full scale of political thought in the country. There were few conflicts in the meetings, and the dichotomies of public debates and niggling about welfare or immigrants, directors or workers, were laid to one side as they concentrated on the question that really united them: the establishment of a world movement to replace the inadequacies of democratic government. They strove to establish a world dictatorship. To that end all means were allowed.

The committee assembled in Stockholm quickly accepted the decision that Anna Eiderbach, Dr. Habermann, and Dolfin had to be eradicated.

Bengt Ohlsson made a plan for the operation. There were local members who could provide support and protection for the hitmen who would come from Bosnia. Members from Italy would provide the infrastructure of vehicles, weapons, radios, telephones, and other items necessary for the task.

Thomas Johnson, Robert Johnson's brother, could barely breathe the day Bengt Ohlsson contacted him. He gave Thomas a list with vague plans about what was going to happen, but Thomas could see it would be a major event. Thomas was the contact man for people coming in for something big. He worked days for a private security organization which gave him a good cover. He might even be able to provide advance warning of police movements—his brother Robert worked as an investigator for Homicide. The feathers in his bonnet were multiplying.

The head of the Institute for Genetic Research was a political appointee, and had surprised everyone when his research attracted international attention, allowing him to take on several students to do the research he had too little time for. His trips to the United States had put him into contact with several colleagues with political leanings which were foreign to him at first. After many discussions he began to feel his own political foundation was changing. In his own country academic education was almost a stigma, something society didn't really need, and would only be tolerated if those involved used their knowledge to further the goals of society.

Research contradicting political ideals was quickly buried, and unfortunately his latest work seemed to be the antitheses of the current paradigm. He had been working on a genetic link to criminal activity, and it seemed his success would be penalized by lower grants for the following years.

He was pleasantly surprised when a member of a Midwestern university in the United States contacted him about a job. It was for a private client, a way for the Institute to earn the funds that they had just been deprived of, and although it was a simple case of establishing paternal identity, it was sensitive and couldn't be carried out by anyone in the United States. The parents, he had been told, were high-profile public people, and it was important the work be carried out by an independent laboratory such as his own. The professor heard the voice of the Dean on the other end of the line tell him his Institute in Stockholm was becoming well-known in the international community, and that he might soon be asked to join the teaching staff for a year's sabbatical.

His latest student was a simpleton, but a good-hearted young man. The job for the customer in the United States wouldn't require anything more than following the simple instructions found on the first page of each of the binders used to guide new researchers at the Institute. He could safely turn over the work to the student and enjoy the difference between the generous fee paid in from the United States and the miserly amount that went to his research assistant.

At the laboratory the research assistant arrived with his life's worst hangover. 'Friends' was a word he had seldom used during the past few years, and the people he worked with were providers of the funds he used for his rent and food, and little else. At work he was considered to be a researcher-wannabe. The assistant had serious problems with the requirements to be able to use mathematics in his work. He was also sloppy in his lab techniques, and his work often required huge amounts of very expensive chemicals since the procedures had to be repeated many times.

He sat at his desk in the lab, looking for an aspirin to alleviate the headache pounding at his temples. A small box had been placed on his desk by his professor with a note that read:

> Here is the blood sample to be used to establish the paternal identity for the parents whose hairbrushes you have already received. Please leave the results and your conclusion with me when you're finished.

The assistant rubbed his temples with both hands. He would have to begin another set of replication procedures and then compare them to two previous sets. Things always looked easier when DNA tests were performed on television. It only took a few minutes for the film makers to show the vials of test material being introduced into some kind of centrifuge, and then the needles that entered a vial, followed by the wondrous results being displayed on the screen as the camera zoomed in on the obvious. He wished that it were that easy in real life. He was faced with hours and hours of tedious, repetitive work that demanded extreme cleanliness and careful documentation. He had yet to find the aspirin tablets. He would have preferred to begin another day, and was about to put the package into his desk for later when his professor stepped into his room.

"I see you've found the package I left you this morning. I just wanted to tell you how important it is we have the results soon. Can you start today?"

"Uh, yes. Of course. I can begin the procedure as soon as I clean up a little."

"I knew I could count on you. Let me know when you're done," said the professor. "Have a good time this weekend?"

"Perhaps a little too good," the research assistant replied, "but I'll get the work done as soon as possible."

After the professor had gone, the researcher found his aspirin tablets and filled a beaker full of water, swallowed three pills and, using his notebook as a pillow, waited for them to take effect. He then took up the package he had been given earlier and removed a small plastic container containing fragments of bark clearly smudged red, presumably blood.

He would have to be very careful. Bark contained chemicals which could contaminate and devastate the test results he needed to make the comparison. He began the difficult and painstaking process of removing the red smudges from the bark. His eyes ached as he focused through the microscope and scraped off the sample he needed. He removed a small specimen and carefully tested it to see if it was a human blood sample.

He smiled when the cotton swab turned red, reacting with the reagent. It was human blood. Now he could continue scraping. After several hours he had enough sample material to begin the amplification process. He noted the date, time, and the assignment number in his notebook, and wrote this onto a small label that he fixed to the vial which would soon contain the millions of cells needed for the test specimen. Everything was routine from here. The trick lay in finding the cell to replicate. Making a mistake here would invalidate the entire procedure. There would be results provided, but they would be entirely useless for the purpose.

His professor had made this abundantly clear during his training by giving him a specimen to sample containing cells of frogs, fish, sheep, and a human being. He was told to produce a DNA sample on the human being, in this case his own DNA collected by his teacher from a can of soft-drink he'd thrown in the waste basket. He'd kept the sample vial of his own DNA in the refrigerator to remind him of the number of times he had to run the testing procedure before he finally got it right.

Several days later, the assistant opened the pages containing the details of the tests he'd processed on the two hairbrushes. His handwritten notes were smudged, and although legible could lead to a mistake if he weren't careful. He would have to double-check to make sure he didn't screw up the most important assignment he had ever had.

He looked at the notebook again to make sure, then went to the refrigerator to take out the two vials with the test samples. The assistant found the female sample quickly, but hesitated a minute before he took out the male specimen, checking the vial number again against what had been entered into his notebook. The ink on the label was smudged from the moisture of the refrigerator. He was unsure, but prodded by the professor to provide quick results, he placed the glass vials onto a tray and began the work of comparing the samples to what had come from the bark. He put the three vials into a machine which would soon spit out the telltale histograms making it possible to determine kinship. The PCR tests took several hours to complete, and by the time the smell of morning coffee wafted through the lab, his results were available.

The female who had contributed the blood sample on the bark was the daughter of the woman who had left hair on the hairbrush he had been given. The result was clear and could never be disputed.

The result of the male whose cells had been replicated from the other hairbrush was just as clearly negative. He was definitely not the father. The researcher checked the test results again. He could see from the results that they were definitely from a human male, and for some reason he seemed to recognize the pattern emerging in the histograms on the screen. The assistant wondered if his professor had given him a new test, providing him with a test sample that he'd worked with before, but he discarded the thought and continued his report.

He felt like God. Sometimes clients were happy, sometimes they were devastated, but they all accepted the truth he provided. He always tried to be at the client meetings when the professor presented his findings. He had learned small gestures to increase the validity of his work, peering over the rims of his glasses, twitching his mouth as he dryly announced the results of the kinship in question.

This client would just have to accept the negative kinship result for the father, and he secretly hoped it was a case where the man was wrongfully accused of fathering a child. He also hoped he could be present when the results were presented to the client, and tried to imagine how he would control the timbre of his voice as he softly let loose the bombshell.

The researcher kept working on his report for the rest of the afternoon. Everyone else had left for the day when he had finished it. He stretched and yawned, then saved the report to the hard disk, printed it out, and went by the professor's room to leave him a copy. He approached the server room, and a janitor stopped his swabbing of the floor for a moment to make room for him to pass.

"Bye," said the assistant.

The janitor nodded his uncombed locks of hair and smiled a broken-toothed grin. An unpleasant odor of sweat, garlic, and something else wafted toward the researcher as he passed, and he hurried by the janitor to leave for his apartment.

Minutes later the janitor unlocked the door to the server room and went inside. He blocked the door with the mop and bucket. It took him less than a minute to exchange the USB memory stick he had attached to the backside of the server. The memory stick containing a copy of the researcher's report was on the desk of the Mossad before 8 a.m.

Chapter 32

A few miles away from the genetic research laboratory, the Mossad began their follow-up meeting about the fate of the Lebanese hitman they had hired to solve the Habermann problem. It had gone well, and they would be able to report to the S-Office the target had been neutralized as desired. Now the question remained: what could they negotiate out of it?

"We've been offered the ID of a Hamas bomber," said the Mossad's Section Secretary, "but I think we can get more."

"Good," said the Section Chief. He focused on a tiny piece of dust on his dark blue pinstriped jacket, then dusted it off. "And so what can we get?"

"More bombers?" asked the Secretary and laughed. "We don't even have to ask them to set up a Holocaust museum, they're already doing it. I don't know. Maybe we could get them to finance us with a foreign aid grant." He laughed again.

"Let's get serious for a minute," said the Section Chief. "We can take the Hamas bomber and let them know that in the future they owe us something."

"And the American working with the police? Is he still in Sweden?" The Section Secretary turned to Rachel Goldsten.

Rachel grimaced and nodded. "He was on site when the police found Dolfin. He has a ticket booked for Mannheim, then Newark in the United States."

"What about the woman?" asked the Secretary. "Is there any update on her?"

Rachel Goldsten glanced up from her report. "Yes, we've got

her targeted. We know where she lives, what she looks like, and I'm sure we'll have no trouble completing the mission if we have to. The Swedish Iron Guard is still looking for her, but we've discovered that the Iron Guard from the United States has found her and is already watching her."

"So they're not working together," said the Section Chief. Winkles formed on his brow, and he asked, "What are the American Nazis doing?"

Rachel grinned and shook her head. "They've collected a DNA sample from her, so we assume they're trying to establish her identity. We don't know what they'll do with the knowledge they've got. We do know how they got it. We have an agent working at the Institute where they conducted the tests. He works there as a janitor and has access to their computer room. Their researcher finished the DNA testing yesterday. Here's his report."

Cleaning the Institute's server room was part of the job for the janitor. He wore jeans and a sloppy brown shirt which hadn't seen a washing machine for several weeks. He hadn't been to a barber for more than three months, and his hair was oily and uncombed. He bathed only every third day to make sure that he kept attempts at friendship at work to an absolute minimum. He came from a mixed marriage, Jewish father and Arabic mother, a woman of extraordinary beauty. The agent was more like his father, an Israeli policeman. She had been working as a waitress in a café when they met.

The agent had grown up in the Gaza strip with her, his father visiting almost every other day, but never really at home as other fathers were in his neighborhood. Then, when he came of age, his father had come to collect him and move him to another family. He had been given an education, and then was recruited by the Israeli Army, and after that the Mossad. He had a skill for languages and was selected for foreign assignments, ending up in Sweden to work among the many Arabic-speaking refugees staying there.

His cover was working as a cleaner for a company with many

state agencies as customers, like the universities where he met many Arab women also in the same job, and he listened to their gossip quietly, relaying what he heard to the office in Stockholm. As a janitor he was perfect, carrying out each step of the cleaning routine for each area that he had been assigned. No one had ever complained about his work, and he was always finished in his area before the others. He never asked for extra time off, and had only been off work for two days of sick leave during the two years he had been employed. He also had a doctorate in computer science and four years of training in cryptology and network management.

It took him less than an hour to find and access administrator rights to the server, and he located the professor's and researcher's libraries with no difficulty. He inserted a USB memory stick on the back of the server, and with a few key strokes a small program had been uploaded onto the server which copied and downloaded the professor's and researcher's entire collection of files onto the memory stick at 6 p.m. every evening.

All he had to do now was to collect the memory stick every time he cleaned the room, exchanging it for a new one.

The client would not be present for the researcher's presentation. The agent from the Iron Guard who had left the blood sample had already left the country, and was now safely back in Michigan enjoying the celebrity and extra money his trip had provided.

The U.S. Iron Guard set up a special chat site for the professor to access when it was time for the results. They would not need to hear the researcher's voice or scientific explanations. They had their own expertise in genetics to reference. There would be questions to the professor dealing with the degree of accuracy obtained and the risk that the results had been contaminated.

It was late Monday afternoon in Stockholm when the professor logged onto the chat room as Supplier, and it took only a few minutes before he was joined by a chatter at the other end named Curious.

Supplier: I have some results from the tests you ordered.

Curious: Good. Please relate them at once.

Supplier: The tests indicate the female who supplied the sample on the hairbrush is the mother of the female who left the blood sample.

Curious: We expected that. What about the male?

Supplier: The tests indicate the male who supplied the sample on the other hairbrush is not the father of the female who left the blood sample.

The chat room went silent for several minutes. The professor clicked again and again on his mouse to update the chat room dialogue, but there was no answer from the other side. Fifteen minutes went by with no answer, then:

Curious: Are you sure? Please explain the method used to determine this and the exclusion statistics.

This was not exactly what the professor had expected. He had examined his researcher's short report about methods and exclusions, but the client seemed to expect another result and questioned the veracity of the work done. He hoped that the researcher had done a good job. He keyed the address to attach the researcher's report, and added it to his next message.

Supplier: Look for yourself. My lab report is attached.

There was another silence, this time much longer. Nearly half an hour had elapsed when the message came from the other side.

Curious: We have examined the lab report. It seems to

be in order, but we want to do another series of tests at another laboratory in order to achieve an independent second opinion.

Supplier: This may be difficult. I noticed the hairbrushes didn't have very many cells to sample, and the blood sample required extra work because of the bark contamination on earlier samples.

Again, another long silence. He imagined there was another correspondence being carried out at the other end between his client and someone with enough scientific knowledge really to understand his results. It made him a little nervous.

Curious: What do you mean, bark contamination?

Supplier: As indicated in the report, the blood sample we received was on a piece of fir bark. It caused difficulties in our testing in the beginning.

The answer came back like a shot.

Curious: What do you mean 'our' testing?

Supplier: I meant that I had a lab assistant do the testing. He knows nothing of why, or who you are.

The silence on the other end was ominous, an indication that he had made a mistake. The terms of the agreement had been that he, and only he, would be involved in the testing. He knew he couldn't explain his way out of the dilemma he had just created, but he didn't know how to resolve it. He waited for another half an hour and the chat room was still silent. He sighed as he typed in his last message.

Supplier: Have to go now. Talk to you later?

He waited for another five minutes, and when he got no response he logged off and shut down his machine before going home.

What the professor could not see was the feverish activity on the other end.

The U.S. Iron Guard had been summoned to a committee meeting in the United States, an unusual occurrence. They almost always held their meetings in Canada or the Virgin Islands, trying to avoid the prying eyes of the FBI and others who might try to eavesdrop, but this had been deemed an emergency.

By the end of Monday evening the committee had assembled and the details had been put forward by the Chairman. Most of the committee's members were shocked, first to find out that their Führer's wife had had a child, then that it wasn't the Fuhrer's child. It seemed like an episode from a modern-day reality show hosted by a woman who could find only the most miserable examples of humanity to put on stage. It took them several minutes to absorb the information.

The Chairman was the first to speak. "I think we should get a second opinion. I'm not sure that the results can be relied upon."

"Which results do you mean?" asked the geneticist. "Do you mean Eva's results or the Führer's?"

"There was mention of bark contamination in the samples. Who knows how this could have affected the results? I think we should get another test done."

"How do we do this?" asked the geneticist. "There was already a lack of materials to do the first testing. How do we find enough material to do another set of tests?"

It was a good point, and no one seemed to have an answer to the problem it posed.

"And anyway," said the geneticist, "if the bark contamination was important it should have interfered even with the comparison made with Eva's DNA, which it didn't. I think we can assume that the testing, if done correctly, has left us with results we don't like, but that we'll have to trust. We'll have to base our decisions on a single sample. It's not good, but it's probably better than no sample at all."

The Chairman agreed reluctantly. "It would appear that our colleagues in Germany now have no reason to terminate the woman, Eva's daughter. She's not going to be a problem since she can pose no threat to anyone, even if her identity were revealed."

"Yes," said the member from the West Coast, "and they also run the risk of exposing us should this operation get out of hand, like it seems to have done already. The Guard in Stockholm must be informed. They are the ones running the highest risk right now. I think we should inform them of the results we have managed to obtain. My suggestion is that they just call off the whole operation. Who can contact the Munich Guard?"

Chapter 33

Security was a priority with the Iron Guard. With the exception of their occasional meetings, there was no way for one cell to contact another cell directly. Each cell only knew how to contact one other unit directly. The U.S. Iron Guard would first have to contact the Guard in Argentina to have them send the message forward. Argentina would in turn send the message to Greece, and so on until finally the message reached the Guard in Munich. After that the Guard in Munich would set up a date and time on a restricted chat room, and the message would be relayed on to the United States. It took time, but they believed it was a sure way to keep their identities secure.

The only weak point would be if one of the cells were broken. A break in the chain would render communication impossible, but it had worked so far, it was that simple. It also worked for the FBI. The FBI had managed to buy several small companies managing chat rooms for clandestine organizations, giving them first hand access to some of the sites that the Guard used. They had inserted themselves into the chain several years ago.

It took one day, but finally a message came in to meet in the chat room at 3 a.m.

Eagle: Hello Fox.

Fox: Hello Eagle.

Eagle: We have information regarding the woman in Stockholm.

Fox: Stockholm has already begun the operation.

Eagle: We have heard. We still have important information. We have proof she is not the daughter of the Führer. The information we heard in Tarragona was incorrect.

Fox: How do you know this?

Eagle: We obtained scientific proof. DNA samples have confirmed it. The woman is Eva's daughter, but not the daughter of our Führer.

Fox: Can this be certain? Belgrado's message was so clear.

Eagle: There was no such thing as DNA testing while Belgrado lived. Perhaps it was wishful thinking.

Fox: Who was the father?

Eagle: We don't know. We know that it wasn't the Führer's child. She must have had someone else we never heard about.

Fox: No wonder the Führer kept her from the public eye.

Eagle: Now that we know this about the woman, perhaps we should call off the action. She can't cause us any embarrassment or trouble.

Fox: Stockholm reported that the doctor and the nurse have already been taken care of. They were having trouble finding the woman. How did you succeed?

Eagle: American ingenuity. How we did it doesn't matter. I think we should call off all the operations and try to cover our tracks.

Fox: Keep the information about her location with you for the time being. We will ask Stockholm to stop the operation until further notice.

Eagle: Thank you. I think it's the right decision.

Fox: We'll talk later. Auf Wiedersehen.

Eagle: Auf Wiedersehen.

The word was spreading faster outside the Guard than inside. By the time the Iron Guard in Stockholm got the message to stand down and await further instructions, the intelligence community, including the FBI, FSB, CIA, Mossad, and the NSS had already been informed about what was happening in Stockholm.

Commissioner Ekman at the NSS had been informed from both sides. The message intercepted from the German Iron Guard had been short and could not be misunderstood. The operation must be stopped. The message he received from the FBI was a long, rambling attempt to put several pieces of the puzzle together, but without success. The end of their message informed Ekman he should be watchful of a group called the Iron Guard and that they might be involved in a plot to murder someone, a woman.

So very helpful, he thought. *At least they told me they don't really know anything.*

When Sven got into his office at Homicide, he began his day with the usual routine. He turned on his computer, went to get a cup of coffee while he waited for it to boot up, and then looked for relevant emails. There had been very few emails related to his cases for the last three weeks, coinciding with the take-over of the homicides by the NSS. He felt as if he was directing traffic, but on an intersection where the cars paid him no heed whatsoever. His arms waved and his whistle blew, but in the end the only net effect was that he got tired and the traffic seemed to obey the logic of another world.

He went through his inbox for in house mail and found little of interest, just a few memos regarding the next reorganization of his unit. Their activities would soon fall under a larger department, this time with no clear functional description. This had happened before and he felt the familiar dread of change that brought no real advantage to anyone. If the Party lost the election in the coming year then that would all change again, and he would find himself working with new faces and with a new agenda.

The crooks must be having a party, he thought.

At the bottom of the pile was a note from Sara about the medallion, asking if he would have time to meet her about it during the week. She thought she might have found out something. He was about to divert his phone when it rang. He answered with his name.

"Sven, it's Sara. We have to talk. Now."

"OK, where are you?" he asked.

"The Habermann/Eiderbach room," she answered.

He diverted his office telephone to his cell phone and walked toward the Habermann/Eiderbach room. She was on the phone when he popped his head in the door, and she nodded him in, motioning for him to sit down opposite her.

"Right," she said, "I'll look at it as soon as I can," and she put the phone on its cradle.

"The medallion," said Sven, "you wrote that you found something."

"Yes." Sara shifted a stack of paper to find her notes. "It was the inscription: *'Eva und Dolfin, in Liebe Wolf'*—'With Love To Eva and Dolfin from Wolf', Remember?"

"Of course," said Sven. "What of it?"

"Dolfin is the patient at the hospital that both of the murder victims were working with, we've got that nailed down. We still haven't figured out who Eva or Wolf were."

"Eva isn't a very uncommon name, there must be hundreds of thousands of them," said Sven, and raised himself to leave.

"Yes, but not all of them would have their names inscribed on a gold swastika medallion. Suppose it's the famous Eva, an Eva who knows a man who calls himself Wolf."

"Where are you going with this?" asked Sven. "I'm getting lost."

"Wolf was Adolf Hitler's favorite code name for himself. His mistress at the time was a woman whose first name was Eva, the woman he married just before he died."

Sven sat down again. His jaw slackened slightly and the events of the past few days congealed into a small knot of blazing neurons in his brain.

"Of course," he said, "of course. If Wolf is Adolf Hitler, then Eva is Mrs. Hitler, and their daughter is named Dolfin. That's more or less what the American has been trying to get us to believe. But why would Anna Eiderbach have the medallion in her purse? Why wouldn't Dolfin have it?"

In the meantime Sara had used the stand-alone computer to open a page on the Internet containing some history on the life of Adolf Hitler. It took the search engine a few seconds to display the page she was looking for, and she spun the monitor toward Sven.

"There," she said, "read it yourself."

Sven read about Hitler's penchant for code names of all kinds: Wolf for himself, and his retreat high on the Austrian Alps was called the Eagles' Nest. The bunker in northern Germany was the Wolf's Lair. He used the code name of Wolf on several other occasions.

Sara and Sven looked for other pages regarding medallions, and found that Hitler had been fond of giving medallions with his party's symbol, the swastika. Like a king from the Middle Ages, he had invented a way to reward people he thought had performed remarkable and heroic deeds for the country.

I have to tell him now, thought Sara. *He has to know.*

Sara turned from the computer monitor and looked at Sven.

"I found something else," she admitted. "I found the woman called Dolfin. I've seen her. I know where she lives."

"What?" Sven was surprised, but now there was anger in his voice as he stood up and said, "Why wasn't I informed of this before now? How could you just go out and meet with her without letting me know?"

"Sorry, Sven," she said, "I had to do it that way. I was afraid that if I didn't, someone from higher up would make it impossible, so I just did it, that's all. And it wasn't even that difficult."

"How did you do it?" he asked. "My God, not even the NSS knows how to find her, and you manage to do it? OK. Tell me about it quickly, write it down as a report as you tell me, and then we'll go to Ekman and you can tell him yourself."

Sara told Sven about the way she had found Dolfin, carefully omitting Karin's involvement. She mentioned that a personal friend, who just happened to be a doctor, had made the initial contact with the woman. She described the walk to the woods across the street from Dolfin's apartment, and how difficult it would be to make deeper contact with her owing to her condition. She also omitted that Hurtree had been at the meeting.

"And there's something else," she said. "I can put the suspect who could have done the murder of Nurse Eiderbach at the site of another murder in Fruängen, close to where Dolfin lives. I don't know what that means yet. He was caught on a video camera at one of the hot dog stands near the metro station in Fruängen."

"What about the tape in the metro station?" he asked.

"Erased. The wonders of modern technology. We install all these cameras and tape machines for millions, and when we need to use them we discover they don't work."

"Back to square one on Eiderbach," said Sven. "At least I've got a line on the suspect for Dr. Habermann's killing, the guy who flew to Greece. He was fished out of the harbor outside of Athens a couple of days ago. No sign of external violence, but he had a huge percentage of alcohol in his blood."

Sven sat down on a chair next to the door. "So let's summarize. Eiderbach was murdered. Her killer gets killed himself, and oddly enough in the same way. Habermann gets murdered and his killer ends up drowned. And now you've found the Dolfin woman, but we don't know if there's a killer out there looking for her. Did you leave any surveillance on her apartment?"

"If we're going to put uniforms out there then they have to be able to speak to her. That's difficult. I thought it would be better to attract as little attention to her as possible for the present. Maybe the NSS can help us with that."

"Let's go talk to Ekman," said Sven.

Ekman's eyes wandered to the ceiling on several occasions while Sara read the points she had jotted down on a page. Sara remembered a teacher at the Police Academy, a man who almost always consulted the ceiling when searching for answers to the difficult questions his students could ask him. Sara wondered if Ekman found answers on the ceiling in the same way.

"Good." Ekman slammed his hands together as if praying when she'd finished reading. "Excellent work, Sara. From what I can see there's little more we need to do on these cases. Your two murders are solved, the identity of the mysterious woman has been established, although we still have no real proof, like a birth certificate. But I think it's enough for us to be able to clear the Habermann/Eiderbach room and get back to doing some really important work."

Sara glanced over at Sven, who said, "OK, we understand. Cases closed. Right?"

"And that's it?" asked Sara. "We just leave it like that? What about her, Dolfin?"

Ekman turned to Sara with a scowl. "The NSS will take care of her from now on. The murder investigations are closed."

"But the Iron Guard?" asked Sara. "I've been doing some background checking. I found a witness who says he knows someone who has an Iron Guard tattoo. His name is Bengt Ohlsson. He could be a member of the Iron Guard."

Ekman rose, went to a filing cabinet, and took up a well-worn file. He let it fall to his desk with a thump.

"We know a lot about Bengt Ohlsson," said Ekman, and he fastened his gaze on Sara. "I know who his parents were, why his father left his mother, and why Ohlsson was such a failure in school. I can tell you how many times he was arrested for petty theft and when he joined the Guard. I even know the day he got his tattoo. I know where he travels, what hotels he stays at, and even what he likes to eat." Ekman kept his eyes on Sara, opened the file, and took up a pen. "Now what can you tell me about Bengt Ohlsson?"

Sara sat speechless for seconds, then she asked, "But, Sir, if you knew all that, why wasn't he arrested?"

"For what?" asked Ekman. "Belonging to a Nazi organization? Sara, you know what our laws are like. We have to catch them in the act of doing something illegal or have technical evidence before we can do anything. Even then it's not easy." Ekman rose and put the file back in the cabinet. He continued as he returned to his desk, "Sara, you did a great job on the murder investigations, really good. But they're solved now. We'll keep an eye on the Dolfin woman, but my, uh, guess is that her life is not in imminent danger. Thank you for your help."

Sven accompanied Sara down the corridors leading to the secure elevator isolating the NSS wing from the rest of the building. The soles of their shoes squeaked on meeting the well-waxed linoleum floors.

"I'm still wondering if this American guy, Hurtree, was right when he said Dolfin is Hitler's daughter. We don't really have any proof of it," said Sven.

"Proof? What kind of proof would be possible? Do you really think there will be a birth certificate we could find as evidence?" Sara's voice echoed in the corridor. The scent of freshly brewed coffee stole its way out of the kitchen.

"The NSS probably knows all the details. Maybe they're just trying to keep a lid on it," said Sven. "It wouldn't be the first time. But it really doesn't matter. The important part for us is not who the victim was, but who the killer is, and we seem to have that all wrapped up. Anyway, you heard what he said: case closed."

"No, Sven," Sara replied with a tone of sarcasm, "I heard *you* say, 'Case closed'."

"Sara, there are times when it doesn't pay to be too good at your job," said Sven.

"They don't pay us very much anyway," Sara muttered. "Why not be as good as we can be? About Hurtree—if these cases are really closed, I'd like to tell Hurtree he was probably right, and thank him for his help."

"If Hurtree's smart he's already on a flight back home," replied Sven. "But OK, give it a try if it'll make it easier for you to shut down the files. But listen to me, Terrier, you've got to learn when to let go."

Chapter 34

Hurtree left his luggage at the reception before checking out. He took the bus to spend the early afternoon meandering through the Vasa Museum. After buying a hot dog for lunch, he walked around the main floor of the museum. He admired the ancient ship which had capsized on its maiden voyage, remaining in Arctic preservation at the bottom of the frigid Baltic Sea outside Stockholm for over 300 years.

He entered a mock-up of the gunnery deck and slapped the colorful brochure on his knee. *I wonder what the world will think of my discovery 300 years from now.* Then he recognized the world probably wouldn't care at all. He doubted anyone would remember the Nazis in 300 years. People talked about Sweden today, but almost no one knew it had been a major power in Europe 300 years ago. Such was the fate of those who lost wars.

The air was thick with the plastic used to treat the ship after it was raised in the 1950s and he struggled to breathe. He coughed several times to clear the congestion, and ducked to avoid the low beam supporting the ceiling. He wove between a pyramid stack of three pounder cannonballs lying next to a bronze cannon and made his way to the dimly-lit exit.

Thomas Johnson rolled the man in the wheelchair to block the way.

Hurtree stopped. He studied the man standing behind the wheelchair—*No one I know*—then dropped his line of sight to survey the man sitting.

Recognition sent his brain reeling. *It's you. Frank Nord. Iron Guard Sergeant in the drug business. What the Hell?*

Hurtree stood his ground. "I was just leaving."

"No, Hurtree, you are not," said Nord, his voice hard and unwavering.

"Yeah, I thought I recognized you. Are you lost?" asked Hurtree.

"No," said Nord. "You lose."

Thomas Johnson came from behind and said, "We want to know where she is. The Dolfin woman. We heard you saw her. Tell us and we'll let you alone."

"I don't believe you. Mr. Nazi here has a score to settle. He thinks I should have killed him instead of putting him in a wheelchair. He's right. Anyway, tough shit. I won't tell you."

Nord replied in a calm voice, "We'll find out anyway. Once you're dead. Tell us now and I'll let you live."

Hurtree saw the glint of the pistol being pulled from under the blanket on Nord's lap. He took a step back. Eyes full of revenge beamed at Hurtree like two white beacons in the murky darkness.

Hurtree took another step back, his right hand sought contact with the top cannonball on the pyramid stack of three pounders behind him.

"You must be a slow learner." Hurtree steadied his grip on one of the cannonballs. "I should have done more than put you in a wheelchair, you Nazi bastard."

The cannonball was cold in Hurtree's hand and he weighed it behind his back, judging the distance to the man sitting in the wheelchair in front of him.

"I'm glad I got the chance to settle this score, Hurtree." Nord raised the pistol from his lap.

I get one try, that's all, thought Hurtree, and he spun a perfect side-arm pitch and ducked down for a follow-through. There was a cracking sound as three pounds of thirty mile-an-hour solid iron smashed into the victim's face. A tenth of a second later, Hurtree heard the muffled pistol shot and the whine of the ricochet.

Hurtree recovered his stance and took three long strides to reach both men. He grabbed the pistol and trained it on Thomas

Johnson's chest. "Now, like I said, I'm leaving. I hope your boss bleeds to death before you can get him to a hospital."

Thomas Johnson faltered. He looked down at the unconscious man sitting in front of him. The man's bald head drooped and blood poured from his flattened nose onto his lap. Teeth were scattered on the blanket over his legs. Blood covered the cannonball lying in his lap.

Thomas Johnson spun the wheelchair around and ran out of the gunnery deck onto the main floor of the museum. Hurtree followed him out, waving the pistol as he said, "You leave me alone, you sonofabitch. And you leave the woman alone too."

Two security guards pounced on Hurtree. They wrestled the pistol from his hand, and forced him to the floor.

"Stop," cried Hurtree. "This isn't my gun."

He struggled for less than a minute, giving up when he saw Thomas Johnson steal away in the confusion. He allowed himself to be handcuffed. The two guards led him to a detention room. They called for the police and an ambulance, then attended to the wounds of the man in the wheelchair. When the police arrived, Hurtree asked them to call Sara Markham before they left for the police station.

"John, you're supposed to be on your way home," said Sara as she entered the interrogation room.

"I was detained," answered Hurtree.

"They tell me the German lost a few teeth, but he'll survive. You want to tell me what happened?" asked Sara.

"He shot at me. I tossed him a cannonball and he missed it. It was dark in there."

Sara grinned as she imagined the scene. "In the video from the Vasa Museum there are two men. What happened to the man who pushed the wheelchair?"

"Don't know. They wanted me to divulge where Dolfin lives."

"You didn't tell them, did you?"

Hurtree shook his head. "I knew him, the guy with the gun. His name is Frank Nord. He was the drug dealer I told you about. Looks like he's still part of the Iron Guard."

"He has asked us to arrest you for assault."

"It's his gun," said Hurtree.

"With your prints on it," Sara replied, and she pulled her chair to sit next to Hurtree.

"Check the prints on the magazine and the bullets. Check for gunshot residue on him and me. He won't be able to explain that. I guess you don't serve chocolate in this room."

Sara chuckled. "No, but I could offer you a dog biscuit. Thanks for the candlesticks, they're beautiful. You know, you should be glad you're not sitting in a cell. John, this is Sweden. You can't use your adrenaline on the bad guys. I'll speak to the prosecutor, but I'm going to have a hard time getting you off on this. Did they say anything else before you, ahem, defended yourself?" asked Sara.

"They said they'd find out where she was anyway. And they knew I saw Dolfin yesterday. You've got a leak somewhere."

Sara massaged her temples. "Ekman will be enraged," she said. "He closed the case today. Are you satisfied?"

"Sure," said Hurtree, "I learned that a lot of what I thought had happened really did happen. I found out a few things about Schwerlieb that I didn't already know. It may not keep the questions from popping up in my dreams, but I might have answered at least one of them. As far as I'm concerned, Dolfin's last name is Hitler, even though I'm sure there will never be any conclusive proof of it."

"What else could there be to know?" asked Sara. "It seems everything has been solved. Not as clean as I would like it, maybe. It would have been a lot better to put the killers in jail, but finding out that they were killed themselves serves at least some form of justice. I doubt we'll ever know who killed the murderers. But it appears to be someone who had a lot of the background in both of these cases."

"So it's being covered up," said Hurtree. "No one wants to take it to the next level."

"What purpose would that serve?" asked Sara.

"Justice?" Hurtree shook his head. "Is it OK over here to kill murderers before taking them to trial? Oddly enough in the States we'd try to catch someone who did that. Sometimes I think it's strange myself, but if you can't offer justice to crooks, what kind of justice do you really have?"

"Philosophy wasn't my strongest subject in school," said Sara. "Some people think we give the crooks too much of a break already. Anyway, who's going to cry for these guys? From what we know they were professional killers."

"Their mothers, Sara." Hurtree shook his head again. "Even killers have a mother. Some perhaps had a father while they grew up. And Miss Justice—you know, the lady holding the scales? I think I see tears seeping through the blindfold."

Sara called the prosecutor, and after a brief description of the events, signed off on Hurtree's release, citing lack of evidence. Hurtree exited Police Headquarters.

"Mr. Hurtree?"

"Shit," said Hurtree as he turned to face the man behind him, "I feel like I've been interviewed by Oprah. Everybody seems to know who I am. So who are you?"

"My name is Ove Berg," said the stranger. "I work for a group in the National Police Board called Internal Affairs." He flashed a plastic ID badge. "We're investigating one of our employees, and your name has come up. I have a few questions, if you don't mind."

"I'm in a hurry." Hurtree sighed.

"I only need to ask you a few questions," said Berg.

"OK then," said Hurtree. "Will you fix my plane ticket if I miss my flight?"

Berg smiled and said, "No. Have you ever met a policeman named Robert Johnson?"

"No, I don't think so. I met with two, no three of your police. One was a Sven, then there was a really nice woman, Sara something, and the third guy worked for something called the NSS, or something like that. I can't remember his name, so he was probably a spook, but it wasn't Robert anyway. At least that's not what he told me, but you can check that with Sara What's-her-name. She knows."

"Have you ever heard of a group called the Iron Guard?"

"Now I know I'm gonna miss my plane," said Hurtree. "I'll be here another week if I have to tell you everything I know about that bunch. Seems everyone is interested in them. I didn't know what they were up to here, but then they're everywhere."

"So you didn't meet any of them while you were here?"

"Probably, but it doesn't matter now. I don't like them, they don't like me. You should really ask Sara. I already told her as much as I know. Are you sure you can't fix my ticket?"

"No, I can't," said Berg. "What I need from you now is an address and a telephone number so we can contact you in the future, if we have to. You have been most helpful, Mr. Hurtree. Thank you." He extended a pen and paper, and Hurtree scribbled his details.

Hurtree had been forced to book a round trip ticket to be able to enter Germany when he first came to Europe, and there was still plenty of time on the Atlantic ticket to do some sightseeing before he had to return. His real concerns were the flight between Stockholm and Mannheim, and the cash he was burning during his stay in Stockholm. He calculated his available funds would run out in about two weeks. He took up his ticket for the flight to Mannheim.

"How long does it take to get to the airport?" he asked the hotel receptionist.

"About forty-five minutes."

Hurtree shook his head and put the ticket back into his jacket pocket.

"Can I get my room back for tonight?" he asked.

He carried his bags up to the room again and threw himself on the bed. *Hurtree, you stupid asshole,* he thought to himself. *Did you think you were going to get some kind of reward or something? You didn't even get the case out in the open, and just ended up poorer than you were before. You're a jerk.* His alter ego kicked in as a defense. *It doesn't matter, Hurtree. You got the satisfaction of knowing the truth, even if you can't prove it. At least you'll be able to sleep easier at night.*

That part was not true, and he knew it. He let his mind do a survey of the fifty years he had been involved in the case, and quickly concluded he had been the victim of his own obsession, blinded by some kind of ray shot from a weapon called Universal Justice. He felt wasted and empty, a spent bullet lying harmless on the ground.

Chapter 35

Bengt Ohlsson of the Swedish Iron Guard was proud of their recent achievements. The attack on the first target had succeeded without a hitch. Although the second target had escaped their attempt, serendipity saw to it their goal was reached anyway. Dr. Habermann was now no longer a threat to their organization.

They had experienced problems in obtaining the address details for their last target, but they were getting close. The first operative was being extracted and a new operative was being inserted. He sat in a wheelchair, but was extremely competent. He also had history with the American, and he would be able to take care of Hurtree and get the address of the old woman in a short time. The police barely knew what they were doing, and the protective shield was in place and working well.

Bengt Ohlsson was surprised to receive an urgent request to contact the unit in Munich regarding the current mission.

Horst used his code name, Fox, and was waiting in the private chat room reserved for only two chatters when Bengt signed on as Thor.

They seemed to be alone, and they were, with the exception of the chat room administrator sitting in Munich. Unknown to either user, the server was part of a large server park located in Belize and owned by the BND, the German Secret Police.

Fox: Hello, Thor.

Thor: Please explain the urgency.

Fox: Have you succeeded in eliminating the woman?

Thor: No, but we are close.

Fox: That's an inadequate answer. Explain.

Thor: There were some issues. The American would not reveal the location. He injured our operative.

Fox: Your team is incompetent. What is your plan?

Thor: Our operative will be released from the hospital tomorrow. He will complete the mission then.

There was a pause before the answer flashed onto Thor's screen.

Fox: There has been a change in plans. Locate, but do not harm the target. Pick up Horst tomorrow morning at 8 a.m. at Arlanda Airport.

Thor: Understood.

Fox: Horst prefers a SIG Sauer P226. Use 9mm standard police ammunition.

Thor: Understood.

Fox: I hope so. Auf Wiedersehen.

Thor: Auf Wiedersehen.

One hour later an encrypted email flashed on the monitor of the International Desk at the NSS. The duty officer forwarded the email to Ekman. That same afternoon Lars spread the news to the rest of the group to expect the arrival into Sweden from Germany of a high-ranking Nazi. Their surveillance of Dr. Habermann was finally paying off.

"We are about to increase our knowledge base on the Iron Guard enormously," said Ekman to the group of NSS officers assembled in front of him, and he spread both his arms to indicate how much. "We can expect the entire Iron Guard will be involved in this. Our profile is now connected to the German, American, and Bosnian groups. Pretty soon they'll have to ask us if they can blow their own noses."

Several young men in the group sniggered.

The local Station Chief of the Mossad sat with senior members of the team, including two people who, for diplomatic reasons, were not usually allowed to be there. There were several files in front of them, including one filled to the brim with paper and yellowed with age, showing the wear coming from being removed and inserted from the filing cabinet several hundred times during the past few years.

He nodded toward Rachel Goldsten to begin.

"And so on to the status of Dolfin. There have been a number of developments and we have to make a decision." Rachel Goldsten opened the file in front of her, removing the first two pages as she began to read. "The question of kinship has now been determined. She is the daughter of Hitler's wife Eva, but she is not Adolf Hitler's child."

There was a murmur from the men and women assembled around the table. "We have a report made up for an American client, the U.S. Iron Guard. It's 100 percent conclusive. No kinship relation to Adolf Hitler." She continued without looking up, "Regarding the issue of the hitman hired to take out Dr. Habermann. He has been, uh, as the Swedes put it, neutralized. Apparently he fell off a boat dock while too drunk to swim." There were small chuckles from the group as she continued, "And then we have the matter of payback. We agreed to help the S-Office regarding the clean-up action, and we were offered the names and addresses of two Hamas bombers, one for each of the assassins."

Rachel closed the file and nodded to the Section Chief that her presentation was complete.

"Let's begin at the beginning," said the Section Chief. "What does the kinship result mean to us?"

"It means we've lost a great opportunity to put the Neo-Nazi movement to sleep," said one of the participants, a woman who sat on the board of several international companies. "It also means we have no reason to spend more time or money pursuing or protecting the Dolfin woman. She's irrelevant."

"You're wrong," said another member of the group, nodding toward the woman. "It would have been fantastic to be able to publish the news Hitler's child survived and is mentally deficient. I'm wondering if we couldn't just publish it anyway, even though it isn't true. It would certainly be difficult for them to counter news like that. How could they deny it?"

"Easily," said an elderly gentleman, a man who spent as much time in airports as he did at home. "The Iron Guard would just deny it and accuse the source of trying to damage their cause for political reasons. Such a step might even be more beneficial for them than for us."

"But what about the news that Adolf Hitler's wife was unfaithful to him? That must be worth something," said one of the diplomats. "It feels like such a waste to know all this and not be able to use it."

"You're a diplomat," said the Section Chief. "You should be used to that by now. Anyway, there are people who've never heard of Eva Hitler, even today. It might create more interest for their movement than distaste. I think we should do as our Director friend has indicated: nothing. The woman called Dolfin is irrelevant. Taking out Habermann's killer gave us one Hamas bomber in exchange, and when we add the nurse's killer we should be getting another Hamas bomber. My feeling is that we should cash in our chips on this deal while we're still ahead."

The older gentleman agreed, but asked a final question. "Is there any risk anyone else will make this public? Would it serve the interests of anyone else to spread knowledge of Dolfin?"

"You're right," said the Section Chief. "We should run through the other players before we close the file. The client who arranged the DNA tests, the U.S. Iron Guard, will they make it public?"

Everyone shook their heads.

The Section Chief continued, "The German Iron Guard. We have to assume that they'll find out sooner or later. How about them?"

Again, all heads shook in negation.

"Then we have the Swedish S-Office, the ones who wanted us to clean up. We have to assume they'll find out about this. Will they go public?"

This time only a few heads shook back and forth, and Rachel asked, "Do we really think we can predict what they will do? I mean, there have been times when they've acted very unpredictably. So can we really be sure they won't make this public?"

"What would they have to gain from it?" asked the Section Chief.

"It might be hard for us to know what they could gain from it," said the Director. "The Swedes don't always use our form of logic when they act rationally." There were smiles, but the uncertainty remained.

"I think we can assume the other international players won't get involved in this, not even the CIA or the FSB. They might use the information in the future if they ever figure it out, but I don't see this happening any time soon," said the Section Chief, and the chuckles turned to outright laughter. "So we only really have one problem, and that's the Swedish intelligence community."

He shifted his eyes to view Rachel Goldsten before he continued, "We can at least prepare for what might happen there. In the meantime our janitor should be instructed to remove the data collection program and the USB from the server at the Institute for Genetic Research. He should get back to business at the other site. Any surveillance we have on the woman known as Dolfin can be removed. Her safety is no longer our concern. Do we know if anyone has managed to make the connection between the nurse's killer and his death? We left a trail of breadcrumbs for them to follow, so do we know if they did it yet?"

Rachel Goldsten gulped, then replied, "An investigator at the NBI, Sara Markham, has built a file on the Iron Guard. They call her the Terrier. She doesn't quit. The NSS has already closed their case, but she keeps on anyway."

The Section Chief drummed his fingers impatiently on the table. "And the American?"

Rachel Goldsten studied the fine grain of the mahogany of the table in front of her. Her face flushed red. "We ran out of operatives. We've been following him, but I had Moshe follow someone else today. Hopefully nothing happened to him."

Olov Björnsson at the S-Office was surprised to hear the Mossad had managed to neutralize the agent in Athens so quickly, but the Mossad always seemed more efficient than other agencies in the intelligence community.

The drowning wasn't connected to foul play, Björnsson had been told. He secretly assumed the agent might have been held under water until his lungs were filled. Now he would have to reveal the name and address of one of the two Hamas bombers. It was unpleasant, since it jeopardized the agreements made with all terrorists who were allowed to enter Sweden: as long as they carried out no local activity the Government offered protection and immunity from persecution. The S-Office would have to be careful. His one-page memo to the Minister was even shorter than the previous one dealing with the case.

> The risk any relationships of previous governments to the German Nazi Party during the Second World War could be made public has now been minimized. We have heard via our source in the NSS there is also confirmation the woman called Dolfin is not Adolf Hitler's daughter, although there is evidence she is Eva Hitler's

daughter. She poses no threat to us or anyone else at present.

The name and address of a member of the Hamas organization now living in Stockholm was relayed to the partners who helped in this crisis. They were most grateful.

Björnsson watched with satisfaction as his words turned the Minister's face into a large smile as she read the memo.

"This really is good news," she said. "Are you sure there were no lives lost?"

"My information was the killer in question lost his life in a drowning accident. He was drunk at the time."

"That's a loss of life," she said.

"Yes, technically I suppose it is, but accidents will happen, even if you don't want them to," said Björnsson.

"And what about the man from Hamas? What will happen to him?"

"I don't know," said Björnsson. "He might be put into a training course to readjust his political thinking."

"Don't be so smug," said the Minister sourly. "We're talking about a human life."

"Yes," said Björnsson, "he took several, I think."

She sat for a few minutes, rereading the memo, and then asked, "And what about the father of the woman called Dolfin? Who is he?"

"We don't know," said Björnsson. "All we know is it can't be Hitler."

"Can we really be sure?"

"Genetic testing is never really certain. There's always one chance in a billion another result could have been obtained. But otherwise, yes, as long as the tests were carried out on the right material, we can be sure."

"I still wonder who the father is," said the Minister.

"If Hitler were still alive he would probably share your curiosity." Björnsson watched her shred his memo.

"If Hitler were still alive we would both be in trouble," she said as she left the conference room, "but he's not. And I need to know more about the Prime Minister's love life. Focus on that for the next few months."

Thomas Johnson felt proud when he was told to meet with Bengt Ohlsson, the head of the Swedish Iron Guard. They would look for each other in a park on the waterfront side of the City Hall in Stockholm. They both bought a quick lunch, Thomas opting for the Turkish Kebab while Bengt bought a Swedish hot dog with a shrimp relish piled on top of mashed potatoes and covered in mustard and ketchup. They waited until they had sat down on a stone bench before speaking.

"I need a quick status on the latest project. You are the coordinator. Fill me in," said Bengt.

Thomas mumbled between bites of the kebab. "You know" another bite "about the nurse?" Bengt nodded. "You know about the doctor—that we missed, but he was robbed and killed anyway." Bengt nodded again. "You know our hitman was taken out at an underground station, and we don't really know who did it." Thomas took another bite of the kebab.

Bengt suddenly concentrated on Thomas's face. "No, I hadn't heard that."

"The police have managed to keep it quiet. The papers haven't managed to get hold of it yet. According to my brother, the cop, the police recognized our guy from Bosnia because of the tattoo on his arm. When his body was taken from under the train, the people at Homicide started to search for identities on the system, and he popped up. At least we don't have to provide him with a protective shield anymore."

Bengt finished the rest of the mashed potatoes, wiping off his mouth with the back of his hand. Then "It seems your shield didn't do him much good anyway," he said, frowning and clearly displeased. "Do we know what happened? Who took him out and why? How did they manage to find him?"

"He was living in one of the hotels we use. Could be he blabbed to someone there. All we know is we were about to extract him and someone got to him. We don't know who yet, but to me it looks like Mossad.

"And the woman?" asked Bengt, his voice low and with a hint of menace.

"We know where she lives now. We finally got one of the homeless drunks who hangs out near where she lives to talk, so we have her located. The new operative, Frank Nord, came in from Germany yesterday, but he had an, um, medical issue. I expect this project to be finished by tomorrow morning."

Bengt Ohlsson glanced first into the ground in front of them, then up into Thomas Johnson's face. His voice was now hard and determined.

"The operation is to be shut down. Now. We have received new instructions from the organization in Germany. You will inform any contacts you have for this project as soon as we leave here. You will inform me of your progress."

The friendly smile on Thomas Johnson's face changed to a scowl. He rubbed his hand on his knee, trying to eradicate an invisible spot. "Shut it down?" he asked. "That's going to be very difficult. Everything is in place."

"Shut it down. Now," said Bengt Ohlsson sharply, "and report to me later this afternoon that it has been shut down. Today. When you're done with that, prepare to receive a visit from one of our brothers from Germany."

Bengt Ohlsson handed Thomas Johnson a paper with the name of the semiautomatic pistol and ammunition. "We are to provide our man from Germany with everything he needs for the next few days. Don't mess this up."

Chapter 36

Thomas Johnson met Horst at the airport outside Stockholm. Thomas was surprised such an important person would appear so ordinary. Horst could have passed for a well-dressed businessman in any country. They spoke English, and Thomas was impressed by Horst's knowledge of the language.

Horst handed him a list of names and addresses, and they consulted a map of the city to set up his visits. Thomas noticed the Iron Guard tattoo on Horst's left wrist, and he wondered if he would be allowed to get one himself after the operation was finished.

From their vantage point on the roof of the Customs building, several hundred meters from the parking area at the airport, Lars Ekman and Sven used high-powered binoculars to watch Thomas and Horst get into the black Audi. They saw Thomas Johnson hand over a brown leather briefcase to Horst, then dial a number on a cell phone. Sven pointed at the laptop monitor as the telephone connected to the network.

Lars Ekman clicked on the number and saved it to a file. From now on this telephone would be a beacon, giving Ekman the geographic position of the telephone to within thirty meters. They would also be able to listen in on all conversations the telephone was used for. The GSM telephone was impossible for ordinary people to listen in on, but for those with a translation unit, the telephone became an open microphone.

The program provided another feature. Ekman used it to send

what looked like an empty SMS to the telephone number. Horst tried to read the message, and before he gave up in frustration a tiny program had been downloaded onto his telephone which turned it into an open microphone in the car. Ekman redirected control of recording locations and conversations to the office in Stockholm. The NSS team in Stockholm could track the two men wherever they drove, listening in on every conversation they made from their vehicle and every word said in the car. The team would make lists of the numbers called and the names of those called. A team of assistants would summarize the content of the calls, and everything would be added to a database, giving them a detailed overview of the entire trip.

Ekman and Sven got into an unmarked car and drove toward Stockholm.

"There's only one thing wrong with all this," said Sven as he watched the information being compiled grow on one of the windows of the laptop he held on his knees.

"What's that?" asked Ekman.

"We're still following them," said Sven. "Imagine if we could get in front of them."

"I was going to suggest we do just that," said Ekman. "I know at least one of the places they are sure to visit."

Horst and Thomas Johnson began their visits at the Institute for Genetic Research, just fifteen minutes south of the airport. The cell phone Thomas had given Horst was loaded with enough cash for several hours of conversation. He called the head of the Institute, telling him he represented the client in the United States and he expected to be able to meet with him soon. The professor provided him with the address of the laboratory where his assistant toiled with new DNA tests.

Horst was shown the laboratory reports of the DNA analysis creating the ruckus. The assistant went to the refrigerator and collected three glass vials, placing them on the table in front of Horst. He used his most learned voice to explain the intricacies of DNA analysis. He held up each vial as he explained how each sample had been obtained.

Horst examined the original hairbrushes and the bark where Dolfin's blood could still be seen as dark red blotches. He seemed satisfied with the explanation, and asked if it was possible the tests could in any way have shown any other result.

"Only if another person's DNA had been used," said the researcher, and his voice exuded wisdom and self-confidence.

When Horst had gone, the assistant replaced the vials in the refrigerator. His mistake glared back at him. There, hidden behind another set of vials, was the male sample from the hairbrush which should have been used for the DNA tests. He became queasy, and swallowed hard several times to fight back the impulse to throw up.

His own words to the German echoed in his head again and again. He hurried over to his computer and accessed the database with the DNA comparisons. His stomach cramped up as he recognized he had used his own vial of DNA for the male specimen during the comparison.

The assistant first wondered if he should inform the visitor, then realized it was too late. The visitor was already gone. He thought briefly about telling the professor about the error, but decided against it. The visitor seemed to be completely satisfied with the results of the testing.

Fear over what might happen if the mistake was corrected became larger than the assistant's sense of conscience. *It is obviously better just to let this slip into oblivion*, he reasoned. No one had been harmed by the error, and he would be more careful next time.

That same morning, Sara woke to the persistent ringing of her cell phone. Her head ached, and she fumbled with an aspirin fizz while searching for her phone.

"It's Sara."

"Hi, it's me, Karin."

"And I thought I got up early." Sara swirled the glass,

encouraging the aspirin to dissolve quicker. "What's the matter?"

Karin giggled, then replied, "We've, um, I've been up all night. So it's not early for me, it's late."

"Are you drunk?"

"Yes, with love."

"Is it the doctor you met on the ferry to Finland?"

"Shh, he's standing right behind me. Oh. And he's, um. Yes, it's him." Karin giggled again.

"My God, you sound like a schoolgirl. I have a splitting PMS headache. What's this about?"

"I'm leaving Sweden. We're going to Australia."

"What? That was quick." Sara swallowed the contents of the glass. "Have you gone mad?"

"No." Karin hesitated, then, "Yes, madly in love. It's real. We both feel it. Never been like this before."

"Well, congratulations. Thanks again for helping me with the person number. I would never have found that woman without your help," said Sara with a tired voice.

"Yes, of course. That's partly why I'm calling. I've been visiting her since we found her. I go there after work. She has no one now that I'm leaving."

Sara held the telephone away from her ear and looked at it in surprise. "Are you going to ask me to take your place?"

"Yes. Thank you. I knew you'd do it."

"Karin, I didn't say yes. Not even maybe. Do you realize what you're asking me to do?"

"Yes, and I can't think of a better person to do it."

"So I lose my best friend and you ask me to take over an obligation I can't possibly handle. Are you crazy?"

"We're leaving tomorrow."

"What? What's the rush?"

"Tom. He's been given a huge grant from an Australian drug company to study the effect of a new drug for prostate cancer. He starts next week."

"Wow. And you? What will you do?"

"A lot of what I've been doing the past few days." Karin giggled again.

Sara shook her head. "I'm going to miss you."

"I'll miss you too," Karin's voice broke then, "but we'll stay in touch. You know that."

"Of course," Sara replied, and she let a sigh fill out the rest of the sentence.

"I have to go now," said Karin. "Tell me you'll visit Dolfin in the afternoon. I'll be sending you some tips on dealing with autistic patients."

"I don't know." Sara closed her eyes. She filled another glass with water and dropped in a new aspirin. The tablet dissolved with a fizz.

"Sara? Are you still there?"

"Yes. So I guess it's good luck to you and Tom. Keep me in the loop. I'm really very happy for both of you."

Karin answered in a whisper, "He's such a catch. You should look for someone like him. I'll see if he has a friend."

"I'm already married," said Sara, "to my job."

"Bye for now, girlfriend. I'll keep in touch."

"You do that," said Sara. She blinked, and a tear rolled down her cheek. "Good luck with everything," she sniffled into the telephone before she shut it off.

That afternoon Sara drove to Dolfin's apartment in Fruängen. She saw the light on in the kitchen window, but no one answered when she buzzed the apartment number, shouting Dolfin's name into the intercom. She shouted again.

She left the apartment building and crossed the street to enter the park where she had first seen Dolfin. She spotted Dolfin sitting on a park bench overlooking the small pond populated by ducks, geese, and seagulls. Sara sat next to her, carefully avoiding her eyes, and quietly murmured her name.

Dolfin's hair was a wild briar patch of white strands, and she smelled as if she hadn't bathed since they last met. She looked haggard and gaunt; her chin seemed to have grown into a sharp point as her mouth receded.

Suddenly she made contact. "Dolfin help."

"Dolfin help," said Sara.

"Karin."

"Sara."

"Sara help."

Sara began the long story of what had happened to Karin, and what had brought them together. Dolfin sat silently, staring into the treetops and making no sign she was listening or understanding any of what Sara related. Minutes became an hour, and Sara opened her heart to Dolfin as if she had been her own mother. She confessed to feelings and deeds she had barely spoken of, even to Karin.

A fetid odor made her turn her head, and Sara made up her mind to see to it Dolfin had a thorough shower. She got up from the bench and offered Dolfin her hand. She promised herself and Dolfin she would get her into the health system again and make sure she received some kind of treatment for her ailment.

Sven and Lars Ekman arrived outside Dolfin's apartment in Fruängen. They sat in the car listening to a relay of the conversation between Horst and Thomas Johnson in the black Audi. Sven glanced at the map on the laptop monitor and saw the blinking symbol representing the cell phone in the Audi approach. Sven raised his eyes to look out the window for a moment and saw Sara walking together with an elderly woman, leaving the duck pond to enter the park.

"What the hell? That's Sara," he said.

"What's she doing here?" asked Lars Ekman.

"I don't know yet, but she'll have to answer that question soon," said Sven.

Sara was on Dolfin's left, holding on to her arm. When they

reached the part of the park which was Dolfin's favorite, she tore herself loose from Sara's grip and began to run, her clumsy body waggling toward her tree. Sara watched as Dolfin embraced the tree, murmuring incomprehensibly.

After a moment, Dolfin stopped hugging her tree and approached Sara, averting her eyes until the last moment. Sara removed the photograph of the children from her purse and held it up to Dolfin, bringing it in front of her eyes as she walked by. At first there was no reaction from Dolfin and she continued walking toward the road, but after several steps she gave out a squeal and Sara saw her slam her head onto her shoulder.

Sara ran to Dolfin and grasped her arm again. They began crossing the road.

Thomas Johnson was behind the wheel of the black Audi. He stopped to let the two women cross the street and turned into the parking lot. Sven and Ekman were parked under a tree only fifty yards away.

"Here comes the Audi," said Sven. "Are we just going to watch them or do something if they attempt to make contact?"

"If we take them before they've attempted contact then we tell them their communications network has been compromised. But if we wait until some harm comes to the old woman then I'm not sure I could sleep for quite a while," said Ekman.

Sven sat still and watched the two women approach.

"Wait," said Ekman, "we can ask Thomas Johnson to help us with a few questions. Tell him we found out about him from his brother. Robert is already being investigated by Internal Affairs. Then we can take them in for possession of an illegal weapon."

"Let's do it," said Sven.

The women strode toward the Audi. Sara felt eyes probing from inside the car. She tried to catch a glimpse of who was behind the darkly tinted glass. She couldn't explain why, but she slowed her pace and went into defensive mode.

Dolfin was unaware of any danger. She shook herself loose of Sara's grip and took the lead as they continued toward her apartment, approaching the silent murmur of the idling Audi.

Sara heard the doors of the Audi open, and when she looked up she saw a well-dressed man get out of the car. She saw him approach Dolfin, accompanied by a burly skinhead dressed in black. She tried to signal to Dolfin, but there was nothing she could do. Dolfin had retreated into her own world.

The two men approached Dolfin, first Thomas Johnson, followed closely by Horst.

"Shoot," Horst cried out in German.

Thomas Johnson hesitated. Beads of sweat broke out on his forehead. His hand wavered. He closed his eyes, and then opened them to look at the ground in front of him. Determination rose in his mind. He raised the semiautomatic pistol and steadied it with his other hand. He aimed at Dolfin.

Sara took one step to the side, drew her pistol, and trained it on Thomas Johnson's shoulder. "Police. Drop it!"

Horst shouted in Thomas's ear, this time in English, "Shoot. Now."

Sara saw movement out of the corner of her eye, but she kept her Sig Sauer aimed at Thomas Johnson's shoulder. "I said, drop it."

The first shot came from her right, a warning shot in the air that echoed off the walls beside them. Ekman's voice rang out. "Drop it."

Thomas Johnson spun to his left to face Ekman, pistol still raised, and he began to draw a bead. Ekman's second shot caught Thomas Johnson in his arm. He staggered backward, trying to take aim again. Sara's shot hit his right arm at the same time Ekman's third shot stopped his heart.

Horst was already opening the driver's door of the Audi. He clambered in and pushed the starter button. The engine sprang to life, and he looked up to face Sven's pistol on the other side of the windshield. "Out. Hands in the air. Now!"

Horst climbed out of the car, his hands raised. "There has been a misunderstanding," he said. "I do not understand what happened."

Sven kept his gun trained on Horst. "Shut up. Hands behind your back."

The too-ta, too-ta of the ambulance grew in volume as Sven cuffed Horst. Sara holstered her pistol and caught sight of Dolfin hiding behind a lilac bush to one side of the parking lot.

"Dolfin help," Sara said.

"Dolfin help. Sara," said Dolfin, and she crept into Sara's arms.

"It's alright, Dolfin." Sara stroked her hair. "You're OK."

Chapter 37

They put Horst into a squad car and drove him to a holding cell in the center of the city. Ekman turned off the air conditioner cooling the interrogation room and let Horst sit alone for an hour. He watched Horst, waiting for him to show signs of nervousness or fear. When he saw none, Ekman entered the room and sat facing him.

"Can I get you something to drink?" asked Ekman.

"No, thank you. I need to get to the airport. I'll miss my flight," said Horst.

"You don't have to worry about that. I need to know what happened out there. Why were you trying to drive off?"

"I'll miss my flight."

"You have other things to worry about than missing your flight, Horst. Like your connection to two murders and an attack on an elderly woman." Ekman splayed the fingers of his right hand out in a fan.

"I don't know what you're talking about," said Horst. "I didn't attack anyone."

"But I was there, Horst. Remember? I saw it all."

"Did you see me attack anyone?" asked Horst. "My driver told me he was going to ask her for directions. We were trying to get back to the airport."

"Horst, you're Iron Guard," said Ekman, and he pointed to the tattoo on Horst's wrist.

"I'll miss my flight," replied Horst, his eyes meeting Ekman's with a mocking glance.

"And the gun? How do you explain that? You're going down for illegal possession of a firearm." Ekman's tone hardened.

"Whose gun?" asked Horst. "I had no idea my driver even had a weapon with him. How could I know he would try to use it on that old woman? I demand to be released. I'll miss my flight."

Ekman insisted, "We know who you are, Horst. We've been following you since you arrived."

Horst sat with his arms crossed. "This will be very expensive for the Swedish State. I have an important meeting to get to in Munich."

The interrogation room became stuffy. Ekman felt beads of sweat form under his armpits. "You're going down for attempted murder," he said.

"I'll miss my flight."

"You'll miss the rest of your life."

"I'm not connected to the crimes you're investigating," said Horst. "I have no idea what you're talking about."

"And your visit to the Institute for Genetic Research?"

A cruel smile crossed Horst's face. "Business."

"And the researcher's office?" Ekman leaned back in his chair.

"More business."

Ekman leaned forward. "And the attack on the woman in Fruängen? Remember, I was there."

"I was a witness. Do you need a statement?" Horst's eyes narrowed.

"You told Thomas Johnson to shoot her."

"No," said Horst and smiled, "I remember I told your lady police officer to shoot my driver. First in German, then in English. It was obvious he threatened you."

"We'll see what she will testify." Ekman wiped the moisture from his palms on his pants.

"Perhaps she has insufficient language skills. I'll miss my flight if I'm not allowed to leave immediately."

Ekman was beaten. He lacked conclusive evidence to link

Horst with Thomas Johnson. The surveillance material from the cell phone and the chat site wouldn't hold up in a Swedish court. Ekman knew it.

Ekman started the tape recorder and said, "Tell your version of what happened today. Then I want your contact details." He pushed his notepad and pen toward Horst.

"Can I go then?"

"We'll talk about it tomorrow. I'll listen to your statement again when I get to work tomorrow," said Ekman and his shoulders slumped.

Hurtree prepared again for his trip to Mannheim. He threw his dog-eared notebook into his suitcase. He was about to add a pile of shirts and pants on top, but stopped himself and took up the notebook again. He leafed through it and shook his head when he saw page after page of the same set of questions flash by.

The notebook had become the receptacle for his obsession, the place where he stored his anguish and self-doubt. Now it was over. He had an answer for every question he had echoed on the pages, except the final question about who had taken the photograph. Hurtree thought about that question.

I don't care, he thought, *and I don't think anyone else does either.* Hurtree stared at the notebook with distaste as if he viewed a deed he would rather forget, the memory of all his mistakes.

Goodbye, you sonofabitch, he said in the silence of his hotel room. Relief went through his body as he tossed the notebook into the wastebasket under the desk. He felt free for the first time in nearly half a lifetime.

His phone rang. It was Sara.

"Hi, John, I'm so glad you haven't left yet. I need to talk to someone. Can we meet?"

Hurtree answered without thinking.

"Sure. When and where?"

*

They met at a restaurant near Hurtree's hotel. He cringed as he examined the prices and was about to suggest another restaurant, but Sara stopped him.

"It's OK. I'm buying," she said, and patted her purse.

"You must be making a lot more than I ever did," said Hurtree.

"This doesn't happen every day, John," she said. "And I need to talk to someone. To you." Her voice went to a low whisper. "I nearly killed someone today."

Hurtree dropped the menu onto the plate in front of him. He said nothing at first. The waiter came for their orders and Hurtree waved him away.

"You're serious, aren't you."

"Yes. It was very close. I shot him in the shoulder. Ekman killed him. It was scary. Shit, it could have been me."

"Was he armed?" Hurtree narrowed his eyes and waved away the waiter one more time. "Let's take a walk before we eat."

Pink clouds hung on the horizon, hiding the never-ending sunset. Bunches of young party-goers shouted to each other. No one paid heed to Sara and Hurtree as they strolled aimlessly through the center of Stockholm after leaving the restaurant. "So, was he armed?" asked Hurtree again.

"Yes. He was threatening Dolfin. She was with me earlier today. He had a gun aimed at her. I drew on him. I would have shot him, but Ekman came out of nowhere and fired a warning shot. He turned to confront Ekman, and Ekman hit him in the shoulder. The bastard just kept coming. Then I shot him in the shoulder, but Ekman put one in his chest." Sara felt the adrenaline surge as she recounted what had happened earlier that day.

"Sounds like you never did that before," said Hurtree.

"No. I've had my gun out plenty of times before, but this was the first time I fired at someone," said Sara. "It was so close. I'm glad Ekman was there. I could barely breathe afterwards."

"Sara, I'm still feeling a little queasy about destroying Frank Nord's grin, but what you have been through is much worse."

"Did you ever shoot anyone?" asked Sara.

"Yes," said Hurtree, and he dropped his gaze to the sidewalk in front of them. "In the war. It was part of the job. You never get used to it. And you shouldn't."

"It didn't bother me when it happened, I didn't have time. I did everything automatically. It was afterwards I got scared." Sara grasped Hurtree's arm as they strolled back toward the restaurant.

"That's good," said Hurtree. "That's the way it's supposed to work. So is Dolfin alright?"

"I think so. I called someone for help from the Social Office. The lady was very kind. They're going to take care of her. She'll be put in a home for the mentally handicapped."

Hurtree nodded his head. "Who was the guy Ekman shot?" he asked.

"The brother of someone I work with. Thomas Johnson. He was taking orders from a German. Sven said he was Iron Guard. Ekman took him in for questioning."

"Did you say Johnson? Someone from your Internal Affairs Department questioned me about a Robert Johnson. Sounds like your workmate was well connected. If you were in a shootout with a member of the Iron Guard, you're lucky to be alive.

"I know," said Sara.

"I'm lucky I got the chance to thank you for helping me throw out my notebook."

"What?"

"I used to have a notebook about Dolfin. It ran my life for way too many years. I just threw it out, thanks to you."

"Sven told me I had to learn when to give up," said Sara.

"It's great if you can do it," replied Hurtree, speaking more to himself than to her.

They continued in silence for another block. Hurtree looked inside another restaurant, checked out the menu and prices, and asked, "How about something to eat, Terrier?"

"Do they serve dog biscuits?" asked Sara.

Chapter 38

John Hurtree was on his way back home. He sat on the airport bus, using the time to run through a mental list of items he had to have with him.

His foot nudged his suitcase. He tapped his jacket for the bulge of his wallet, then took it out to make sure his passport was there. The clutch of keys jingled in his jacket pocket, then he withdrew his airline ticket. He methodically checked the date again and the time, and glanced at his watch. As he looked at the ticket again, a sickly feeling began rising up from his bowels.

He was one day late and hadn't rebooked.

When the bus arrived at the departure hall, Hurtree marched straight to the ticket office. He had practiced the explanation he would use at the counter during the final moments of the bus trip, and felt confident he could get his ticket changed. He stammered as he began telling the ticket agent he had been required to take part in a police investigation and forced to stay one day more than originally planned. The ticket agent was sympathetic, and punched a few keys on her computer terminal. She smiled, then told him his ticket could be rebooked, but that the European portion had to be paid for again.

Hurtree was devastated. His eyes wandered aimlessly to the posters advertising airlines to European destinations. He grabbed a few brochures and went upstairs to a café to sort out his options.

The first brochure was from GoGermany, a new budget airline flying only to Munich and Berlin from various European capitals. He was pleasantly surprised to learn he had enough money to get to

Munich, the flight costing less than what he had paid for the bus to the airport. He could actually afford to fly to Munich and still have enough money to get to Mannheim where he could take the flight home to the United States.

I must be living right. I'll even have time for one last look at Munich, he thought. He studied the timetable and noticed he would be able to book and purchase a ticket that same day if there were empty seats.

He hurried back to the GoGermany ticket counter and arrived at the same time as Horst, who was accompanied by Sven and Lars Ekman. Sven shouldered his way in front of Hurtree.

"I'm in a hurry," he said, flashing his ID badge over his shoulder, "I'm sure you don't mind."

"No," said Hurtree, "I might not live long enough to get on board anyway, so I'm not in as much of a hurry as you are."

Sven recognized Hurtree's voice and turned toward him. "Ah, hello, John. Glad to see you're finally going. Thanks for the help, by the way. Welcome back some time."

"Don't mind if I do. Are you going to Germany too?" asked Hurtree.

"No, not us," said Sven. "This man seems to have missed his flight, so we're arranging transport for him."

Horst raised his hand to shield his face, and Hurtree saw the tattoo: three vertical lines intersected by three horizontal lines, the triple cross of the Iron Guard. Hurtree could hardly believe what he had just seen. He moved a little to one side to be able to look closer at the man's face. Horst felt the attention and turned toward Hurtree. His eyes narrowed and focused, but when he saw Hurtree he laughed, barely audibly.

"Aisle or window seat?" asked the ticket agent. "And your passport, Sir." Sven handed over Horst's driver's license to the agent.

It was Hurtree's turn next, and he asked to be booked on the same flight to Munich. He asked for a seat next to the man who had just bought a ticket if possible, and got a seat two rows behind him, across the aisle. He checked in his baggage and went through security and then strode immediately to the gate.

The international organization of the Iron Guard was beginning to crumble. One of the members in Sweden had been shot and was being connected to several murders. It was obvious the Swedish group had been compromised. Even the German group was out in the open, with their leader having been taken in for questioning in Stockholm. There was no deportation within the EU, but the Swedish police had done the next best thing, and Horst had been told not to return to Sweden.

How much else had the authorities learned? Was there any risk of the newspapers getting hold of these stories? Questions fired back and forth throughout the organization as each group assessed their own risks. A game of finger pointing had broken out.

Hurtree's flight taxied toward the gate in Munich airport, and he glanced up at the original flight tower, only three stories high. He recognized it from the war, and was surprised it was still standing, amazed to see that pockmarks from machine gun bullets remained. It was a strange monument to leave standing, and he wondered which authority kept the Germans from tearing it down.

He lost track of Horst while he waited for his luggage.

Hurtree had enough time to wander through a few beer halls and an attempt to visit Schwerlieb's son one last time. He booked a simple hotel for two nights and went to the taxi stand outside the arrival hall. He remembered most of Schwerlieb's address from the first time he had left the photograph. Sitting in the back seat of the taxi, Hurtree called Charlie Peters at the CID in Heidelberg, quick-dialing on his cell phone.

"Hi, Charlie, it's me, John Hurtree."

"I'm surprised to hear your voice," said Peters. "Tell me you're back in Philly."

"Not yet, but I'm working on it. Missed my flight. Are you guys still interested in following the Iron Guard? I found out a few things in Stockholm you might want to know."

"So you're not back in the States yet. When does your flight leave?"

"I just booked it. I leave in two days. My flights got all screwed up when I missed my flight from Stockholm."

"John, I told you to quit. Drop this thing with the Iron Guard. I won't say it again." Peters's voice left no room for mistake. This was not a cordial warning. There was an unfriendly click on the other end as Peters hung up.

In a few more minutes the taxi pulled up on the street where Wilhelm Schwerlieb lived. Hurtree paid the driver and began searching for the house. He recognized it immediately, in spite of the early evening dusk. The sun set quickly in this part of Europe, and Hurtree knew that in another thirty minutes it would be dark. He went to the door and rang the bell.

Schwerlieb opened the door, waving him off at first. "*Nein. Nein*," said Schwerlieb. "*Nix*."

Hurtree had not prepared for this and stood there as the door closed in his face. He rang the doorbell again. This time a short, sturdy woman appeared, explaining in harsh German that he wasn't welcome and the police would soon be called if he stayed on the doorstep.

Hurtree managed to say in German "Iron Guard" as the door was closing. The door opened again, and this time the chain was unlocked. He was shown into a room off the hall, and the woman, who could have competed in Olympic shot-put events, asked him to sit down. She asked simply "*Und?*" It was a sign Hurtree should explain why he was there.

Hurtree's answer rambled, a mixture of faulty German and unplanned English. What he really wanted to do was to speak to Wilhelm Schwerlieb. He needed to explain a few things about what Schwerlieb's father had done in Sweden in 1940. The woman listened without saying a word, and Hurtree had the feeling there was someone outside the room, listening to his explanations. After he had said "Sweden" the door opened and Wilhelm Schwerlieb stood in front of him.

"I remember you," said Schwerlieb. "You are American. You were in the U.S. Army."

"Yes, that's right," said Hurtree. "I returned some items to you several years ago when I quit work: a medallion, a photograph, and a few personal papers."

"I remember," said Schwerlieb. "What made you return? Have you found other items?"

"No," said Hurtree. "I returned to set my mind at ease. There was a murder—no, two murders in Stockholm recently, and it seems they might in some way be connected to a trip your father made to Stockholm during the Second World War. I found out a few details on the trip, and I think you will be interested in what I found out. I doubt the police up there will provide you with the details. They seem to be more interested in covering up the whole thing."

Schwerlieb's son, Wilhelm, had never been to Sweden. He'd avoided the place as if it had been smitten with the plague. His mother had told him of the first wife, the Swedish Baroness, and how his father had been so dedicated to her that after her death she had been interred in a crypt on their own private land. His father had even named the estate after her, Karinhall. It was such an insult. Wilhelm supported his mother during those bleak years while she was incarcerated by the military after his father's suicide.

He and his mother were subjected to many interviews with the military. Their prying questions concerned things he seldom knew anything about. He told them nothing. The photograph came up one day, and he held his ground, even though he knew everything about everyone in it. After he and his mother were freed, he had put it out of his mind, removed the photograph from his memory, and tried to manage life with his mother until she passed away.

His life went into a normal loop, and Wilhelm Schwerlieb became much like every other German, learning a trade and going to work every day. Once in a while he would be contacted by functionaries who had escaped the tribunals, or the newer ones who saw him as some relic from the past, an interesting person to be associated with. He never took part in their meetings or read any of the literature that somehow showed up in his mailbox. He tried to put a distance between himself and the Iron Guard, even though he accepted two elderly women assigned to cook for him and clean his apartment. He noticed they were also capable of acting as substantial bodyguards when necessary, which was very seldom.

Schwerlieb lived the life of the middle class inhabitants of the suburb he lived in. He was isolated from politics and had an interest in sports. He seldom went out, but when he did so he found that the women who were attracted to him had mistaken ideas about his political future, and that other women were put off when they heard his last name.

Schwerlieb seldom watched television except for soccer games and knew very little of current affairs, except that most of Hitler's dreams of a united Europe with no borders for its citizens had finally been realized, although not in the way Hitler had imagined. People, money, and goods could move with no hindrance within its borders, as it had been imagined in *Mein Kampf.* They had even accepted a common currency for the most part, the Euro. It wasn't the Deutsche Mark, as had originally been planned, but it wasn't the French Frank either. The Euro was a compromise, typical of the spirit of modern Europe, but close to the goals and dreams which had born the seed.

So convenient it has become, Schwerlieb thought, *a united Europe.*

So tragic, Hurtree thought at the same time, *that so many people had to die because of one man's wickedness.*

Chapter 39

Hurtree and Schwerlieb sat only two yards apart, but with an infinity dividing their ways of viewing the world.

"Could you help me with something?" asked Hurtree. "It won't mean much to you, but I've lived more than half of my life wondering about something."

Wilhelm Schwerlieb surveyed him in silence. Hurtree continued, "Do you remember that photograph, the one of you and the Goebbels kids? Who was the little girl next to you?"

"I thought you would have guessed that by now," Schwerlieb replied. He got up and removed the picture from the mantelpiece. "This is the photograph you returned to me."

Wilhelm Schwerlieb gazed into his own face on the faded black-and-white photograph. He tried to relive that day again, and his hands shook as he held the frame. He could hear the laughter of his friends. He even felt the sun on his face as he and the other giggling children faced the camera, unaware that soon their lives would be cast into a well of despair.

"Did you say you were in Sweden?" he asked Hurtree when he returned to reality again. "You must have found out about the girl standing next to me," and Schwerlieb pointed his finger at the second child from the left.

"Yeah, but she wasn't easy to find. So who is she?" asked Hurtree.

"She is a very special person, a relic of the past, you might say, with no reason to exist except to remind us about what went on in those days," said Schwerlieb. "Her name is Dolfin."

Hurtree inhaled a sharp breath. "But why was she so special? Your father wouldn't talk about her, you won't talk about her. Why won't anyone talk about her? I just want to answer this one question."

Schwerlieb leaned forward and spoke as if the walls of his own house had ears. "She was my playmate. For a while. Until she disappeared one day shortly after that photo was taken. She is the child, Adolf and Eva's child. She's Dolfin Hitler."

Hurtree swallowed. The room swirled and he closed his eyes for a second. "And you have known this all these years?" asked Hurtree incredulously. "I'm amazed the secret was kept so long."

"Actually I didn't find out she survived the war until just a few weeks ago. Some, uh, colleagues discovered her existence. I think they were trying to, as you say it, tie up loose ends."

Hurtree finally had the confirmation he had been searching for. "Well I'll be damned. So I was right all the time. Everyone else has been telling me to stop searching, that it didn't matter even if I did find out. I'll be damned. So your father took a picture of you and Hitler's child. Damn."

When Wilhelm Schwerlieb had first heard from the Iron Guard about Dolfin's existence in Sweden, he had refused to accept it as possible, even though he knew it might be. His stomach knotted as he remembered again that the Goebbels children had been killed by their own parents in the bunker in Berlin. Schwerlieb had been lucky his father had seen this coming, and had seen to it that he and his mother had been safely out of the way at Karinhall as the end came.

Wilhelm Schwerlieb turned to Hurtree after he replaced the photograph on the mantelpiece. "We were very happy that day. That's why we were all smiling. The weather was so warm and clear. The poor Goebbels children, they were all killed, of course. And my strange friend, Dolfin. Did you find out what happened to her?"

The photographer had taken their picture on the huge veranda overlooking the entire world, and now, when Schwerlieb regarded the picture again, he didn't see the photo as much as his father standing out of view next to the photographer.

"I found her," said Hurtree. "I've actually been very close to her. I even spoke to her, but she didn't speak back. She's, uh, got some mental difficulties. Perhaps you knew about that already." Hurtree took out his camera from his jacket pocket. "Look, I even took her picture."

"Dolfin was always a little strange," said Schwerlieb as he leaned over to view the image. "She always seemed to be preoccupied with something else. She barely spoke, but she liked to play with my toys."

"It seems your father brought her into Sweden. He signed her in as next of kin at the hospital where she stayed until it was closed. She still lives close to it."

"Was there anything else you learned?" asked Wilhelm.

"Yeah, but it all had to do with the Iron Guard being involved in a couple of murders up there. I don't think your father had much to do with that bunch even then. I wanted to tell you what I found out in case you might still be wondering. It seems you already figured it out. Hell, you probably knew about it the whole time," said Hurtree. "Anyway, I'm leaving for the United States the day after tomorrow. Good luck to you, and thanks for letting me in." Hurtree left a note with the number to his cell phone.

"I didn't let you in," said Schwerlieb, "it was my housekeeper."

The street was dark when Hurtree left the house. He had forgotten to ask Schwerlieb for the number to a taxi, so he walked to the nearest street light, hoping he could read the telephone number off the taxi receipt he held in front of him. He squinted in the orange light of the mercury-vapor street light, struggling to read the receipt.

A man approached him from behind, and Hurtree began to phrase how to ask for directions to the part of Munich where his hotel was located. The man was very friendly, and seemed to understand the broken German Hurtree tried on him.

"I can help you out," replied the man in English. "My friend can take you there right now."

"Well thanks," said Hurtree, "but I think I'll walk. It can't be that far." As he spoke, a car approached from around the corner and stopped in front of them. The back door opened and another man got out. Hurtree felt a chill when he saw the triple cross tattoo on the man's wrist. It was too late. Before he could turn to escape he was shoved inside the car, and the men from the Iron Guard sat next to him.

Hurtree found his cell phone in his pocket and pushed the key for the menu, once again for last calls, and then again to dial the last person he had called, Charlie Peters. He knew Peters would have gone by now, but he hoped to leave at least some kind of trace on the messaging machine.

"So what do you think of Munich?" asked the man in the driver's seat.

"It's really nice," said Hurtree. "I hope I can get back next year."

"Yes, and where did you come from?" asked the driver.

"I'm from the United States. Philadelphia."

"No, I mean were you traveling anywhere else before you arrived in Munich?"

"No, not much. I went to Stockholm to meet some friends, that's all. Have you ever been there?" asked Hurtree.

"Not me," said the man beside him, "but I know someone who just returned from there. Perhaps you would like to speak to him."

"Oh no, that won't be necessary," said Hurtree.

"Wrong, Mr. Hurtree. I think it is," said the driver as the car whisked them through the dark streets of suburban Munich. "I'm actually quite sure of it."

They arrived at the dimly lit backside of a run-down industrial building. The weather-beaten sign announced it had been an industrial bakery many years ago. As they pulled up, a garage door opened and the car drove inside. When the garage door closed, they all got out, and two men held Hurtree by the arms as they walked toward an office where a single light illuminated the room.

Hurtree was told to sit on a wooden chair and someone directed a desk lamp into his eyes, blinding him as he looked up, trying to see the person behind the desk.

"I know who you are, Mr. Hurtree," said the voice behind the light.

"OK," said Hurtree, "that's good. I'm getting so old nowadays I sometimes forget."

"Don't try to be funny, Mr. Hurtree. Especially if you want to keep getting older."

"Sorry." Hurtree looked first intently at the floor, then raised his eyes, trying to view the person sitting in front of him. The blinding light from the desk lamp made his eyes smart and rivulets of tears ran down his cheeks.

"I know who you are, and where you've been. I need to know only a few things from you, and then you can go. I know you have had contact with the Swedish police recently. I need to know a few details about that."

"About what?" asked Hurtree.

"About why you were in contact with the Swedish police."

Hurtree had already decided he would co-operate with his abductors. He knew they were members of the Iron Guard, and he was certain that he would soon be hearing about Frank Nord. Hurtree remembered the face of the man who had been with Sven and Lars Ekman at the airport. Could the man behind the light be him?

It doesn't matter who he is, thought Hurtree. *I'll answer their questions as well as I can. Trying to conceal something in this situation is meaningless.*

"I was there to satisfy my own curiosity. I got involved in solving two murder cases, and the police seemed to think I made some kind of contribution, although I still don't know what that was," said Hurtree.

"I would like to know how much they know about the Iron Guard," said the voice.

"I'm not sure," said Hurtree, and he squirmed on the uncomfortable wooden chair, "I couldn't tell them very much, because I don't know very much myself. They had read some kind of file from one of your murder victims, a Doctor Habermann. I think they found out something there."

There was a slight pause. "We didn't kill Dr. Habermann," said the voice.

"The police seemed to think you did anyway," said Hurtree.

"Did they tell you any details about the other murder case?"

"No," said Hurtree. "It was very frustrating. They just asked questions, like you're doing right now, and I just had to answer."

"And what were they asking about?" The voice behind the desk lamp was calm and controlled.

"They wanted to know some of the details about a photograph I gave to Wilhelm Schwerlieb when I retired. It was a picture of some Nazi kids. I didn't know too much about it, but from what I found out one of the kids was the daughter of Adolf Hitler. But then I think you guys already know that."

"You will make no assumptions of what we know," said the voice sharply. "Did they tell you what they plan to do with this knowledge?"

"No," said Hurtree. "In the first place they didn't seem to believe it since there wasn't any proof available, and it didn't have any relevance to their murder cases anyway. As far as I can figure out they seem to be covering it up. They have closed the cases as far as I know."

The man behind the desk rose and left the room. Hurtree could hear him speaking to others outside, but he couldn't make out what they were discussing. After several minutes of heated conversation, the man returned and sat in the safety of the darkness once again. Hurtree tried to catch a glimpse of him, but failed, and tears rolled down his cheeks again. He focused even more intently on the floor in front of him.

"You injured one of our colleagues while you were there.

He has asked us to detain you until he is released from the hospital."

Hurtree squirmed in his seat. "I defended myself. I could have shot him, but didn't."

"He is a fool. He achieved nothing and damaged our organization. I have decided to let you go, Mr. Hurtree. You will relate nothing from this meeting to anyone. You should be careful about telling others, because we have friends in places you cannot imagine. As for the child in the photograph, I doubt there is anyone who will believe you, and it isn't true. The part about Adolf Hitler being the father. We have proof of it."

Hurtree was puzzled by the generosity, but nodded his head in agreement, and the man in the dark continued, "There is a taxi waiting for you outside. Please do not try to look at me as you leave. You have behaved well so far. It would be a shame to ruin it."

Hurtree crept into the taxi and gave the driver the name of his hotel. He shivered during the entire trip back to his hotel. He couldn't sleep until he heard the sound of the birds screeching on the roof of the hotel, fighting over the remains of a rat they had found in the alley.

Chapter 40

The same day his brother met Horst at the airport, Robert Johnson was surprised when his ID card failed to function at the security turnstile. The guards eyed him with flat, unemotional faces. He heard the doors behind him click as they locked.

"There must be a fault in the system again," he said to the guards behind the bulletproof glass window. "Just call Sven at Homicide, he'll vouch for me."

The guards pushed a few buttons, and he could see them speaking to someone as they waited. Nervousness crept up from his knees. Within minutes his brow was covered with sweat as he waited in the security sector. Robert watched as his colleagues passed through the security check beside him unobstructed. He felt trapped like a fish in a fish bowl.

Two uniformed police officers came up behind him and stood there as a plain clothes officer came from the other side of the checkpoint. He understood immediately. He was being investigated for something. His life was about to become hell.

The Internal Affairs Department was a small group of investigators with many years of experience and a single item on their agenda: the investigation of police officers suspected of criminal activities.

They weren't popular with most of the police, who feared them. They were the ones who kept everybody in line. They spent most of their time investigating cases where the public had reported policemen for excessive violence during an arrest. Occasionally they worked on cases where officers had been involved in robberies and were paid to look the other way. Sven had never heard of a case where an officer had been involved in a murder. He gathered the binders on Nurse Anna Eiderbach's murder and placed them on a cart for transport to the archive.

He knew the effects the IAD investigation would have on Robert, but he felt he had no choice. It would have been negligent not to have someone look into the string of unfortunate events. If there really was something sinister lurking in the background and he didn't report it, then he would have been reported for negligence.

Robert felt a faint glimmer of hope when he was shown into the investigating officer's own room instead of an interrogation room. His hopes were squashed as the investigating officer entered, carrying a thick file with his name on it. They exchanged barely audible greetings and his ordeal began, one piece of evidence at a time.

The investigator gave him a chance to explain each item. Robert's answers sounded hollow in his own mind. He wasn't lying, but his answers echoed in his head, sounding like falsehoods. Robert Johnson felt like a bug sitting in a glass jar. He could see the officer speaking, but couldn't hear what was being said.

It seemed slightly comical at first and he smiled, thinking the scene must have been difficult to stage. Robert wondered if the officer was miming or just speaking too softly. After several seconds he began to hear a high pitched buzzing sound in his head and his vision blurred.

Robert passed out from not having drawn a breath since the interrogation began. He was sent home and told to return the following day. In spite of being totally exhausted, he couldn't sleep. Thoughts of what was to come gnawed at his mind. He tried to sleep but didn't succeed until well into the morning hours.

The interrogation began in earnest as soon as he arrived the next morning. The questions never seemed to end, and Robert had trouble answering some of them. He knew nothing about his brother's connections to an organization known as the Iron Guard.

The first time he had heard the name was during the murder investigations.

"Can you explain how a piece of evidence, a gold medallion, was lost during transport?" asked the officer.

"The medallion must have been lost at the Coroner's office. It was being registered as lost evidence when I went back there," said Robert, feeling relieved. "I put it into our evidence room that same day."

The officer scribbled something onto the paper in front of him. "You were instructed to search surveillance films for signs of a murderer leaving Central Station. You said you didn't see him. Is that true?"

"I saw him, but I was trying to carry out an investigation of my own. I wanted to put all the pieces together so I could present the whole story at one time and take all the credit." Robert's voice wavered. His forehead beaded up with the moisture of fear.

The officer stared at him and pushed over the printout from the hotel listing his credit card guaranteeing payment of the room for the murderer. "And this?" he asked. "How do you explain this?"

"I loaned my credit card to my brother. I have no idea what he used it for. He told me he was going to take some girl out to dinner and needed to impress her."

"I have to remove you from duty until we get a few things cleared up," said the officer. "You're not under arrest, not yet, but I suspect you were involved in two killings, and you can't provide me with credible answers to my questions."

Robert looked up, clearly shaken. "You don't think I had anything to do with the murders?"

"I don't know what to think," said the officer. "Up to this point, your answers aren't very convincing. My investigation will clear that up." His cell phone vibrated in his shirt pocket, and he answered as he was leaving the interrogation room.

"Yes? Yes," and just as the door was closing, Robert Johnson could hear the officer say, "Yes, Commissioner Ekman, you can come around for a meeting right now if you wish."

*

At the meeting, Ekman made it clear the NSS had already been following Robert Johnson's brother for some time, and that the search for Anna Eiderbach's killer had involved a number of foreign agents. Ekman verified large parts of Robert Johnson's story, and although it appeared Robert was devoid of exceptional human intelligence, he couldn't be accused of any wrongdoing except the lack of excessive diligence which should be natural in his position.

"Our information indicates he has used poor judgment several times. I won't be surprised to hear he's been transferred to the freight dock soon, but that's fortunately not my problem," said Ekman.

Hurtree woke up hungry. When he had arrived at his hotel in Munich the night before, he had gone to bed hungry, confused, and afraid. He was unaccustomed to facing a situation he was incapable of handling. As he brushed his teeth, his cell phone rang. It was Charlie Peters from the CID.

"So you're still alive," said Peters. "I'm waiting downstairs and it's time for breakfast. I want to know what happened last night, so get your ass in gear, Hurtree."

This is more like it, thought Hurtree, and he met Peters in the breakfast room, already on his second helping.

"Nice hotel," said Peters. "Good breakfast. Now give me some details before you get killed."

"You know, if I liked having orders barked at me before breakfast, I would have got married. You'll have to wait until I at least get some grub in me." Hurtree heaped a first helping from the breakfast buffet onto a plate.

Between bites, Hurtree began relating his visit with Schwerlieb, how he got in the door, the meeting with the Iron Guard, and his ride back to the hotel. Peters looked at him in amazement.

"You are one lucky sonofabitch, Hurtree. I should be fishing your body out of a river, and you just say you're hungry. I told you to drop this business. If you don't stop now, then someone's going to make it their business to see to it that you do. Jesus, Hurtree, listen to me. Stop. Desist. Follow orders, for Chrissake."

Hurtree spread marmalade on a croissant and asked for more coffee as the waitress walked by. "I did quit," he said, "but no one's noticed it yet."

"We know where you were last night. We followed your cell phone trace to an old bread factory. Was there anything special about the place, or were they just using it temporarily?"

"I don't know. They put a desk lamp in my eyes the whole time. There could have been busts of Hitler and Nazi flags behind the guy I was talking to and I never would have known it. The only thing I'm sure of is they were Iron Guard. I saw the tattoos. Schwerlieb doesn't seem to be connected to them. It's more like they are protecting him and he's barely aware of it. I still feel sorry for the poor bastard. It can't be easy being the son of one of history's most infamous war criminals."

"We stopped following him years ago. The Iron Guard is another story, though. They still get their fingers into all the cookie jars I have, and then some," said Peters. "Are you satisfied now? Are you really going to go home and get out of my hair?" Peters stroked his bald head.

Hurtree took a long sip of his coffee. "Shit, Charlie, I was thinking of moving over here. I get tired of Philly. There's too much violence there today. And I miss the beer. Speaking of, can I buy you one last beer before I leave? My flight goes out about noon tomorrow and I think I left an empty beer mug here a few years ago. I'm sure we can find it if we look hard enough."

In Stockholm, Sven waited for Robert Johnson to appear in his room.

"I hear you've been cleared of suspicion," said Sven.

"I still feel dirty," said Robert. "Interrogations make you feel guilty. I'll need a few days just to get back to my old self again."

"I want to talk to you about that." Sven closed the door to his room.

Robert stood at attention in front of Sven's desk, and as he looked down he saw Sven had a thick file with Robert's name on it.

"I got your file from Internal Affairs, and this will be part of your personnel file even in the future," said Sven. "You don't have to worry about what you just went through. That part of the file will begin with your clearance. What you do have to worry about is me. I was the one who had to talk to IAD, just so you know. I had to do it, Robert, because of your own stupidity. I hope you can see that. If you do, then there's a chance you can get beyond this. Otherwise you might as well start looking for a job at the same security agency your brother worked for."

There was little Robert could say in his defense. He knew he had made some serious errors and was glad to have kept his job. His anger at what his brother had done knew no bounds, and he began to practice what he would tell Thomas the next time they met. His chest constricted and he could barely breathe. He was trying to relax to regain his composure when Sven continued.

"Sorry to have to tell you this, but your brother was shot before we could arrest him. He was armed and shot at one of our officers," said Sven, and he watched as an incompetent detective broke down in tears. He wrote on the report *Suggest transfer*.

The head of the NSS updated the Prime Minister after his return from the trip to Israel. He was unhappy to have been cheated out of the photo-opportunity of him standing at the Wailing Wall. His irritation showed through his reactions to the NSS report including information received from various sources concerning the German Question, as it was becoming known in the circle of ministers, and he listened halfheartedly.

While he listened, the PM fixed his vision on the view of the lake outside his office. It was a warm, sunny day, and the wind stirring the surface of the lake had subsided. His thoughts went to the lake outside his home where he would be setting out his nets in just a few hours. It would be a good day for fishing.

The head of the NSS repeated his question. "And so what should we do?"

"About what?" asked the PM. "I didn't understand your question."

"We have information the woman who has been living here since the Second World War is apparently not Adolf Hitler's child. Should we allow the Press to play with this?"

The word 'Press' brought the PM's attention to the forefront. "I don't think so. No. Definitely not," he said. "I can't see anything positive in letting this out. Did we solve the murders?"

"It's complicated, Prime Minister. We know the identity of one of the killers, but he was killed by someone else and we haven't found out by whom yet. The other one died in an accident in Greece."

"So we can't point to a success story there. No, it's just not going to sound very good if this ever gets out. Stamp everything secret."

The head of the S-Office got her report too. It was short and pithy.

"So now he's banging the head of Revenue, even on the trip to Israel. Oh, I like that," said the Minister. "Have there been any more developments about this Hitler's child business?"

"It seems the whole thing has been put into the freezer. We can't use anything we got there."

"And the people from Hamas?" asked the Minister. She was thinking of a visit she would soon be making to the portion of Stockholm where Palestinian refugees were well represented.

"We haven't got any news yet," he said. "I doubt if we'll ever know. They're very discrete."

"I have to be able to deny, you know that," said the Minister.

"Then don't ask any questions," said Björnsson.

Sara Markham sat in her car waiting for a stop-light to change. She answered her cell phone.

"Oh, hello, John. Did you make your flight yet?"

"Almost. I'm on the way to Mannheim Airport now. I just wanted to tell you I was contacted by the Iron Guard while I was in Munich. I don't know who it was, but you can tell your boss he's got them worried. They kept asking me how much the Swedish police knew about them," said Hurtree.

"When you say 'contacted' what do you mean? How did they know how to find you?"

"I must be wearing a neon sign or something," said Hurtree. "It was like this: I visited Wilhelm Schwerlieb at his house, and when I left there, they more or less abducted me. It was probably the housekeeper. I don't think this guy, Wilhelm, is a Nazi at all, or if he is then he does a good job of hiding it. His housekeeper could be, though. She reminded me of one of the women doctors at Dachau, but forty years too young."

"Were you injured?" asked Sara, her voice wavering with concern.

"No, just my pride," said Hurtree. "I hate being such an easy target. I should have seen that coming. Anyway, it was just a heads-up to let you know the score. By the way, they warned me not to tell anyone. Told me a spooky story about having friends in high places."

"I'm sure they do," said Sara. "I'll tell Sven you called anyway. The murder cases were closed, and from what I hear Dolfin is safe. She lives in an assisted living quarters and has help every day."

"So I was right," said Hurtree. "That was my gut feeling all along, that you guys would put a lid on this. Someone must be pretty frightened upstairs."

"No one seems to think this is important any more. Did you find out anything more about the photograph, like who took it?"

"Shit," said Hurtree, "I knew I forgot to ask something. Anyway, it doesn't matter. I know the score on who Dolfin is and who her parents are. The guy from the Iron Guard told me she wasn't Hitler's daughter. He seemed pretty certain about it, but he didn't convince me. I heard the truth from Wilhem Schwerlieb."

"I still want to thank you for your help. I'm sure Dolfin will thank you some day, when she has the capacity to do so," said Sara.

"And if you ever get over here again, I hope you let me know so we can get together," and they both said goodbye.

Hurtree put his telephone back in his pocket. The Mannheim Airport bus had nearly arrived at the departure zone, and he went through his ritual for the third time that day. Passport, money, plane tickets, keys, baggage. This time he was sure he had everything in order, and was early enough to go to the tax-free store to do a little shopping.

Chapter 41

Artillery shells exploded on the surface as Adolf Hitler and his mistress were married in the *Führerbunker,* just hours before the Soviet Army overran that part of Berlin. It was a wedding with little joy. The sound of the detonations overhead caused many of the participants to show signs of fear, which they quickly hid from their leader, a man who hated weakness and fear more than anything else.

His mistress had arrived only one day before, surviving a strafing which nearly killed her and the pilot who flew her from Sweden. It was chaotic, but she had defied Hitler by traveling to be at his side as the end grew near. Eva had taken her camera with her to make sure at least one more picture could be added to the family album. She asked Goebbels's wife to hold the camera and push the button once she had adjusted all the necessary settings.

When the wedding had been officially recorded, Bormann and Adolf went into one of the chambers of the bunker. When he emerged, Adolf announced that Martin and some others would be leaving the bunker to take up the fight elsewhere. He held a short speech, coughing several times, clearly not in his best rhetorical form.

Silence prevailed as Hitler and his bride closed the door on their underground bedroom. Within minutes a shot rang out.

Eva was carried out of the bomb shelter in a rug. A sergeant stood outside beside the body of a young woman. They removed Eva and rolled up the dead woman in the rug, then poured gasoline over it. The smoke behind them joined the conflagration signaling the end of Nazi Berlin. Bormann then took Eva beyond the Russian lines to an airfield Adolf had used after he had become aware of plots to kill him. The airfield was in the forest, and they made their way through the lines using moonlight and stealth.

On one occasion they were close to being discovered, but the soldiers were too busy having their way with Hitler's secretary and some other women who had tried to escape earlier. No one took notice of the two figures creeping past them toward the small Fokker reconnaissance biplane standing at the edge of a copse of firs.

After four hours of flying at treetop level, they were out of what used to be the German Reich, landing on an island in the Baltic for fuel before continuing.

It wasn't until Eva had a chance to develop the roll of film documenting their wedding that she learned Goebbels's wife hadn't pushed the shutter button. Eva had been cheated of her husband, and now was denied proof of their marriage.

It was as if all those years of being his mistress had not existed. She had trained as a photographer before she had met him, and her skills were behind hundreds of photographs of them together, but Adolf had insisted such embarrassing evidence be archived with him. He was extremely nervous they might fall into the wrong hands and would take no risk his career be destroyed because of a few pictures generating the wrong questions.

Now she had nothing to prove to the outside world she actually had been the wife of one of the most powerful men in the world; she, little Eva—photographer, mistress, mother, wife, and now widow. As she grew older there were days when she felt it was just as well no one else knew of her secret. After the trials at Nuremberg and the disclosure of the atrocities there were very few people who spoke well of her husband. There were even quiet evenings when she would secretly admit to herself she had been married to the world's worst murderer, and she felt ashamed she had never seen it.

She wondered if Schwerlieb had really been as naïve as he had maintained in his defense during the trial. Eva read about

Schwerlieb's trial many years after, and could not grasp how anyone in his position could possibly have managed to remain ignorant of the factories of death used to kill so many unfortunate souls.

She remembered how pleased he had been to receive his own copy of the photograph of his son and the other children. He had been so jovial that day, a day like any other, and yet only weeks before he had ordered the bombing of targets in Britain, causing the deaths of thousands of innocent civilians.

As Hurtree left the tax-free shop with a liter bottle of thirty-nine-year-old Islay Single Malt Whisky, his cell phone rang. He looked at the number and noticed it was a German caller. He felt sure it was Charlie Peters on the other end.

"Hi there, you old fart," he snorted into the phone.

"Hello, Mr. Hurtree. My name is Wilhelm Schwerlieb. You visited me the day before yesterday."

"Oh, yes, of course. Sorry, I was expecting a call from someone else."

"I understand. I wanted to inform you that this morning I heard my housekeeper bragging about what happened to you when you left here. I want you to know I had nothing to do with that. I'm no Nazi, Mr. Hurtree, and I have no connection to the Iron Guard, as they call themselves. I have asked the housekeeper to leave my house."

"Well that's good to know, Mr. Schwerlieb, but I didn't really think it was you behind what went on last night. Hey, while I've got you on the phone, I forgot to ask you something yesterday. Could you help me with it?"

"Perhaps." Schwerlieb's answer floated through the earpiece of Hurtree's cell phone.

"It's the photograph you showed me on the mantelpiece over your fireplace. I've always assumed your father took it."

"No, my father stood beside the photographer, Mr. Hurtree. It was Dolfin's mother, Eva. She was a professional photographer, you know. That's what she did before she met Adolf for the first time."

Hurtree asked him another question before Schwerlieb's answer had a chance to sink in.

"And then there's something else. There was a medallion in the box that I left you, a small gold ring with a swastika in the middle."

"Yes, I was given one. We all had one. Uncle—we always called him Uncle—gave them to us. The one you saw in the box was my father's. Mine was inscribed *Wilhelm, in liebe Wolf*—To Wilhelm, with love, Wolf."

"Yeah," said Hurtree, "I remember the medallion, but I never saw the inscription. Did this Dolfin girl have one?"

"Oh, yes," said Schwerlieb. "Both she and her mother had one. They both bore the same inscription: *Eva und Dolfin, in liebe Wolf.*"

Hurtree went quiet as he pondered over what he had just heard, then, "But, could there be only two such medallions with that inscription?"

"I would think so, yes. Why? What's so important about the medallion?" asked Schwerlieb.

"The police in Stockholm found a medallion with just that inscription in the purse of the nurse who was taking care of the Dolfin woman, the one who was murdered."

"What was her name?" asked Schwerlieb. Hurtree could hear an urgent tone in his question.

"The nurse? Anna something. Eiderbach, I think."

"But that's impossible. Anna Eiderbach was my nanny. She was killed in the first bombing of Berlin in 1940, right outside our apartment. I know it because I saw her body. It was horrible. She couldn't have been the nurse in Stockholm. My nanny was a good woman, but she would never have received a medallion." Schwerlieb paused, then continued in a whisper. "My God," he said, and Hurtree could barely make out the continuation. "My God, imagine if it was her?"

"Who?" asked Hurtree. "Who are you talking about?"

"Eva," he said, "Dolfin's mother."

"But she died in the bunker in Berlin. Everyone knows that," said Hurtree, then suddenly the holes in the history written to explain her fate flashed into his mind. "I mean, the Russians said it was her. They were the ones who had the bodies of both of them."

"And if it wasn't her?" asked Schwerlieb. "What if she was the nurse who flew up to Stockholm with my father at the beginning of the war. When I think of it, Eva was never around after Dolfin disappeared. I only saw her once after that, when her sister Gretl got married. My God. Imagine if she came back to Berlin to be with Adolf at the end, and that he found a way for her to escape after they were married."

Hurtree shook his head as the possibility sank in. Schwerlieb continued, "My father must have arranged for her to use Anna Eiderbach's name and documents to get her into Sweden. It was Dolfin's mother and not just some nurse caring for her all those years."

Hurtree grasped the enormity of what Schwerlieb was saying, and his eyes glazed over as reality filled the chinks in the story he had believed for half his life.

"But that means…" Hurtree stumbled through his answer "that means…" and his voice trailed off as his mind explored other twists and turns in the realm of the possible. In the background a woman's voice called out flight information in one language after another. He looked up and saw his own flight beginning to board.

Schwerlieb filled in for him. "That means the nurse who was killed was Dolfin's mother, Eva. My God, they killed her."

"Who?" asked Hurtree. "Who killed her?" but his question barely managed to reach Wilhelm Schwerlieb, who said goodbye and switched off his cell phone. He had a score to settle.

When Hurtree returned to Philadelphia he read an article explaining how a group called the Iron Guard was being investigated by the authorities in Germany. They were suspected of being responsible for burning out immigrants in Germany, Sweden, and Greece.

There were reports of an unidentified informant who had

provided details on large parts of the organization, and Europol was now investigating the group all over Europe, including their involvement in a murder in Sweden.

Sara visited Dolfin at her new home once a week. One afternoon, Dolfin removed an object from a drawer in her closet. She dangled it in front of Sara: a small golden medallion with a swastika in the center bearing an inscription. *Eva und Dolfin, in liebe Wolf.*

"*Vati.*" Father, she confided to Sara. "*Vati.*"

The End

A Note to My Readers

Many thanks for purchasing this book, I hope you enjoyed it. Your purchase makes you a member of a group who gets *increased content* on my website, www.jonstenhugg.com, available under the tab for More Content. John Hurtree and Sara Markham each have a blog, and you will be able to read them and leave your own comments. When you open the tab, enter the code XWC3481FA to register your membership, and read what Hurtree and Markham said that couldn't be published. This code will also allow you to access the first chapter of my next book a week before it is published.

Acknowledgements

I could never have written this book alone. First, my wife Ann provided me endless support during the years this book was written and rewritten. After Ann, the list of those who helped make it possible is in no particular order, and includes generous writing friends. I would like to send a warm thank you to both Gini Grossenbacher and Kathy Boyd Fellure. In Elk Grove, Gini Grossenbacher and her group of hungry helpers include Robert Pacholik, Dennis Mahoney, and Daniel Babka. Then we have some members of the Amador Fiction Writers group, with founder Kathy Boyd Fellure, and her group of lunchless heroes: Kitty Haspel, Sarah Armstrong-Garner, Pam Mundale, and Gwen Bodhan. All these people are excellent writers themselves, and they were generous enough to nudge me away from some of the glaring errors a new writer makes. Their constructive suggestions brought me no end of grief as I revised and rewrote the book, but finally joy as I reread the final version. I am happy other readers never have to be subjected to the first draft.

For more information about the author and his work visit
www. jonstenhugg.com

Lightning Source UK Ltd.
Milton Keynes UK
UKOW04f1455220515

252137UK00001B/3/P

9 781781 323304